# ALSO BY
# DARCY COATES

# GHOST CAMERA

# DARCY COATES

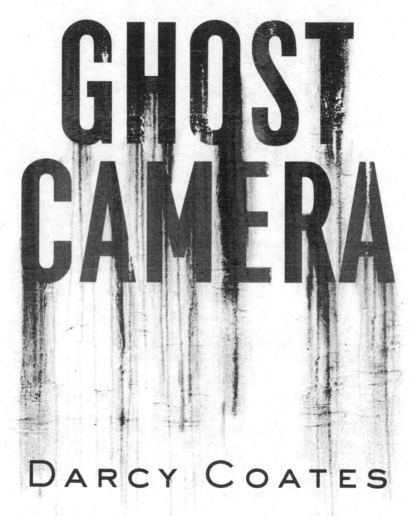

*Poisoned Pen*
PRESS

Published by Poisoned Pen Press, an imprint of Sourcebooks
P.O. Box 4410, Naperville, Illinois 60567-4410
(630) 961-3900
sourcebooks.com

Originally self-published in 2014 by Black Owl Books.

Cataloging-in-Publication Data is on file with the Library of Congress.

Printed and bound in Canada.
MBP 10 9 8 7 6 5 4 3 2 1

# AUTHOR'S NOTE

The heart of this collection, *Ghost Camera*, is not new. In fact, it's one of the first stories I ever wrote. I remember stumbling my way through it as I tried to learn a host of new skills all at once—writing skills, editing skills, pacing, narrative, characters, dialogue. Everything was brand new and both daunting and thrilling.

The story came out as a novella that took me a shade over seven months to edit. Each revised version was printed out on reams of paper that I went over with red pens and yellow highlighters while crouched at my parents' coffee table. (These days, my editing all happens digitally, and I'm relieved to say it usually takes a lot less than seven months.)

Once a story's complete, I try my hardest to never look at it again. I fear discovering things I wish I could change. What would happen then? Either I would be trapped knowing there was a flaw in one of my books (awful, unendurable) or I would feel compelled to re-edit it. And if I let myself edit old books, nothing new would ever get written. Life would become a Sisyphean cycle of revising each old title, one at a time, before starting from the beginning again.

And so I have a rule: once a story is published, that's it—it goes into a metaphorical locked box and is never critically examined again. Like a child that spies a monster lurking in the corner of the room, I close my eyes and tell myself that if I can't see the problems, they don't exist.

Because of this, old stories tend to take on mythical forms in my mind. I remember the story and the characters, but what was the writing like? Did I do a good job, or would I be ashamed if I had to look at it again?

*Ghost Camera* was one of my oldest stories and therefore also one of the most mythicized. And not in a good way. In my mind's eye, it was a hulking, shambling thing, its gait uneven and with spindles sticking out of its back. Monstrous and terrifying to this poor author who hadn't faced it since writing it a decade ago.

Despite that, it somehow remained a fan favorite. After it went out of print, I began to receive a slow but steady trickle of emails asking where it could be found. When I asked readers if they had any requests, one answer was repeated over and over: they wanted *Ghost Camera* back.

And so my editor and I dutifully scheduled a revised version of *Ghost Camera* to be added to the publication schedule. Fearing that a short-ish novella of dubious quality would be a bitter disappointment to everyone involved, I begged my publisher to let me turn it into a collection and to let me revise *Ghost Camera*.

Then I forced myself to open the locked box of prior manuscripts and to confront the monster inside.

And…*Ghost Camera* wasn't the shambling beast I'd dreamed of.

It had flaws, absolutely. It's impossible to be a fledgling writer and not make a mess in some way. But my fear—that the story was so dire it would need to be dismantled and virtually rewritten from scratch—never came true. It actually had something slightly special about it. This was my first proper story, and I'd poured an almost inhuman amount of enthusiasm and delight into it. And those emotions persisted, even ten years later. I made the choice to keep *Ghost Camera* as close to its original form as possible.

The new edits ended up taking much less time than the seven months I originally spent on it. I've rewritten confusing sentences. A few patches of ragged pacing have been smoothed, and I fixed a part where the point-of-view character changes midparagraph. But the *Ghost Camera* you'll read here is almost identical to the *Ghost Camera* I originally published.

In a lot of ways, my first story feels very different from the novels I write now. In other ways, it feels like coming home.

There's probably a lesson here. Maybe I could peel back the covers on some of my other books. Is it possible I would fear them less now that I've confronted my oldest work?

No. Absolutely not. The locked box is staying locked, the way it should.

All my love,
Darcy

# GHOST CAMERA

# ONE

JENINE TACKLED THE LIGHTHOUSE STAIRS TWO AT A TIME, HER lanky legs eating up the distance. The air was cooler there, hidden from the summer sun, and the thick stone walls muffled the noise from the wedding reception.

She wanted to get to the top and take a photo before the cake cutting. She wasn't the official wedding photographer, but the hired man was only taking posed photos. If she got some good candid shots, she could make an album as a present for Helen when she returned from her honeymoon. A photo from the top of the lighthouse would be perfect for the cover.

Jenine reached the top of the stairs winded but elated. The trapdoor was already open, so she slipped into the room above.

The lighthouse hadn't been used since shipping companies changed their routes decades before. A strangely gummy dust, infused with salt by the wind that swept over the bluff, covered every surface and made her shoes stick to the floor.

The now-defunct light hung in the center of the platform, taking up most of the room, with a narrow stone walkway running around it. The waist-high brick wall was periodically studded with support beams, and Jenine had a perfect view of the wedding reception below. She scooted around to find a good angle then took her photo. As she stepped back, her shoe bumped something small and solid.

Someone had abandoned a black-and-gray Polaroid camera. Judging by how dirty it looked, it hadn't been touched in years. Jenine picked it up and examined it gingerly. Other than the dust, it seemed in good condition. Out of curiosity, she raised the camera to her eye, angled it at the wedding guests, and took a picture.

To her delight, it clicked, whirred, and spat out a black-and-white square. Jenine put it in her pocket to develop, slung the Polaroid's strap around her neck, snapped a second photo with her digital camera, then raced down the stairs.

She opened the door at the base of the lighthouse and pulled up short. An aging, sour-looking man blocked her path. His face was weathered and covered in gray stubble, and his eyelids were so heavy she could barely see the pupils behind them.

"You oughtn't be up there," he said, and his voice sounded like sandpaper felt.

Heat raced across Jenine's face. "Sorry, I didn't know it was off-limits. I just wanted a photo—"

"It's not safe," the man said, his face stony. "Little boy fell from up there a few years back. Died."

"Oh," Jenine whispered. She gazed up the length of the tower, and unease dribbled down her back. There was only one place someone could fall from: the walkway around the light, where Jenine had taken her photos. She'd likely been standing where the child had spent his last moments on earth.

She looked back down to see the elderly man shuffling away from her, toward the groundskeeper's cottage behind the church. "Sorry," she called, but if he heard her, he didn't give any sign of it.

Jenine broke into a jog to get back to the other guests and arrived just in time to photograph the cake cutting. As she waited for the caterers to pass out the plates, she touched the Polaroid camera hanging around her neck. She wondered if it had belonged to the little boy. The thought made her feel queasy, and she pulled the camera off and hid it in her bag.

---

It was dark by the time Jenine got home. She opened the door to three mewling, disgruntled cats.

"I know, I know," she whispered as she turned on the lights and waded through the rubbing, crying felines. "I wouldn't like being left alone all day either. How about I give you a special treat to make up for it?"

She dished up three plates of wet food then went to her room to change her clothes. She'd dressed casually for the wedding, but slipping out of the slightly-too-tight jeans and into her pajama pants still felt good. Before throwing her jeans into the laundry, she frisked the pockets to make sure they didn't hold any tissues or stray coins.

"Huh," she muttered, pulling out the Polaroid. She'd forgotten about it in the buzz of the wedding.

The picture wasn't bad, she supposed. It had the inherent graininess and off colors of a Polaroid but showed the wedding reception relatively clearly. Jenine had half expected the film to have gone bad after so long.

She smiled and pinned the picture to the corkboard above her bed. The board stored happy memories: train tickets from her trip to visit her quirky spinster aunts in the mountains. Zoo passes from when she and her best friend, Bree, had spent an afternoon watching the penguins. Letters, photographs, and trinkets hung above her head to give her pleasant dreams.

The three cats, finished with their dinner, filed into her room one by one and took their places on her quilt. Jenine showered quickly, then crawled into bed between the warm lumps of fur.

---

She dreamed about the photo. It was perfectly clear in her mind: the happy bride hanging onto the groom's arm, talking to her father. A cluster of women gathered around the drinks table, already on the verge of being tipsy. The professional photographer arranging the bridesmaids in a line in front of the cake.

At the forefront of the picture stood a little boy. Blood ran down his distorted face from where the top of his skull had been crushed. He stared upward, directly at the camera he had once owned, oblivious to the wedding reception behind him. While the rest of the Polaroid was grainy, his eyes were sharper and clearer than any modern camera would have been able to achieve. They were completely white, bleached of iris and pupil.

Jenine woke with a smothered gasp. She grabbed at her covers, disturbing the nearest cat and causing it to roll over with a yawn. She sucked in a few tight breaths as she oriented herself, then reached for her bedside lamp.

The photograph hung from the corkboard directly above her bed. She carefully unpinned it and held it up to the light. To her relief, the boy was not there. The bride and groom were still talking to her father, the women still indulging in the relaxing powers of champagne, and the photographer still hustling the bridesmaids into a line—but there was no boy.

Jenine exhaled deeply and rubbed the chin of her largest cat, which was kneading her thigh. Something about the photograph was definitely off, though. She squinted and held it up, straining to make out the details.

Because the picture was so grainy, she hadn't noticed it at first, but pale figures stood among the crowd. She counted six of them. Some were partially obscured by people or tables, and some seemed to be huddled among the partygoers, joining their conversations.

Jenine brushed her finger over the clearest figure, trying to understand it. The woman was transparent, looking almost like a human-shaped wisp of smoke.

Then she spotted a seventh figure. Crouched behind one of

the shrubs that bordered the church's lawn was a little boy, his knees pulled up to his chin and his arms wrapped around them. He was hidden so well that he was barely visible except for his head, which was turned toward the lighthouse.

Jenine threw the picture onto her bedside table and clambered out of bed, trying not to disturb the cats again. She pulled on a robe and slippers and looked at her clock. It was just past four in the morning. Too early to call Bree.

She went to her kitchen, turning on every light in her path. She switched on the radio before heating some milk over the stove, then sat on the edge of a wooden chair, mug clasped between unsteady hands, and waited out the early morning hours.

---

Bree opened shop two hours before anyone else Jenine knew. Rosie Posy, Bree's flower shop, was a tiny corner store near the heart of their rural town. It was small, but the shop was brightly lit and overflowing with bunches and boxes of flowers. Bree had forgone university and used her life savings and a substantial loan from her parents to open the shop when she was nineteen. It got by reasonably well, making her enough money to pay her bills and her part-time assistant, Nina.

The distinctive smell of pollen and sap mingled with floral scents hit Jenine as she pushed open the door. Bree was already behind the counter, preparing homegrown daisies while she waited for the biweekly delivery of fresh flowers.

Jenine and Bree made an unlikely set of best friends. Jenine was reclusive and thoughtful; Bree was loud and active. Jenine was ungracefully tall and wore her tawny hair long and straight, but Bree, who was short and stocky, frequently added colors to her black undercut. That morning, it was streaked with pink.

Bree broke into a grin when she saw Jenine. "Morning, Sprocket! I missed you at the after-wedding party last night."

"Sorry, I was tired. Was it fun?"

"Absolutely. What could be more fun than watching Vince throw up all over Tiffany while they were slow-dancing?" Bree leaned forward conspiratorially. "Because that totally happened."

"Eww. See, that is the exact reason I don't do parties."

"Clearly, your fun-o-meter is broken." Bree pointed her scissors at a stool, indicating Jenine should take it. "Talking about things you don't normally find fun—how come you're up so early?"

Jenine pulled up the stool to sit at the counter opposite Bree. "Actually, I wanted to ask you about a photograph I took at Helen's wedding yesterday. Some weird things have shown up in it."

Bree continued to hack at the daisies, pulling off leaves and trimming stems. "Do we mean weird in a hilarious way or weird in a creepy way?"

"Creepy. Definitely creepy."

"Sweet," Bree said. "Let's have a look. Ooh, nice angle. Where'd you scurry off to?"

"The lighthouse," Jenine said, watching Bree scan the image, waiting for her to notice the pale shapes.

"Damn, girl, clever thinking. Hey, there I am!" Bree jabbed her finger onto an orange-and-red blob near the bride.

Jenine forced herself to be patient. "Notice anything odd?"

"Hell yeah. Why did you downgrade your Nikon to a Polaroid? It's the twenty-first century, Jenny. People use digital now." Bree glanced up and placed one hand over her heart, feigning concern. "Are you in trouble? Do you need money?"

"Be serious," Jenine said, waving the picture in Bree's face. "I found the camera in the lighthouse. But look at these!"

Bree, determined to play out her joke, clapped her hands to either side of her face in horror. "Jenny, you stole? I can't believe it! Oh, it can't be! Poor, sweet, innocent Jenny has been reduced to a life of crime!"

"Hnnng." Jenine dropped her head onto the counter in frustration. "The picture, Bree. I think there are ghosts in the picture."

"And she's hallucinating too!" Bree cried, but she picked up the Polaroid to have a second look.

For the first time since Jenine had entered the store, Bree lapsed into silence. Her smile faded into bewilderment, which in turn morphed into intrigue. Without saying a word, she set the photo on the counter, then disappeared into the storeroom at the back of the shop. She returned carrying a square magnifying glass. She placed it directly over one of the pale shapes in the photo and put her eye to it. Jenine held her breath while her friend examined the image.

"Damn, Jenny." When Bree looked up, she had an odd expression on her face: half-nervous and half-excited, with a hint of exhilaration. "I don't recognize any of these people. I never forget a face, and I swear, I've never seen these people in my life."

Jenny pointed to the child crouched behind the hedge. "The lighthouse keeper said a boy had died falling off the lighthouse. I think this is him. And…I think the camera was his too."

Bree let her breath out in a whistle. "If you weren't such an adorkable stick-in-the-mud, I'd think this was a prank." She fixed Jenine with a hard glare. "It's not, is it?"

"Cross my heart." Jenine made the sign over her chest, something she and Bree had done all the time when they were children. "I came to you because you took that course in photography last year. I thought you might be able to tell if it was a glitch or something."

Bree picked up her scissors and began attacking the daisies afresh. She put a little more force behind her snips than she had before. "Well, for starters, Polaroids don't 'glitch' in the way you're thinking about. That's all digital. What can sometimes happen, though, is there can be double exposure, or sometimes light will get on the picture and damage it while it's still developing. So, yes, this could just be a big mistake, but really—look at it." She paused in her cutting just long enough to jab a finger onto one of the male ghosts. "This isn't some blob of light. It's a fully formed, somewhat transparent person."

"Someone who definitely wasn't at the wedding."

"Exactly. I mean, I might suspect double exposure, but look at him—it looks like he's really there. With double exposure, two images are juxtaposed, and you'll get all the awkwardness that goes along with that. Objects will be the wrong size; people will be floating in midair. But he's not. He's the same size as everyone else, standing on solid ground like everyone else. Heck, that little boy is even interacting with the shrub. It's either the luckiest coincidence I've ever seen or we've got something pretty significant on our hands."

Finished with her daisies, Bree scooped them up and propped them in a bucket of water. "Do you still have the camera?"

"Oh, yeah." Jenine pulled it out of her bag and handed it to Bree.

"It's an old model. Looks like it's from, what, the eighties?"

"That's what I thought."

Bree opened the film slot just long enough to check inside then closed it before the light could cause any damage. "Mind if I take a picture?"

"Go for it."

Bree pointed the camera at Jenine and clicked the button.

The light blinded Jenine for a second, and when she blinked, white blobs floated across her vision. "Harsh flash."

"Quit your whining." Bree grinned, placing the undeveloped picture under her desk's place mat to protect it from light. "These things take, what, four minutes to develop?"

"You're the expert on cameras."

"Only on proper cameras. Digital ones. Not these dinky relics." Bree handed the camera back to Jenine and picked up a roll of ribbon, which she began to cut into lengths. "Do you have any plans for tomorrow?"

"No. What about you?"

"Just work. Saturday's a slow day, so I was thinking of closing early and catching a movie."

"You weren't going to visit Travis?"

"Ugh, don't even mention him." Bree threw the empty ribbon roll toward the bin. It missed and clattered to the floor.

Bree and Travis had been dating for nearly four years. At times they were inseparably in love, and at other times they hated each other with a scalding intensity.

Jenine found their relationship bizarre, confusing, and extremely fascinating. She drew her knees up to her chin. "What'd he do?"

"He bought the hottest chili sauce he could find and slathered it all over my sandwich without telling me. It burned so bad I thought I was dying. That butt-face filmed the whole thing and says he's going to upload it and watch it go viral."

Jenine resisted asking for the link and mumbled a commiseration instead. Travis loved pranks almost as much as Bree did. Their next argument would undoubtedly be about Bree's revenge.

Bree finished her second roll of ribbon and threw the scissors down with more force than necessary. "Photo should be done by now, right?" She pulled the picture from under the mat and turned it around. Her eyes grew wide.

"What? What? Let me see." Jenine hopped off her stool to look over Bree's shoulder.

The picture showed Jenine sitting behind the desk, smiling awkwardly at the camera. The bouquets and boxes of flowers in the background were fuzzy, and the odd tints and colors Polaroids specialized in saturated the picture.

The only colorless part of the photo was the woman standing

behind Jenine. Long hair hung limply around her gaunt face and empty eyes as she stared at the back of Jenine's head.

"Oh," Jenine whispered. "Oh."

An itch crawled down her back, making her hair stand on end. She knew the answer, but she still had to ask: "There wasn't anyone behind me when you took the photo, was there?"

Bree gave a wild, high-pitched laugh. "Babe, no. Especially not looking like that. Oh, hell."

"Do…do you think she's still there?"

"Shoot. She'd better not be. Not in my store." Bree looked up at Jenine, her eyes filled with frantic energy. "You want to get out of here?"

"Would you come with me?"

The door slammed open before Bree could answer. They both jumped, and Jenine shrieked.

"Don't mind me. Just bringing the flowers." Burke, the deliveryman, backed into the room, guiding a trolley carrying a dozen boxes of fresh flowers, which he set in front of the counter. Jenine placed her hand on her heart, waiting for its pace to slow.

"That's the lot, Breanna," Burke said as Bree hurried to get his pay out of the till.

"Thanks. See you Tuesday?"

"Sure as rain. You ladies have a good day now."

Bree waited until his truck had rumbled to life and driven away before speaking. "You'd better go." Her voice was steadier, but her fingers still trembled faintly as she picked up both Polaroids. She placed them in an envelope and sealed it before handing it to Jenine. "I know you've got exams you need to study for. Go do that, and promise me you won't look at or think about these photos while you're doing it, okay?"

"Okay," Jenine whispered. She felt as if she were back in middle school, being lectured by the older Bree on how to eat lunch properly.

"And, Jenine, if I were you, I'd burn them."

"I'll think about it."

Bree swept her into a tight hug. "Stay safe, girl. I'll call you later, okay?"

"Sure," Jenine said, hugging back and wishing she could avoid ever letting go.

# TWO

JENINE DROPPED THE ENVELOPE ONTO HER KITCHEN BENCHTOP. Three cats coiled around her legs, and she realized she hadn't fed them that morning. Cooing apologies, she fished food from the cupboard and divided it onto plates. As her cats ate, Jenine's gaze turned toward the photos.

She pulled out her law books instead. She was nearly two years into the three-year course to become a solicitor. She'd been doing well in class, well enough to have a decent shot at getting into one of the two local offices, possibly even one of the bigger firms in the city if she could get a good referral. She scraped her chair up to the counter and opened the textbook while the photos in the envelope tugged at her mind.

*Could the camera be a prank?* Maybe it was a toy carefully styled to look like a Polaroid camera, but with the digital capabilities to add the ghostly figures. It would need to identify the shapes in the photos to place the new images appropriately, but that was still within the realm of digital ability, right?

Jenine slammed her book shut and picked up the envelope. She reached for the seal, hesitated, put the envelope down, then picked it up again. Bree had told her to ignore it, and Bree's advice was usually solid. She was the one who had her life organized; she had a business, her own home, and a *mostly* steady boyfriend. Bree was arguably the more mature of the pair. That meant her opinion should carry more weight than Jenine's.

Jenine tore open the envelope and picked out the second picture. It was exactly how she remembered it: her own face, blinking at the camera, the start of a goofy smile at the corners of her mouth. Directly behind her stood the being with limp hair, hollow cheeks, and dead eyes.

It was more than a digital trick. The ghost was looking directly at the back of Jenine's head—not just in her general direction, but directly at her, focused on her with the intensity of a predator stalking prey.

Jenine placed the photograph flat on the kitchen counter and rested her chin in her hands, pressing her fingers over her mouth.

What were the possibilities? It could be a prank. Some clever, well-designed, well-devised prank.

Or the camera could show actual ghosts, walking among humans, invisible except when captured on film. She bowed her head until it touched the top of the counter. It was cool and solid, something real she could concentrate on.

*Ghosts. Real ghosts. Around me constantly.* She raised her head and picked up the photo again. If it was fake, there would be clues. All she had to do was find them, which was easier said than done. The Polaroid was grainy and the colors looked like they'd been applied with a filter, but as far as she could see, the image was seamless. The ghost seemed to be standing about two feet behind Jenine. The shadows over its transparent face matched the store's lighting. The edge of the counter covered the lower half of its body.

Jenine caught her breath. There was a second ghost in the photo. The picture caught the edge of the window overlooking the street. On the other side of the glass was the boy from the wedding—the boy who Jenine was sure had owned the camera. His face was barely more than a faint smudge in the glaring light.

Jenine put the photo down with shaking fingers. The camera was in her bag. It still had film in it. *I could take another photo, just to see.* Just to see if the images were real. Just to see if the boy had followed her home.

Just to see if anything else was in her house, standing behind her, perhaps, watching her with dead eyes.

She put the photo back in the envelope and hid it on top of the bookshelf, out of sight, then turned the TV on and set the volume loud enough to override the anxious thoughts spinning through her mind.

Then she went back to the kitchen to retrieve the bottle of wine her aunt had given to her as a gift when she'd graduated from college. Jenine had never opened it, but she was jittery and anxious, and half a glass of wine might help her calm down. *Just half a glass.*

She poured the wine into a water tumbler and sat at the kitchen counter. The law books lay forgotten beside her and the TV played the audio from a home renovation competition while she stared at the wall, trying to ignore the camera.

———————

Just after seven o'clock that night, Jenine heard the front door to her apartment rattle open. Even without turning around, she knew who it was. Bree was the only person she trusted enough to have a spare key.

The house was lit up as bright as Jenine could make it, and the news was blaring from the TV. Bree put two shopping bags onto the kitchen counter and leaned over the back of the couch where Jenine was slouched. "Hey, hon. I tried calling but you didn't answer. Rough day?"

Jenine hazarded a watery smile. "The worst. I'm sorry. I looked at the picture."

"Oh, Jenny." Bree wrapped her arms around Jenine's torso, giving her a rough hug. "Look, we'll figure this out."

"That's not all." Jenine pulled her legs up and hid her face behind her knees.

Bree let go of her, rounded the couch, turned the TV off, and flopped onto the lounge next to Jenine. "Tell me your sins, child, for I am greatly forgiving," she intoned.

Jenine snorted with suppressed laughter, then quieted. "I got drunk."

"Still drunk now, babe?"

"No, no, well, not much."

"So, what happened?" Bree's smile disappeared as understanding flashed over her face. "You took more photos, didn't you?"

"There were five Polaroids left. I used them all." Jenine picked up a pillow and began toying with its tassels, blinking furiously.

"Can I see?"

"They're in the kitchen."

Jenine waited for Bree to find them. She focused on the cushion she was holding, feeling the soft fibers of the tassel between her fingertips and tugging on a loose strand.

Bree sat down next to her. She flipped through the pictures, pausing to absorb the details of each snapshot. "Oh, hell. You should have called me."

Jenine shrugged, avoiding her friend's eyes. "It's not like you could have done anything. There's nothing that *can* be done. I can't—I can't get away from them."

Bree sucked on her teeth as she looked through the photos more slowly. Jenine's fattest cat jumped onto the arm of the lounge and sat, watching them with disdainful eyes.

There were five photos: one from the living room, two from the bedroom, one from the bathroom, and one from the hallway, looking into the kitchen. The snapshot of the hallway didn't show much. The hall itself was empty, but there was a whisper of white in the kitchen, mostly hidden by the wall, as though something had tried to hide itself a moment too late.

The photo of the living room only had one being in it. A woman stood in the corner, facing the wall. Her shoulders and knees were bent as though she had a skeletal disease. Her long nightgown was stained in places, and her bald head was turned just enough that the camera caught the glint of one eye. Bree quickly moved to the next picture.

The shot of the bathroom showed Jenine's face, scrunched, anxious and flushed from the wine, reflected in the mirror. Two other beings, both male, appeared in that photo. The first—old, bald, and with sweat stains under his arms—was lurching toward the camera, an outstretched hand reaching for Jenine, while a toothless leer spread across his puffed cheeks. A sheen of sweat coated his transparent skin. The second ghost, a young man with a sunken face and tattoos across his shoulders, was sitting in the tub, eyes turned to the ceiling, mouth drawn in a long line. The water he sat in was tinged red.

The final two photographs were from the bedroom. Jenine's bed, unmade and messy from where she'd abandoned it after her nightmare the night before, filled the center of the room. In the first photo, one of the cats was licking itself on the carpet while a small child stood in the corner and watched it. The child, a girl with a gray dress and hair done into a harsh braid, had a sallow, joyless face and blank eyes. A man lay prone on the bed, his undershirt barely covering his puckered skin. He had one hand raised, gesticulating as if he were speaking.

The second bedroom photo had been taken no more than a few seconds after the first. The man on the bed seemed to have become aware of the camera and looked directly toward it, his face contorted in anger. A new figure had come into view: a woman who had stepped from behind the cupboard where she'd been hidden. Her Victorian dress, with a high neckline and a low hem that fell over her boots, was spattered with dark stains. Her face was cold and severe as she gazed at the camera.

The girl was no longer watching the cat and stood directly before the camera, staring up at it. Her mouth was agape in a silent howl, revealing rotting teeth sticking out of dark gums.

"Shoot," Bree whispered. "Oh, Jenny. You really should have called me. I could've closed the shop early. I could've."

"To do what?" Jenine asked. She threw the cushion toward the TV. It fell short and flopped to the ground.

Bree wrapped her arms around Jenine's shoulders and pulled her into a fierce hug. "Moral support, idiot. And wine. We can drink lots and lots of wine and forget about that stupid camera."

Jenine chuckled. "I think I've had enough wine for today."

"Well, then, we can watch cheesy romantic comedies and eat junk food and talk about how sucky my idiot boyfriend is. And we can have a sleepover. I can borrow your pajamas, right?"

"Hmm," Jenine replied, leaning against Bree. "It's been years since we've had a sleepover. That would be nice." She hesitated. "As long as you're okay with it. I mean, I know I wouldn't want to sleep in a place with photos like…that."

"Hey, don't worry about it." Bree shrugged awkwardly. "Hell, that camera has taken pictures at three different places, and all of them were blighted by the dead. What makes you think my apartment would be any better? It's older than this place, so it's probably lousy with ghosties."

"But still. It makes a difference when you've actually seen them."

"Yeah," Bree admitted. "That's true. But, hey, safety in numbers, right? C'mon, let's get a party happening."

For the next hour, they did just that. Bree tuned the radio to a station that played songs Jenine had never heard of, then pulled bag after bag of sweets and chips out of her shopping. She'd obviously anticipated that comfort food might be required.

They avoided Jenine's room—the photos were still too fresh in their minds—and pulled a spare mattress and blankets into the living room, which had been relatively ghost-free in the photos.

Bree chose a romantic comedy, but they turned it off halfway through because it reminded Bree how much she hated Travis. They lay together on the narrow mattress, staring at the blank screen, letting the silence wash over them. Two of the three cats had curled into tight balls on their blankets during the movie, and Jenine scratched at the nearest one's head.

"I've heard animals can tell when ghosts are around," Jenine said at last.

Bree rolled over. Her hair no longer fell into a tidy, well-groomed arrangement, but stood up in patches. "I guess they've gotten used to them. If—and this is a big if—the camera really does show ghosts, then I think we can safely say there's a lot more of them about than we thought."

"Not everyone who ever died," Jenine said, "or there wouldn't be enough room for them to stand. But, yeah, a lot. Maybe just the ones who have unfinished business."

"Or who were unhappy in life. None of them looked very cheerful."

They stared at the ceiling for a long moment. The third cat arrived and flopped into the space between them.

"They've probably always been there, and we haven't been able to see them," Bree said. "Like cockroaches. They're horrible, and you don't want them about, but you don't lose sleep over them as long as they stay in the walls."

"Do you think they can hear us?"

"Dunno. The bedroom photos make it look like they reacted to the camera."

"Yeah."

"They've got to be harmless, though. No way could people be oblivious to that number of spooks if they were dangerous."

"Yeah."

"You don't sound convinced."

Jenine exhaled. "It's like—I mean, they look angry. Especially that man on my bed. I don't know if I'll ever feel comfortable sleeping there again. He looked furious. Like he hated me." She rolled onto her stomach. "I don't want people to hate me."

Bree reached over and mussed Jenine's hair. "Oh, babe, that's inescapable. If I curled up into a defeated little ball just because people didn't like me—"

"How could anyone not like you?" Jenine laughed.

Bree mussed her hair harder.

Jenine's smile faded as the silence pressed in on them. She swallowed. "Do you think we should show someone?"

Bree didn't answer right away, but stared at the corner opposite her, where the woman had been standing in the photograph. "Who would you show it to?"

"Ghost hunters? They're real, not just on TV, right?"

"Sure. Anything can be a job, just as long as you can find someone who'll pay you."

"So we could take the pictures to one of them. Or maybe a photography expert? Or what about a journalist?"

Bree laughed. "Wouldn't they just call it a hoax? We live in a world of photo manipulation and filters. Anything can be faked."

"So, what if we got fresh film and gave them a live demonstration? That'd be pretty hard to argue with."

Bree considered it. "Yeah. Maybe. You want to be famous?"

"No." Jenine paused, then reached down and patted the cat at her side. "No, I mean—no. I guess I just… I want it to be someone else's problem."

"Yeah. So do I."

They both stared at the corner, examining the neat plaster and trim. Jenine wondered if the woman with the crooked knees still stood there.

"I have contacts in the photography business," Bree said. "Someone will probably be able to rustle up some film that'll fit your camera. It's an old model so it might be hard to come by, but we'll only need a few pictures."

Jenine was the first to look away from the corner of the room. "Do you think ours is the only camera that does this?"

"Ours?" Bree laughed. "It's your camera, babe. Don't lump me in with your problems."

"Be serious. What do you think?"

"I think…well, it's got to be a one-in-a-million—maybe one-in-a-billion—chance that it is. I don't think this is the only one."

"We might be able to find something about it online, then."

"The majestic Google will answer our every question."

"Come on, Bree. I'm trying to be serious."

Bree snickered. "I am, I am. Google knows everything. Just type in 'my camera takes pictures of ghosts, how do I make it stop, please,' and it'll answer you."

Jenine threw her pillow at Bree, but she couldn't stop herself from joining in the laughter. For a few brief moments, she felt like she was in middle school again, carefree and safe at a sleepover with Bree.

---

Jenine woke shortly after nine in the morning. By the way the kitchen had been tidied, she guessed Bree had already been up for several hours. She pulled herself to her feet, kicking aside stray cushions.

She found Bree in the spare room, practicing Pilates in a space she'd cleared on the floor. She was puffing and sweating and had her game face on.

Jenine shook her head and rubbed sleep out of her eyes. "Don't you ever slow down?"

"Life's too short to go slow." Bree contorted her body into a pose that looked neither comfortable nor healthy. "Come, grasshopper, sit, and I will show you the wonders of early morning exercise."

"I'm good. Don't you need to be at work?"

"It's a Saturday."

"So? You always work on Saturdays."

Bree shook her short mane out of her eyes as she rolled onto her back and began pumping her legs. "Decided I'd prefer to keep my weekends to myself. I called Nina. She doesn't mind picking up the extra shifts."

Jenine sat down on the floor and pulled her legs in under her. "You're doing this so you can stay with me, aren't you?"

"Well, I was going to play the role of the anonymous martyr, but if you must spoil my fun—yes."

"Don't, Bree, really. I don't need a babysitter."

"Who says this is for you, doll?" Bree let out a huge puff of air and pulled herself into a sitting position. Jenine had always thought Pilates was a gentle, delicate sort of exercise, but Bree's regime was significantly more taxing and aggressive than any she'd seen before. "If you want the pure and honest truth, I'm not so thrilled about this ghost stuff either. You saw that gal in my shop. Hell, I don't want to be sitting around there all day with just her for company."

Jenine smiled. "Sure."

"I mean it. If I had to choose between spending the day with you and a ghastly, hideous being from another plane, you'd win. Just barely, though." She winked and began folding up the blanket she'd been exercising on. "Got any plans for today?"

"Legal reading. But I don't think I'll get far with that."

"Good, because I called one of my contacts, and he's got a few packs of old Polaroid film he'll sell us. Give me a minute to shower and we can go get them."

# THREE

THEY TOOK BREE'S CAR, A TINY PINK THING WITH ADS FOR HER flower shop plastered across the doors. Bree's phone rang not long after they left the suburbs.

"Should we answer that?" Jenine asked the second time it played the K-pop ringtone.

"Nope." Bree's face could have been made out of granite.

"Is…is it Travis?"

"Yep."

"Oh." Jenine stared at the ringing phone as it flashed inside Bree's bag.

Bree and Travis had argued before, sometimes having huge screaming matches, but they'd always made up quickly. Travis would come around with a bunch of flowers he'd stolen from the neighbor's garden or bring tickets for an indie band, and Bree would keep up the pretense of anger for two minutes, tops. Their most recent spat was different, though. Bree was really, truly mad at him in a way Jenine had never seen before.

"Have you spoken to him since yesterday?"

"Yep. Don't ask." Bree turned the radio on and grinned. "Oh, I love this song."

That put a stop to the conversation for the rest of the hour-long drive.

They arrived at a house with a garden choked with weeds, an empty, crooked birdbath, and peeling paint. Piles of dead, rotting vegetation sat in the corner of the yard, the remnants of a spring-clean that had never been completed.

"This is it?" Jenine asked.

"Looks like it." Bree was in high spirits as she bounded out of the car and up the driveway.

The transaction took less than a minute. An aged, balding man answered the door, and he seemed genuinely happy to see Bree. He handed over an envelope in exchange for a handful of cash, then waved them off.

They sat in the car while Jenine opened the packet and fit the ten Polaroids into the camera.

"We'd better test it," Bree suggested. "Take a photo of the house. It looks ancient; I'll bet there's a bunch of spirits hanging around."

Jenine aimed the camera and clicked the button. Bree took the undeveloped Polaroid that whirred out of its slot and tucked it into the glove box before the light could damage it. "Want to stop somewhere on the way home?" she asked as she put the car into gear.

"What did you have in mind?"

"Doesn't matter to me. The beach. A park. Disneyland."

"Disneyland?" Jenine laughed. "As if I could afford the ticket. We can't all be rich like you."

Bree scoffed, but her face was serious. "It's cool. I'll spot you."

"What? Don't even joke about that."

Bree pursed her lips but didn't push it.

Jenine stared out the window at the houses speeding by. The fresh, hot day had just enough breeze to stop it from being unbearably warm. The weather was too nice to spend the day indoors, but Jenine suspected that wasn't why Bree had suggested they stop somewhere.

"You really don't want to talk to Travis, do you?"

Bree considered her answer carefully. "No. I think we might be over this time."

"Because of the prank?"

"No." Bree shook her head, and even though she was smiling, tears gathered in her eyes. "No, no, this was just a…a culmination, I guess."

Jenine waited, letting the silence stretch out as a gentle encouragement to continue.

Bree wiped her eyes, smudging her makeup. "He called me this morning, before you woke up. I…said some stuff I shouldn't have. He blew up. Started dragging up all these things I'd thought we were over. Old stuff. I got mad. He called me toxic. Said I'm unhinged. That I'm ruining his life."

She fell silent, dragging in thick gulps of air. Her mascara was smearing, and her fingers twitched on the wheel from agitation.

Jenine tried to say something helpful, but her mind was blank. She managed to mumble, "I don't think you're unhinged."

Bree laughed and rubbed her eyes. "You're all right, babe. You know that? You're all right. Let's go somewhere. You pick."

They ended up taking a detour to a seaside park. Bree stopped the car under a tree and stretched, rotating her shoulders to loosen them. "You're lucky I have an emergency picnic kit in the back of my car."

"Seriously?" Jenine squirmed to look behind her. "Where do you even keep it?"

"Where the spare tire should be. Hey, did you want to check the photo before we get out? I want to know if the new film works the same as the old."

Jenine opened the glove box and pulled out the square card. One part of her expected to see ghosts milling about the building as they had been at her home. The other part expected the photo to be empty, just a boring, aged house in a boring, aged suburb.

What was actually in the picture made her shudder. A woman, all pale grays and blacks, was pressed up against the car window. Her hands, ending in discolored nails, were splayed against the glass. Thin hair floated about her wrinkled face, and her white, sightless eyes stared intently. Her mouth was open wide in a silent scream, much wider than it ever could have opened in life, and the blackness inside seemed to go on forever.

Bree grimaced. "Yuck. Lovely. I guess at least the camera still works."

"Right," she replied automatically, staring at the woman's dress, which looked uncomfortably familiar. Her mind turned back to the very first photo she'd taken with the camera, back at the wedding. A woman with a shock of white hair had been standing beside the cake table, wearing a dress with a very similar floral print. *She couldn't possibly be the same woman, could she?*

Bree got out of the car and stalked to the trunk. "Give me a hand, won't you?" she yelled, wrestling her picnic basket out.

Jenine shoved the photo back into the glove box, then turned to open the door. She froze. Two handprints had been left on the glass. They were so faint they almost looked like a trick of the light, but when Jenine leaned closer, she could make out the unmistakable outline of splayed fingers.

Bree called her again, and Jenine scooted out of the car as quickly as her feet could move her.

---

Bree had been surprisingly resourceful when setting up her emergency picnic basket, which was stocked with canned soup, packages of cookies, and long-life fruit juice. Jenine couldn't help but imagine it was intended to double as supplies for an apocalypse.

The park was shady, and one side overlooked the ocean.

They found a tree in a relatively empty corner and unpacked the basket. Bree had brought every type of cutlery imaginable except for a can opener, so they ate the cookies and drank the juice while watching a group of children play tag at the other side of the park.

"This is nice," Jenine said to break the silence. "We haven't done this for ages."

"I know. You're always too busy with the law books."

Jenine choked on her cookie. "What? When have I ever turned down a chance to hang out? You're the one who spends all day in your store."

"You hardly ever visit me either." Bree sighed, throwing herself backward onto the grass. "You think you're too good for me now that you're getting your big ol' barrister degree."

Jenine took a second to realize her friend was teasing. She laughed. "Solicitor, you goof."

"You skipped my last birthday party!"

"Left early," she corrected. "I stayed as long as I could. You know I hate crowds."

"You didn't notice when I got my hair cut."

"I did too!"

"Nearly two weeks after the fact, babe." Bree laughed and poked Jenine's thigh. "I swear, you're worse than Travis."

Jenine couldn't stop herself from laughing.

The park was starting to fill up as it got closer to lunchtime, and Jenine watched the distant shapes crossing the field of grass. She found herself thinking about their futures: wondering how many of the couples would still be together in twenty years, which of them would die prematurely, and how many would still be talking to each other in a decade. *Half, maybe?*

"We're good friends, aren't we?" she asked Bree.

"The best."

"I wish we could keep doing this forever."

"Who says we can't?" Bree sat up and wrapped an arm around Jenine's shoulder. "It's not like I'd let something silly like mortality get in the way of our friendship."

"I was being serious."

"Okay." Bree kicked her feet out in front of herself. "Maybe we won't always be together. Maybe you'll get that cool job in the big city. Maybe I'll start a new flower shop in Antarctica. But I'd like to think that we're the kind of friends who could meet up one day when we're eighty and talk like we'd just seen each other yesterday."

Jenine rested her head on Bree's shoulder and smiled. Bree seemed to have a knack for verbalizing exactly what Jenine needed to hear. She closed her eyes and listened to the wind whipping through the branches above them and the shrieking children in the play area. She felt comfortable. Safe.

An ice-cold finger grazed Jenine's neck. She jerked forward and clamped her hand over where she'd been touched.

"What's up?" Bree asked.

Jenine swiveled around, but there was nothing behind her except the tree. "I thought—I thought I felt something."

"Insect, probably."

Jenine kept her hand pressed to the back of her neck. Her skin tingled as though she'd been zapped with a low-voltage electric current. "Do you want to stay much longer?"

"Nah," Bree said. "It's about time we got going. You mind if I camp out with you again tonight?"

"That would be nice." She helped Bree pack her picnic basket and shove it into the trunk. The sun was hot and the air smelled of summer, but she couldn't stop shivering, even after she got into the overheated car.

Bree got into the driver's seat and turned the key in the ignition. Jenine reached out a hand to stop her from putting the car into reverse. "Hang on. I want to try something."

She pulled the camera out of the glove box, aimed it at the tree they'd been sitting under, and took a photo.

"Ready to go?"

Jenine tucked the Polaroid into her pocket. "Sure."

---

"I'll pick up some clothes from my place on the way home," Bree said as she exited the freeway. "Your stuff doesn't fit me properly, anyway."

"Sorry."

"Not your fault you're a beanpole," Bree teased. "I'll grab my order forms while I'm there. I can use this weekend to make a list of everything I'm running low on."

"You don't need to be in the store for that?"

"Huh? No. I've got it memorized."

Jenine sucked her teeth ruefully. She needed a to-do list if she had more than three tasks on her plate.

Bree's apartment sat above the flower shop. The street was quiet for a Saturday afternoon; a handful of parked cars were scattered down the curb, but most of the stores in their small town closed early on the weekend. Bree drove past two free spots in front of the shop without slowing down.

"Aren't we stopping?"

"Changed my mind," Bree said. Her tone was abrupt, and her mouth had set into a thin line.

Jenine swiveled in her seat to watch the flower shop disappear behind them. "Hey, isn't that Travis's car?"

Bree didn't reply, and Jenine felt acutely uncomfortable. "Oh."

She wondered how long he'd been waiting there for Bree to come back. Bree hadn't answered her phone all day. He had to be worried, and it wasn't like Bree to ignore him for so long.

"I might have to borrow your clothes again," Bree said. Her voice had softened, but a frown had set in above her eyes.

"Yeah, sure. Are you—I mean—"

"I'll talk to him eventually," Bree said. "Just not right now."

"And…and you didn't need the order forms?"

"I'll do them Monday."

───────────

They got back to Jenine's place late in the afternoon. The air was still hot, but the humidity had dropped to a more comfortable level. Bree moved into the kitchen while Jenine put the camera on top of the fridge. The three cats wove themselves about her legs, mewling and bumping against her.

"Okay, okay, slow down," Jenine whispered as she got their food out of the fridge.

The mattress and blankets were where they'd left them that morning. Jenine didn't see any point in putting them away if they were just going to come out again in six hours, so she kicked them into alignment and picked up the empty chip bags and glasses from the coffee table.

"What do you want to do first?" Bree asked. "Take some time to study, or look up a ghost hunting expert?"

Jenine rubbed a hand over the still-chilled part of her neck. "You think we're ready to talk to a professional?"

"Now that we know the film works, sure. It seems like the obvious next step, doesn't it?"

Jenine nodded slowly. Having Bree stay at her place helped, but it wasn't a permanent solution. "Let's find the expert first. They probably won't be able to come out for a few days, anyway."

"Laptop?"

"In my bedroom."

Jenine got out two mugs while Bree fetched the computer. She made tea for herself and coffee—extra strong, no sugar, and lots of milk—for Bree. Her friend had set up the laptop on the kitchen table and was opening the browser by the time she brought the mugs over.

"Is there a technical name for someone who investigates ghosts?" Bree asked, fingers poised over the keyboard.

"If there is, I haven't heard of it."

"We'll try 'ghost researcher,' then, and narrow it down to people in our area."

Surprisingly, the search brought up quite a few results. Bree opened the top link, which led to the blog of a researcher named Richard Holt who lived less than an hour from them.

"'Ghosts…damned or desperate?'" Bree read, scrolling down the page. "'The truth about the Mallory Haunting. Haunted items vs. haunted locations.' Hey, this could be good."

"Does he have a number?"

"Yeah." Bree had opened the *Contact Us* page. "Looks like he charges an hourly fee for consultations, though."

"Okay, sure." Jenine felt silly for expecting someone to help them for free. Her funds were tight, but she could probably get a loan from the bank or sell the TV, if it came to that.

Bree had her cell phone out and was dialing the number. "We'll split it."

"What? Hey, no. You don't have to—" Jenine withered under Bree's glare.

"We'll split this thing fifty-fifty. That means any profits from interviews or book deals or whatever too. Sound fair?"

"Oh, sure, okay." She doubted they were likely to make a profit off the camera, but the idea was tempting. She still couldn't shake the feeling that Bree was doing her a favor, though.

"Yes, hello?" Bree said into the phone. "Okay, great. Sorry for calling on a weekend. My friend and I have a ghost problem we'd like to talk with you about."

Bree put the phone on the table and pressed the speaker button just in time for Jenine to hear: "Well, that's my specialty. Haunted item or haunted location?" Richard's smooth voice reminded Jenine of the relationship adviser who had a segment on evening radio.

"Item," Bree said.

"Good. They're normally easier to investigate. Would you like me to make a house call, or would you prefer to visit my office?"

They exchanged a glance. "House call would be easier, if you're traveling by us. We're in West Harob."

"I have a few clients down that way. That shouldn't be a problem. I have Tuesday afternoon free, if that suits you?"

Jenine whispered, "What about the flower shop?"

Bree waved her away. "Tuesday's great."

"Excellent. I'll take a few details, if you don't mind. What's the item, and how long has it been manifesting spectral phenomena?"

"It's an old Polaroid camera my friend found two days ago. The pictures all have ghost…spirit…things in them."

The line was silent. Jenine and Bree exchanged a glance.

"Uh…hello? Still there?"

"I'm afraid I won't be able to help you," Richard said. The mellow tone had disappeared from his voice, which had become curt and vaguely defensive. "I recommend you destroy the camera."

"Wait, what? So you can't get here on Tuesday? We can reschedule—"

"I won't be able to help you," he repeated, his tone lower,

colder. "The best thing you can do is break and burn the camera. Goodbye."

The line went dead. Jenine sat back in her chair and rubbed her arms, feeling prickles trail up her neck.

"What the hell?" Bree snapped, tossing her phone onto the table. It bounced but didn't break. "What a jerk."

"We could try someone else."

"Yeah, we're going to do that. We're going to find someone who isn't a total jerk to prospective customers."

Jenine cringed. "Hey, maybe cameras are out of his area. Maybe he only does cursed dolls or whatever."

"Yeah, uh-huh." Bree was mad. Jenine had seen her similarly angry a few times, mostly because of Travis, and she knew it was best to let her friend work through it.

That day, Bree's method of working through it seemed to involve finding an alternate expert as quickly as possible.

"Here," she said, pulling up the second search result. "Irene Sumner. Looks like...okay, so she specializes in haunted houses, but she should be able to handle a little camera, right?"

Irene answered quickly, and Bree put the phone on speaker. "Hey," she said, unaware she was letting anger seep into her voice. "We have a camera that takes pictures of ghosts. Could you look into it for us?"

"Oh, oh," Irene said. She sounded like an older woman, and her voice was so soft that Bree had to increase the phone's volume. "I'm sorry, darling. I really only handle haunted buildings. I haven't had all that much success with haunted objects, I'm afraid."

"Okay, thanks anyway." Bree spoke through gritted teeth but managed to put a bit of cheer in her voice. "Have a lovely afternoon."

"I could recommend someone, though."

Bree's jaw unclenched, and she leaned forward. "Yeah? That would be great."

"There's a gentleman who specializes in this area. He's done a lot of work, published some great theories, and he lectures at one of the local colleges. He's got a website you can look through too. His name is Richard Holt."

Bree's smile returned to its plastic state. "Right," she said. "Is there anyone else you could recommend? Anyone at all?"

"Sorry, sweetheart, he's really the best. I mean, I would have suggested Jackson. He was a lovely fellow, really knew how to speak to spirits, but he moved to Canada last year."

"Okay. Great. Thanks for your help."

Bree hung up and turned to Jenine with a grim expression. "Richard Holt is a jerk," she said.

"Uh-huh."

"I'm not calling him again. I'll find someone else."

"Sure. I…I'll get us some food."

Jenine listened in on the next two phone conversations while she cut fruit and searched her cupboards for crackers that hadn't gone stale. The first call was with a middle-aged woman who breathed heavily and spoke with a nearly incomprehensible accent. She'd closed her business two years ago, and Bree ended the call with an exasperated sigh. The call to the next ghost hunter seemed promising—until he brought up Richard Holt's name.

To Bree's credit, she remained polite and calm until she'd hung up. Then she threw her hands in the air with an exasperated groan. "Why's everyone in love with this Holt jerk?"

Sensing Bree's bad mood was breaking, Jenine brought over their food, then sat forward in her chair and leaned her chin on her hands. "Maybe he really is the best."

"Why hang up on us, then?"

Jenine shrugged.

Bree blew a gust of wind through her pursed lips. "Okay. We'll call him again. Not that he deserves it."

He answered on the second ring. The smooth tone was back into his voice as he said, "Richard Holt speaking. How can I help you?"

"Hey, yeah, we called you a bit earlier. About our camera."

"Oh. Yes. Of course." The tightness returned to his voice, but he didn't hang up. "Did you destroy it?"

"Hell no. We don't want it broken. We just want to know what's happening. And we thought it might, I dunno, be useful for your type of people. Ghost investigators, that is."

"No, I'm afraid it won't. The best thing you can do is to get rid of it."

Bree pursed her lips as she glanced at Jenine. "Oh yeah? What's making you say that? Do you have a camera of your own that you're doing experiments on? Are you trying to stop us from stealing your thunder?"

She got a frustrated sigh in response. "Not at all. I'm trying to help. Destroy the camera."

"Yeah, well, maybe we'll take this straight to the media. I'm sure they'd love proof of life after death."

"Don't." His voice was sharp. "Whatever you do, don't give it to the media. Don't show anyone else. Just…please. You have to trust me. What you have is a dangerous, sick aberration. It needs to be destroyed before it can do any further harm."

"I'm going to level with you, Holt," Bree said. She leaned over the table, placing one spread hand on either side of the phone as she loomed over it. "I don't like you, and I don't trust you. Both of those facts are making it pretty hard for me to follow your recommendations. If you can help us, go ahead, but otherwise I'm going to have to hang up and do whatever I damn well please with the camera."

Richard was silent for a very long time. Bree sat back in her chair, folded her arms, and waited.

"Okay," he said at last. "All right. You win. What's your address?"

# FOUR

Yawning, Bree stretched her arms above her head, remind-ing Jenine of one of her cats. "Well, I'd say that went fine. Mr. Holt got to eat crow, and we get the supposed expert popping around this evening. Win-win."

"For us, at least. He didn't sound happy."

Bree stood up and carried her empty coffee mug to the sink. "I'll bet it's because he's got his own camera. He doesn't want us showing him up." She paused and pursed her lips. "On that note, we'd better hide it. He's a little too obsessed with its destruction for my liking."

Jenine picked the camera up and turned it over in her hands. "In a drawer?"

"Works for me."

As Jenine stashed the camera inside the coffee table's drawer, Bree rubbed her hands over her jeans. "You got anything else planned for today?"

"I've really got to do some reading," Jenine apologized. "I've got an assignment on Wednesday."

"It's cool. I can place orders for the store. Mind if I borrow your laptop?"

Bree set up the computer on the coffee table and sat on a cushion in front of it. Jenine made good headway on her notes, and Bree was considerate enough to move quietly whenever she refilled her coffee mug, which was often; Bree's creative output was heavily dependent on how much caffeine was in her system.

It was nearing dinnertime and Jenine was close to wrapping up her work when she felt a breeze on the back of her neck. The sensation was as cold as a gust of air from the freezer, and it sent goose bumps along her skin. She jerked away from the chill, but the room behind her was empty.

Soft fingers brushed her arm, raising the hairs there. "Bree?" Jenine jumped up from her seat and rubbed her hands across where she'd felt the sensations. "Bree, I'm freaking out."

"What's up, babe?" Bree leaned back from the computer, a pencil balanced between her upper lip and her nose. She had at least twenty tabs open to packaging sites and was holding a piece of paper covered in neat notes.

Jenine crouched down next to her. "Things keep touching me. I don't know what."

"What, like—" Bree frowned as she made the connection. "You don't mean ghosts, do you?"

"I don't know!" Jenine combed her fingers through her hair.

"Something cold. Like fingers. It happened at the park and again just now."

"Do you think a photo might show something?"

Jenine glanced at the drawer where the camera was hidden. Part of her wanted to try it, but the thought of seeing more of the entities sharing her home made her feel sick.

Bree wrapped an arm around her shoulder. "Hey, it's okay. It's probably just that you're on edge. You're reacting to every little noise, every breeze, and wondering if it might be a ghost. Just try to relax, if you can. Can I get you something else to drink?"

"No."

"Okay, then, how about you help me pick out some new ribbons. I'm low on gold."

Jenine nodded and tried to focus on the screen as Bree rattled through the options. She was grateful for the company. The warmth of Bree's shoulder, the sound of her voice, and the simple fact that she didn't have to spend the night alone was enough comfort to make her feel drowsy. She would have to do something about dinner soon, though. She considered taking the easy route and having a pizza delivered. She could even splurge a little and get the cheesy garlic bread Bree liked.

Bree's hand ran through Jenine's hair, grazed over the nape of her neck, and traced over her shoulder. Long fingernails scratched her skin, leaving burning cold trails in their wake.

Jenine jerked forward. "Cut that out!" Her voice was higher than she'd intended.

Bree stared in shock. "What, you don't like the ruffles?"

"Don't scratch me like that. It's a horrible joke."

"I…I didn't."

Jenine glanced down at the table. Bree had both hands resting on the laptop—and her nails were short. Whatever had scratched her had been long and sharp. She touched a hand to the burning part of her neck, and her fingers came away with a smear of blood on them.

"Oh…" She felt as if she was about to be sick. Her throat closed up, making it hard to breathe, and tears stung at the corners of her eyes. "Oh…"

Bree's face was set in hard angles. She wrenched open the coffee table drawer, snatched up the camera, and aimed it. Jenine didn't even have time to react before the flash blinded her. The camera whirred, and a second later the undeveloped image shuddered out of its slot.

Bree slid the Polaroid into the drawer, then hooked one arm under Jenine's and pulled her to her feet. "Come on."

She must have sensed Jenine was queasy, because they made it to the sink just in time. She held Jenine's hair back and rubbed her shoulder as she gagged and retched.

"You okay?" she asked as Jenine slumped, shivering, against the counter. Jenine nodded, and Bree offered her a glass of water to rinse her mouth. "Listen, Jenny, I don't know what happened back there, but it's going to be okay. That expert will be here soon. He'll know what to do. Just stay chill for me, okay?"

"Okay," Jenine mumbled, allowing Bree to lead her to a

kitchen stool. Bree squeezed her arm, then went to retrieve the laptop and the photo.

Jenine leaned forward in her chair, arms braced on the counter and her eyes closed as she willed her heart to slow. She wasn't sure she wanted to see the image Bree had captured.

*Wait...*

She'd completely forgotten about the photo she'd taken at the park. She stood and fumbled in her pocket for it.

It had come out well. She'd taken it from inside the car, facing the tree she and Bree had been sitting under, about twenty feet away. A couple of the picnicking families were visible at the edges of the picture, fishing food out of their baskets and playing with their toddlers. The ocean was mostly hidden by the thick bushes that grew along the park's fence. Two spirits were present in the picture. A boy peered out from behind the trees Jenine and Bree had eaten under. He seemed to be trying to hide but had leaned out just far enough to watch the camera.

The second spirit was a tall, gaunt man walking toward the car. His clothes gave Jenine the impression that he came from some remote part of the country where shops were uncommon, and mail came once a week. He held an ax in one hand; its handle was long, and its blade looked wickedly sharp. He'd been taking long strides toward the car when Jenine photographed him, and the skin around his bleached eyeballs was creased in a scowl. A stain on his overalls, large and dark, splattered up from his waist across his shoulder, leaving flecks of dark liquid on his cheek.

Jenine slapped the picture upside down on the counter. She could feel her heart thundering in her ears as she rubbed her sweaty hands together.

"Feeling any better?" Bree slipped into the seat next to her. She'd brought the Polaroid she'd taken, but placed it face down, out of Jenine's reach.

"Of course," Jenine lied. She indicated the picture. "Did you look at it?"

"Yeah."

"Is it…is something there?"

"Yeah."

"Can I—"

"Nope." Bree's tone rejected argument. "Not when you're this stressed. It'll only make things worse."

Jenine leaned her elbows on the table and cradled her head in her hands. Her heart was slowing, but the tightness in her chest wouldn't relent. "This sucks."

"It sure does."

Sharp, quick knocks came from the apartment's door, and Jenine flinched at the noise. It was too late for any other visitors; their ghost expert had arrived.

"I'll get it," Bree said, disappearing from the kitchen.

Jenine remembered the camera and slid out of her seat. Bree had left the Polaroid on the coffee table, so she stashed it back in the drawer as Bree opened the front door.

"Mr. Holt?"

"Yes, hello." The man's voice was tense, tight. "May I come in?"

Flustered, Jenine sat on the lounge and tried to smooth her hair back as Bree led a middle-aged man into her living room. In his black slacks, cardigan, and glasses, he looked like an old-fashioned professor. His face was developing wrinkles but seemed mild and gentle. Jenine imagined he could have been a comforting presence if he hadn't been so tense.

"I'm Breanna," Bree introduced them, "and this is Jenine. Apparently, you're some sort of expert on ghost stuff."

"*Ghost stuff.*" He chuckled as he sat opposite them, but it was a hollow sound. "Yes, I am considered an authority. I've worked on a few cases that made it to the news. Which one of you found the camera?"

Jenine raised her hand. "At a wedding. It had been left in a lighthouse."

"I see. Have both of you taken photos with it, or…"

"Both," Bree said. "But Jenny more than me. Why?"

"May I see the photos?"

Bree glanced at Jenine, who nodded. Bree fetched their collection of pictures from the kitchen and handed them to Richard. He glanced at each one for just a second, then placed them back on the coffee table. Once he was done, he pushed the pile toward Bree, almost as if he didn't want to touch them.

"You have what I like to call a *ghost camera.*" Richard sighed. "It's the third one I have come across in my career."

Jenine sat forward on her chair. "Really? But…I've never heard of them before. If they're as common as that, why aren't they publicized? Tested? Displayed in museums?"

"They have a rather dark history, I'm afraid," Richard said. He crossed his legs and placed both hands on the top knee, a pose that was simultaneously relaxed and guarded. "People who know about them tend not to discuss them. It's... I suppose you would call it bad luck."

"That makes no sense." Bree gestured toward the pictures. "We have certifiable, reproducible proof of ghosts. Why wouldn't people be interested in it?"

Richard wet his lips and inhaled deeply, as though he wished he could avoid answering. "The ghost camera has unique properties. Not only does it make the spirit world visible to us, but it makes *us* visible to *them*."

Jenine glanced at the pictures. More than half of the ghosts were looking directly at the camera.

"Normally the spirit world and the mortal world are intangible to each other," Richard continued. He held one palm out flat and laid his other on top to illustrate his point. "We share the same space. We cohabitate without realizing it. Like light and air, two substances can take up the same area without having any effect on each other. Well, barely any effect, anyway."

Jenine glanced at Bree. She no longer looked accusatory, but fascinated. Richard's voice was smooth and compelling and easily commanded the attention of the room. *Definitely an ex-lecturer,* Jenine thought.

"When I say light and air don't interact, that's not strictly true. Light can warm the air, and air can slow the progress of light. That's also similar to the human realm and the ghost realm. The vast majority of the time, they're intangible to each other, but there will be little instances, micro-events, that you may not even be aware of, where they influence one another. You might wake up in the middle of the night and not know why. Perhaps small items move when you're not in the room—never by much, just a few centimeters at a time—that you don't realize. Or your pets will stare intently at a wall—just an empty wall—as though they can see something you can't."

As if on cue, the largest of Jenine's cats leaped onto the lounge. Jenine reached out to rub its head, massaging the thin skin over its skull.

"Imagine two pieces of paper, one sitting on top of the other. This is a flawed analogy, mind, but please bear with me." Richard shifted forward in his seat, the natural excitement to teach burning through his initial reluctance. "Those pieces of paper are close, very close, so that when you look at them, they might appear as one. Yet they're separate. You can slide them, move them, divide them. Now imagine that a single drop of water falls onto the top page. It seeps through to the second page, binding them together. Yes, they can still be peeled apart, but not as easily. It almost, not quite but almost, fuses them together. That can happen in life sometimes. The spirit world will, in patches, sync with the earth and allow ghosts to interact with us. Of course, the drop of water dries quickly. It may take a few hours, or even a day or two, but it will dry, and the pages will separate again."

Bree was scowling, but her eyes were fiery. "You're saying that's what happens with the ghost camera?"

"I'm getting to that. Keeping with my analogy, everyday paranormal events are light sprinklings of water. Sometimes a location can be tainted when a life that passes over is so troubled that it drips water on the paper, so to speak, and creates a haunted location that, depending on the strength, can last for decades. These are your classic haunted houses." He sighed. "What you've found, the ghost camera, is like a glass of water that tips onto the paper every time you take a picture."

Jenine drew her cat into her lap and rubbed along its back. It purred in response: a comforting, safe sound. The enthusiasm was dying out of Richard's voice. He was sounding and looking older, as though the words were draining the life out of him. "Each additional photo dampens the paper further. Breaks down the fiber. Makes it harder to separate. I apologize—I've carried this analogy much too far, haven't I? Essentially, from what I have been able to deduce, the ghost camera makes the user visible to spirits. It marks you. Not just temporarily, like water on paper, but permanently. The more photos you take, the easier it is for them to find you."

Shivers snaked up Jenine's back. She petted her cat more vigorously, desperate for the warmth and comfort between her fingers.

Bree was at the edge of her seat. "Okay. Why is that bad? What happens when they 'find you'?"

Richard opened his mouth, then closed it. He swallowed and glanced around the room, looking everywhere except at the two friends. "They kill you," he admitted.

"What the hell?" Bree stood up, towering over the sitting man. "Bull. You're lying."

He continued in a rush, as though she hadn't spoken. "That's why you have to destroy the camera. Don't show it to anyone. Don't give it to anyone. Destroy it. That's the only way to stop others from being tainted with its curse."

Jenine felt as if her world were collapsing. She didn't realize she was squeezing her cat until it squirmed out of her grip, its eyes narrowed at her. "You...you can stop it, though."

"Yeah." Pacing the room, Bree pointed one finger at Richard but refused to look at him. "You said you found two cameras before, right? You know how to beat it."

Richard sucked air in through his nose. His voice wavered as he stumbled over his words. "The first person came to me two days before his death. We destroyed the camera, and I thought that would be enough to stop it, but he still died. Official diagnosis was a heart attack. The police found him hiding in the cupboards under his sink."

"Bull," Bree repeated, seemingly unable to stay still. Jenine's hands felt empty without the cat, so she picked up a cushion instead.

"When the second victim came to me, I tried everything within my power to free her. And I mean everything." Richard's face was drawn. Beads of sweat had developed on his forehead and cheeks. "Bathing in holy water, exorcisms, expulsions. Blessings by Romanian white witches. We burned sage around her. We tried to hide inside churches, in rural areas, anywhere. We did experiments on the camera and tried to communicate with the ghosts, and I called every expert I thought might be able to help. Only three were aware of ghost cameras, and none knew of any cure. She died."

"So, so, so..." Bree's panic was visible on her face and her voice was tight and high. She stopped pacing. "What do we do?"

Richard finally met her eyes. His were sad and resigned. "Depending on how many photos you've taken, you may still have a few days or a few weeks. Maybe as much as a month, if you only took one picture. You'll know it's near the end when you feel them touch you."

Jenine's fingers fluttered to the part of her neck crusted with dried blood.

Richard continued, "At that point, I would suggest taking a few sleeping pills."

Bree looked from Jenine to Richard. She had her arms folded, fists balled under her armpits, and her eyes were huge. "Will that help?"

"No, but you won't be awake for the end."

Both Jenine and Richard jumped as Bree's anger exploded out of her like water rushing through a broken dam. "You're lying!" Bree threw herself at Richard and grasped the front of his cardigan in her fists.

"No!" Jenine yelled.

Bree shook him hard, as though he might change his story with enough coercion. Jenine grasped Bree around the waist and tried to haul her back. For a second she thought Bree might really hurt the man, but then she relaxed, released her hold, and let Jenine draw her back.

Bree's face was as white as a sheet and her cheeks were wet. She stared at Jenine for a second, then looked back at the professor. "Oh… I'm sorry. I'm so sorry," she said. "I didn't mean—I'm so sorry."

Richard adjusted his cardigan and smoothed back his gray hair, which had come loose from its careful arrangement. His lips were tight and pale, but his voice was even when he answered. "It's all right. I understand. It's difficult news to receive, and I certainly don't like giving it."

"There's got to be something you can do," Jenine said. She sat next to Bree and wrapped an arm around her friend's shoulders. She could feel them trembling—she wasn't sure if it was from fear or anger—but Bree remained mute.

"I wish there was. I truly, truly do. But I didn't lie when I said I tried everything. I had an entire week with the last case, and when we weren't trying new methods of breaking the curse, I was researching. Ghost cameras aren't a new phenomenon; I found evidence of them as far back as the early 1900s. They've become rarer with the invention of digital cameras—for whatever reason, ghost cameras are only analog—but they still pop up every now and then. Every single case of a person using the camera to take a photo has resulted in death. The more photos they took, the sooner and more violent their deaths were."

Bree shuddered and slumped. She grasped Jenine's hands

in hers and squeezed them tightly, rubbing the palms with her fingers. Jenine squeezed back.

Richard looked at them, and his mouth tightened. He looked as though he were on the verge of crying, but he maintained a steady voice when he spoke. "You took a large number of pictures. I'd strongly recommend the sleeping pills when they start to touch you. You don't want to see what happens after that." He stood and turned toward the door.

Bree raised her head and glared at him with red-rimmed eyes. "That's it? You're just going to leave us to it?"

He hesitated in the doorway, shoulders hunched and eyes on the floor. "I wish I could help," he repeated.

"No. There's got to be a way to beat this!"

He turned back to them, emotions struggling over his face. "Look. I'm sorry. I really, really am sorry. You seem like nice people. I wish to hell this hadn't happened to you. But I can't help you any more than I could help someone with an incurable disease. Goodbye."

The door slammed as he left.

Jenine sat, numb, then carefully drew her legs up and hugged her knees to her chest. Bree leaned her head against Jenine's shoulder.

"I don't want to die," Jenine said stupidly.

Neither of them seemed to have anything else to say, so they huddled and shivered together as thunder crackled in the distance. A single raindrop tapped the roof, then a second and a third, and soon the sound of single drops blended together into the steady thrum of a breaking storm.

# FIVE

As she listened to the rain falling outside her apartment, Jenine tried to come to terms with her new knowledge. She was going to die. And not in sixty years, when she was old and had lived a full life, but in the immediate future.

She tried to take stock of her emotions and found they were missing. She felt numb, as if she were watching herself act in a movie. The professor-looking man had strolled into frame, told her she was a dead woman walking, then strolled out, leaving her to shrug at the camera. It wasn't real. It couldn't possibly be real.

Bree seemed to be dealing with the news in a very different way. She rocked, gripping Jenine's arm, her eyes dull as she stared at the floor. She looked sick.

Bree was a perpetual achiever; obstacles only existed for her to vault over. Seeing her look so helpless was a new experience for Jenine, but there it was: proof that Bree Abernackle was human.

"Bree…"

She shook her head and pushed herself off the couch. She stumbled, then crossed to her bag in the corner of the room and pulled out her cell phone. Jenine waited, uncertain what she should say or do.

Bree disappeared into the bedroom. When she came out two minutes later, her face was all hard angles, and her eyes were damp. She dropped the phone into her bag and leaned her hands on the kitchen counter, breathing deeply through her nose.

Jenine approached Bree from behind and placed a hand on her shoulder. Bree turned, offered a thin smile, and said, "He didn't answer."

"I'm sorry." Jenine wanted to smack herself as soon as the words left her mouth. Of all the things she could have said to someone who'd just found out she was about to die, "I'm sorry" had to be the most insipid choice.

Bree scrunched up her face and pulled Jenine into a hug. "Don't be. Not your fault. Anyway"—she pulled back and swallowed to clear the tightness from her throat—"we're not done yet. Holt doesn't want to help us, but that doesn't mean we can't figure this out ourselves."

Just like that, Active Bree was back.

"Here's the plan," she said, collecting their empty mugs and picking up the laptop in one deft sweep. "We're going to get a hot drink. We're going to do five minutes of meditation to clear our

heads. Then we're going to find a solution. So what if we don't
have help from the so-called expert? There's got to be a way to
beat this, and we'll figure out what it is. I promise."

———————

They sat next to each other at the coffee table. Bree leaned over
the laptop as she researched the camera. Jenine guessed it wasn't
going well, based on the quiet grumbles and hisses of frustration.

Jenine's job was to examine the Polaroids and note down
anything significant or unusual. They didn't know what they
were looking for, but they couldn't afford to miss any crumb, no
matter how small it seemed at first glance. Jenine had an eye for
detail, and Bree felt better when she could do a more proactive
job like researching, so the split worked well.

Jenine gathered the Polaroids—they had taken nine—and laid
them out in front of her in chronological order, then placed a
notepad and pen at her side. She counted at least twenty-eight
distinct ghosts trailing through the images, though several
specters appeared more than once.

She rubbed her hand across her face as she realized her collection was one short. "Hey, Bree, where's the photo you took earlier
today, when I felt something touch me?"

"Over there." Without looking up from the computer, Bree
pointed to the far corner of the kitchen counter.

Jenine fetched the Polaroid and drank in the image. Her own
face took up a lot of the picture: pale, frightened, wide-eyed. A
ghostly hand grasped at her shoulder. The hand belonged to an

impossibly tall man, so horribly bony he must have been starved. His mouth was open, and every visible tooth had been sharpened to a fine point.

She grimaced and lined it up with the others, chronologically last.

*Think of it as a law school assignment. There's evidence here; it just needs to be found.*

One element stood out as immediately significant. In the first picture, none of the ghosts were looking at the camera. Out of the five pictures taken in her home, the ghosts only seemed to start paying attention to her partway through the series. The turning point was the set of Polaroids taken in her bedroom. It was like flicking a light switch: in one image, they didn't seem to know she was there. In the second, all three spirits stared toward the camera, open animosity filling their faces.

After that, every single ghost was either looking at or trying to approach Jenine.

That matched what Richard Holt had said: the more photos she took, the easier the ghosts could find her.

Jenine felt shivers course down her spine. She turned to another mystery: the recurring specters. In the photo she'd taken immediately after filling the camera with fresh Polaroids, the ghost—the woman who had left finger smudges on the car's window—looked remarkably similar to one of the women in the wedding photograph. That raised questions: How did ghosts travel? Did they have to walk, or could they disappear and reappear in new locations? *Maybe if I keep running, keep moving, they won't catch me?*

She scribbled that thought on the notepad, then froze. For a second, she thought she felt a cold breath drift across the back of her neck. She swiped her hand over the area but couldn't feel anything. Bree glanced at her, a silent question creasing her eyes, and Jenine smiled reassuringly.

She turned back to the pictures. She found a second instance of a duplicate ghost quickly—a man at the wedding appeared later at the park. The second ghost in the park photograph was also familiar. A child stood behind the tree, his empty, white eyes wide.

Jenine picked up the wedding photo to make certain it was the same boy. He was also in the flower shop picture, barely visible through the window. Jenine sifted through the other images, this time looking specifically for the child with the empty eyes, and her skin began to crawl.

The boy appeared in seven of the ten images. Never featured prominently, he was almost always hiding behind a large object or looking through a window. He was unmistakable, though. His wide, hollow eyes watched the camera from beneath thin hair being blown by nonexistent wind.

Jenine was simultaneously repulsed and heartbroken. *Why is he following me? None of the other ghosts are trying to hide.*

She picked up the wedding photo again. Even then, she'd suspected the boy might have owned the camera. Now, that felt closer to a certainty.

"Jackpot," Bree whispered. Jenine scooted close enough to look over her friend's shoulder. Bree pointed at the screen. "Check this out. Among the droves of fiction, edited pictures, hoaxes, games, and irrelevant nonsense, there's a forum thread that matches our camera perfectly."

Bree had found a paranormal forum. Jenine skimmed the first post, which was from 2008. The author described a situation similar to Jenine's. He'd found a camera abandoned in the attic of a house he'd inherited and had taken some pictures just for the fun of it. He'd attached them to the post, and Jenine suppressed a shudder.

They were eerily similar to the photos she'd taken. Pale figures stared at the camera with empty eyes. Some reached out. One appeared to have a rope around her neck.

The replies varied from curious to downright incredulous. Jenine supposed that was to be expected. The fifth post took the pictures more seriously, though. It read:

An old colleague of mine used to talk about photos like this. He called them "death pictures." He collected them as a hobby.

Jenine scanned the rest of the post, but it focused on analyzing the pictures and coming up with theories about the ghosts' former lives. A few others continued the conversation for about a week, but the original poster never replied.

The thread picked up four years later with a post by a girl named Becca:

Hello, sorry to revive an old thread, but it's very relevant to my situation. I bought a lovely vintage camera from a garage sale (previous owner is deceased), and it shows ghosts in both of the pictures I developed. It's freaking me out! Is there anyone I should be contacting about this? One of the pictures was taken inside my home, and there are these white, ghostly people everywhere. Would a medium help?

A reply had been left the next day:

Hi. Full disclosure here, I know nothing about the paranormal. A friend sent me the link to your post, thinking I might be able to help. I'm a professional photographer with thirty years of experience. I've heard plenty of wild tales in my time, and that includes stories about "ghost cameras" (or "death cameras," as some call them). They're not only meant to show ghosts, but supposedly the user always dies shortly after taking them. Personally, I think it's an entertaining story, but ultimately just that—fiction. If such a thing really existed, it would be all over the news.

Becca replied soon after:

Thanks for the industry advice. It's pretty hard to discard it as fiction when I'm staring at pictures of dead people, though. Should I not take any more pictures? Is there anyone I can get in touch with about this? I've been searching the internet and I'm desperate for help.

Shortly after, there was a new post from a user called RHParanormal:

Hi, Becca. I may be able to help. I've extensively studied the area of possessed items, and I have had contact previously with one person who had used a ghost camera. Where do you live? Don't use the camera again, but call me, and I can talk you through what to do next.

The post ended with his phone number.

"Hey, is it just me, or is that number familiar?" Jenine asked.

"Bloody hell," Bree muttered. "RHParanormal. Richard Holt. I suppose Becca is the second person he claimed he tried to help."

There were no more posts in the thread. Jenine rubbed at the goose bumps on her arms. "What do we do now?" she asked.

"Keep looking." Bree was already back on Google, now expanding her search from just *ghost camera* to include *death camera*.

Jenine glanced back at the pictures laid out on the table. She felt queasy. The people in the forum had only taken a couple of shots each. She'd taken eight. She stood up and stretched her shoulders, trying to look nonchalant. "Actually, it's past dinner. I don't know about you, but I can't think with an empty stomach."

Bree shot her a smile. "Sounds good."

"Anything you want?"

"Whatever you have, babe. I'm not fussy."

Jenine started rifling through her cupboards. She grabbed a tin of fish, intending to make tuna sandwiches, then hesitated as a bleak thought occurred. *What if this is my last meal? Do I really want it to be tuna on toast?*

She tossed the fish back onto the shelf and picked out a bag of tortilla chips and a tub of salsa. She dumped them both in a bowl, poured the remains of a packet of shredded cheese on top, and put it in the microwave.

Bree was muttering to herself again, which meant she'd found a thread to follow. Jenine peered at the computer screen, but it was too far away to read. She turned back to her task and retrieved a tub of sour cream out of the fridge. She was peeling away the seal when an invisible hand grabbed her forearm. The touch burned like a thousand ice-cold needles being pressed into her skin, constricting the flesh and muscles and sending jolts down into her wrist and up into her shoulder.

Jenine screamed and dropped the sour cream. It sprayed over the tiled floor and her jeans, but she hardly noticed. The hand hadn't let go, and every second it held on, the pain increased.

She slapped her free hand at where the invisible wrist should be, but she touched only air. The grip tightened, and the ice spread through her body, rushing up her arm and into her chest.

Jenine, desperate, threw herself back and felt the counter's edge bite into her hip. A scream strangled in her throat as the pain in her arm turned blinding. Then, as abruptly as it had grabbed her, the invisible hand let go.

She found herself on her back, lying in the spilled sour cream. Bree was yelling her name and shaking her shoulders. Jenine felt sick, but she doubted she had enough in her stomach to bring up, so she rolled to her knees. A headache, the kind she got when she tried to eat ice cream, gnawed at her skull.

"Jenny?" Bree's voice was unsteady. "Talk to me, Jenny. What happened? What can I do?"

"I...I..." Jenine rubbed her hand over the aching skin. A bruise was forming on her forearm. It showed the distinct outline of a palm and fingers.

Bree looked down and let out her breath in a hiss. She hooked one arm under Jenine's shoulders and pulled her up. "C'mon, we're going to the car."

"Huh?"

"I found something that might help, but we can't do it here. Hang on. I'll get the camera."

Jenine hovered in the hallway, waiting for Bree. The hairs on the back of her neck were raised, and she had goose flesh down her arms. The house felt ice cold. She let her eyes rove over the furniture, the fixtures, and the photos she'd hung in the hallway. They felt alien, as though a stranger had come in the night and replaced everything with imitations. It was surreal. She rocked onto the balls of her feet and wrapped her arms around her chest, panting.

Bree reappeared, holding not just the camera but also a slip of paper. One look at her face told Jenine she'd made a decision. Bree's panic from before was gone, replaced by brute focus. "Into the car, quickly," she said, ushering Jenine to the door. "We're going for a drive."

The rain was coming down in thick sheets, flattening Jenine's hair and sending a trickle crawling down the small of her back. They ran for the car, feet slapping on the cooling pavement, Jenine's breath coming in short, hard bursts. Bree pulled open the passenger door and practically threw Jenine in, then slid around the front and into the driver's seat. She started the car, set the heat to high, and switched on the radio, turning up the volume until it was loud enough to drown out the drum of the rain.

"Where are we going?" Jenine had to yell to be heard as the car split away from the curb.

"To see the jackass."

Jenine frowned. "We're going to Travis?"

Bree snorted in laughter and turned the radio down a notch. "The other jackass, babe. The one who's going to help us, whether he wants to or not."

"Richard Holt?" Jenine shook her head. It felt fuzzy, as if someone had stuffed it full of cotton wool. "I don't understand."

"I found a blog that was talking about ghost cameras. This woman has a theory that you can talk to the ghosts to find out what they want. EMF tools, sensitive audio devices, whatever you can use to pick up their voices. She thinks some of the ghosts will help us if we can just communicate with them."

Jenine glanced at the bruise on her arm. It had turned a dark, mottled blue. If that was how they communicated, she wasn't sure she wanted more of it. "Has she ever tried it?"

Bree's laugh was shorter and harsher than before. "Nope. It's the best I could find, though." Without tearing her eyes away from the road, she passed the slip of paper to Jenine. "I wrote Holt's address down. Can you look up the directions?"

Jenine's hands were shaking so badly, the task took her several minutes. She could feel Bree watching her and was grateful she didn't say anything.

The road rushed away beneath them as one radio track blended into another. The drive should have taken slightly more than an hour, but even with the slick road, Bree managed to shave precious minutes off the estimated time.

The rain had only gotten worse by the time they reached Richard's home on the outskirts of the suburbs. It looked a lot like its owner: tall and meticulously neat. A low fence and pruned shrubs surrounded its perimeter, half hiding the shadowed building from sight. Lights glowed from several windows.

Bree parked on the street and reached for her door, but Jenine hesitated. "Are you sure we should do this?"

Bree's fingers rested on the handle. "You don't think we should?"

"He wasn't very happy to see us last time. Even if he has equipment to hear ghosts, he might not let us use it."

"I'll convince him."

Jenine hazarded a smile. "You're not going to threaten him with your tape gun, are you?"

Bree laughed and got out of the car.

# SIX

RICHARD OPENED THE DOOR, THEN CLOSED IT IMMEDIATELY. Jenine had just enough time to see he was wearing a heavy red dressing gown—his professor-ish streak ran deep, apparently—and his face blanched as soon as he saw them.

"Come on!" Bree yelled, banging on the door as the rain plastered her hair across her forehead. "Talk to us for a minute. It's raining! You can't just leave us out here!"

*He certainly can*, Jenine thought, wondering how long Bree would persist in the face of a locked door, but after a minute, Richard relented and let them in with a heavy sigh.

He didn't look happy, but he carried himself as professionally as he could in an oversized maroon gown and tasseled slippers. He gestured for them to come into the foyer and said, "Wait here." Then he disappeared into a side room.

Jenine gazed around the room. It was filled with expensive-looking furniture. She and Bree stood on a plush rug, which absorbed the water dripping from their clothes. She didn't dare sit on any of the seemingly antique chairs or touch the artifacts that had been carefully arranged on the polished side tables.

Large classical paintings hung on the walls, interrupting the dark wallpaper. They seemed wrong, somehow, and Jenine approached the nearest one. It showed a nineteenth-century family picnicking beside a scenic river. The man and woman reclined against the trees near their son, who lay on his stomach and gazed into the river. A blanket was cast between them, filled with plates of sumptuous food.

The scene looked so tranquil that it took Jenine a second to realize what was wrong. The family was dead. Gaunt and gray, they stared, slack-jawed, into the distance with empty eyes. It was as though the artist had taken three bodies from the morgue, dressed them in luxurious fabrics, and arranged them into casual positions before laying out a rich feast of fruit, breads, and wine as a twisted joke.

Jenine flinched as the door behind her opened. Richard returned, carrying two towels. He handed one to each of the friends.

"I'm not getting rid of you, am I?" he asked, resignation thick in his voice. "I don't blame you, but really, truly, there's nothing I can do."

"Don't be so sure of that." Bree toweled her hair aggressively, making it spike up at odd angles. She paced about the room, glancing at the paintings on the wall. "I want to try something. You're a paranormal researcher, which means you'll have audio equipment that's sensitive enough to pick up ghosts' voices, right?"

Richard snorted. "Of course I do. But if you're hoping to talk to the spirits, I'm afraid that won't work. I already tried with my last client. Ghosts don't think like us. I expect you're hoping to reason with them, but they're far too…what's the word? Instinctual, for that."

Bree raised her eyebrows questioningly. That was all the prompting Richard needed.

"Ghosts are no longer human. You have to remember that, above everything else. The best way I can explain is that they're like imprints of emotion. If someone is murdered, dies tragically, or has a mental break and ends their own life, the emotions and thoughts experienced immediately before death will be what makes up the ghost. Once they're created, they have no ability to learn or grow. A man who finds his wife has cheated on him, kills her, then turns a gun on himself will only ever be able to feel those last few strong emotions. Wild rage, resentment, self-loathing. He will never be able to let it go. Not until his energy becomes too weak to sustain him, and he dissipates."

"You lost me," Bree said.

Richard shrugged and put his hands in his pockets. "Ghosts are, essentially, energy. It's the same sort of energy that makes us alive, compared to, say, a rock. When a human experiences a significantly strong emotion as they die, they can imprint their energy on the spectral plane. However, it will slowly dissolve. Depending on the strength of the initial energy imprint—and how much energy it can find to consume—the ghost may last for a few years or a few decades. Very rarely do they last more than a few hundred years. This is why we don't have any caveman ghosts. They simply dissolved over time."

Jenine nodded, thinking about the spirits in the photos. She'd seen one who appeared to be from the Victorian era, and a few looked as though they'd come from the '20s or '30s, but otherwise they were dressed in modern clothes.

"So you're saying they won't want to speak with us?" Bree asked.

"Exactly. They're energy—pure, raw, instinctive emotion. They're past reason."

Jenine could see Bree chewing that over. Their gazes met for a second, then Bree frowned and grabbed Richard's elbow. "Can we talk? Let's talk. Come on."

She ushered him through the door to their left as Jenine watched in stunned silence. The door closed, and she could hear their voices—Bree talking animatedly, almost frantically, and Richard's subdued responses—but she couldn't make out any words. She turned back to the paintings as she waited.

The woman by the river had turned to face the room, her lips peeled back to show rotting teeth. Jenine started, took a step back, then leaned forward again for a better look. *Wasn't she gazing into the distance before?*

Jenine glanced at the other paintings. The one to the right showed two puppies lying on the ground, eyes closed. They looked as though they were sleeping. If they hadn't been juxtaposed with the corpse picnickers, Jenine wouldn't have looked twice. She leaned closer, and a shudder of disgust rolled through her as she saw the small cluster of flies gathered about the puppies' eyes.

The door opened and Bree and Richard marched back into the room. Bree looked relieved; Richard seemed to be trying hard to keep any emotion from showing.

Jenine was just grateful to no longer be alone with the morbid images. "Hey," she said to Richard, trying to lighten the mood, "do all ghost investigators collect horrible paintings?"

"Pardon?" He blinked at her as though she'd disturbed him from an important train of thought. "You don't like them?"

*It's got to be an art movement I just don't get*, Jenine thought as Richard led them out of the foyer and into a dining room. *Like how cubism's lost on me. Maybe those paintings are considered some artist's finest works.*

The dining room was decorated luxuriously, just like the foyer. A modern kitchen was visible through the archway and a large mahogany dining table and several large sculptures adorned the room. The sculpture nearest Jenine featured a mostly nude woman with a snake wrapped around her torso. She was caressing the serpent lovingly, even though its fangs were embedded in her neck.

"Wow," Bree said, turning in a circle to admire the space. "If ghost hunting is this lucrative, maybe I should change my career."

Richard laughed. "Actually, I started out in investing. I made some lucky picks, and now my dividends pay the bills. Paranormal investigating was initially only a hobby, but now that I can afford to, I do it full-time." He began pulling boxes out of a display unit tucked against the back wall. "This will just take a minute to set up. Would it bother you if I asked about the camera?"

Bree was instantly defensive. "What about it?"

"I take it you haven't destroyed it yet." Richard gave a heavy sigh. He pulled a large, old-looking machine out of one box and placed it on the table, then glanced at the handbag Bree had tossed into the corner of the room. "Do you have it with you right now?"

"Maybe."

"Go and put it in my study. Second door to the left in the foyer. I don't want the camera anywhere near this."

Bree picked her handbag up but otherwise didn't move. "Why's that?"

"Remember what I said about the camera being like water that connects two sheets of paper?" Richard was plugging cords into the machine. "It's a channel for hundreds, possibly thousands, of ghosts. Having it in the same room would be like trying to hear a whisper at a concert. Better to put it away, so you can only hear the ghosts that are fixated on you."

"Fixated?"

"The ones you photographed." Richard turned on his machine, and it let out a high-pitched whine that subsided when he adjusted some knobs. "They've seen you, and now they're following you. There are plenty of other ghosts around, but they don't know you're there until you take a picture of them, or until—" He stopped, cleared his throat, then busied himself adjusting various sliders.

"Until what?" Jenine leaned forward.

"Never mind. It's nothing to concern yourself with."

"Oh, no, I think it is," Bree said. "How will the others be able to see us?"

"Let it go."

"No."

Richard exhaled a sigh between his teeth. "As this...*curse*, I suppose you might call it. As your curse progresses, you'll move closer and closer to their dimension until they're able to see you, even without the camera."

Jenine swallowed. "Is that...bad?"

"That's why I recommended the sleeping pills," Richard said. "If this doesn't work, you won't have to feel them—or see them."

He broke off and stared into space. He seemed to be on the verge of saying something more.

Jenine took a stab in the dark. "That last woman, Becca, she didn't take any sleeping pills, did she?"

Richard jolted at the woman's name. His face scrunched up as though he was trying to repress memories. "No, no she didn't. I was with her at the end. There—" He took a gulp of air and moved to get another box out of the cupboard. "There wasn't anything I could do to help. I'd tried, I'd made promises, but she still... I hope you understand that it has been very difficult to help you both. After Rebecca—well, it's a situation I've explicitly tried to avoid." He paused, then glanced at Bree. "Please. Put the camera in the study."

Bree chewed her lip for a second, then she nodded, tossed her bag over her shoulder, and marched into the foyer. Jenine sat on one of the dining chairs to wait, her towel draped over her lap and her damp hair sticking to her neck.

"Can I ask you something?" Jenine leaned forward and lowered her voice. "After everything you went through with Becca, what did Bree say to change your mind? She didn't…threaten you or anything, did she?"

Richard let his face relax into a wry smile. "Unless emotional blackmailing counts, no."

"What then? Why didn't she want me to hear?"

He sighed and ran a hand through his hair. "She said she couldn't stand knowing she'd encouraged you to take more pictures. She said she wanted to try anything, no matter how slim the chance, to buy you some time. She said she didn't want to die with your blood on her hands."

Jenine groaned. *Stupid, kind Bree.* If she had any sense, she would have been spending *her* last days with Travis.

"This isn't going to work, is it?" she asked Richard.

He considered his answer carefully before speaking. "Technically, nothing's impossible…"

"But you don't think it will work."

"No." He looked ten years older than he had that afternoon. "No, I don't believe it will."

The door swung open and slammed against the wall as

Bree reentered. She was toweling her hair, which was wet again. Apparently, she didn't trust Richard enough to leave the camera in his study and had returned it to the car. "Did I miss anything?"

"We're just about ready now." Richard plugged in the last cable, which was connected to a microphone. "I built this device myself several decades ago. Under normal circumstances, it's not strong enough to pick up much more than faint murmurs, but—well, I don't expect that will be a problem tonight." Sweat beaded on his forehead as he glanced between Jenine and Bree. "I'll start the communications, but you'll have a chance to ask them questions, as well. Speak clearly, and try not to interrupt them when they're talking. That seems to make them angry. And keep your voice soft. They don't have any trouble hearing whispers." He pressed a button, and the machine hummed into life.

Jenine and Bree scraped their chairs closer together. In the silence, Jenine could hear the rain roaring through the trees and drumming on the windows. The machine gave out a faint, almost inaudible, whirring sound. Then a third noise became audible. It was faint and crackled as it came out of the speakers, but it was a woman's voice, talking rapidly.

"You don't understand. You *do not* understand! You don't understand…"

Richard motioned for the friends to stay quiet, then he leaned close to the microphone. "My name is Richard Holt. Can you hear me?"

The voice abruptly fell silent.

Jenine counted the seconds: *One, two, three, four.* Then the woman spoke again. "*You don't understand.*"

"Tell me what I don't understand," Richard said, keeping his voice slow, clear, and calm.

"Who are you? I don't talk to you. I want the girl." The voice was winding up, becoming higher and tighter.

Jenine could hear a rumbling sound in the background but couldn't make out what it was.

"I'm her friend," Richard said. "She would like to know why you follow her."

"You don't understand."

"Explain it to me, then."

"Give her to me." The voice had grown stronger. It was harsh and demanding.

Richard paused for a second before replying. "She would like to end this business with your realm. She wishes to be left alone."

There was silence for a second, then the voice broke out into something resembling laughter. It was the single worst sound Jenine had ever heard. The steady "ha, ha, ha, ha" was completely devoid of joy but filled with cold intent. The woman kept making that same sound, like a broken record, and the rumbling noise in the background grew in volume, becoming clearer. Other voices—dozens, maybe hundreds of them—added their empty laughter and rattling voices to hers, until it grew into a cacophony of pure noise.

Richard pressed his finger to his lips, urging Jenine to stay silent. Bree hooked one trembling arm around Jenine's shoulders and pulled her closer.

"She will never be alone again."

"She is ours."

"Give her to us."

"We want her."

"Cool her flesh. Break her bones."

"*Give her to us!*"

The lights around them flickered and the bulb directly above the machine burst in a shower of hissing sparks. Jenine gasped, and as if she'd flicked a switch, the machine was silent again.

They froze, barely breathing, as they waited to see if the machine was still working.

"Give her to me," the woman hissed, and Jenine felt her heart miss a beat. The voice was no longer anxious, but hungry. "Give her to me, and I will take such good care of her. Such good care. Like one of my own babies. See how much I loved them? My friends didn't understand my love. They didn't understand at all. But you will, darling, and I will free you too."

Richard's fingers shook as he folded his hands on the table, but he kept his voice composed. "She isn't yours to take. She belongs here, among the living."

The ghost howled. The sound ripped out of the machine, swallowing the room in the wailing noise. It was impossibly loud and sharp enough to break bones. Jenine clamped her hands over her ears and squinted as two more lights blew out in a burst of sparks.

In the flickering, struggling light cast by the remaining bulbs, she saw a tall, gaunt woman standing behind Richard. Her hair flowed out in a wild halo about her head. Outstretched arms ended in long, cruel nails. Dark stains coated her hands and smeared up to her elbows.

Her eyes locked onto Jenine and she crowed, "Come, my darling. I will take such good care of you. They didn't understand, but you will, my darling. I will make you understand."

The ghost reached for her, clawed hands outstretched.

Jenine shrieked and kicked away from the table. She landed on her back and scrambled away from the wild-eyed specter. Her back hit something. She looked up to see the statue of the woman with the snake biting her neck. The snake was alive, twitching and pulsing as it tightened its grip and dug its fangs deeper. Blood, bright and hot, dribbled out of the wound and dripped onto Jenine's shoulder. She shied away and covered her head, frightened to look, afraid to close her eyes, feeling as if her heart might give out at any second.

"Jen!" Bree shook her shoulders. "What's wrong?"

Jenine blinked. She could still hear the ghosts coming through the machine, but the spectral figure was gone. She looked into Bree's eyes and saw the confusion and fear swimming there. Bree hadn't seen the ghost. Bree hadn't seen the statue move. *Is it all in my head?*

"Up," Richard said briskly, looking pale as he gripped Jenine's arm and pulled her to her feet.

Bree wrapped her arms around Jenine's shoulders. "What's happening to her?"

"She can see them," Richard said, his mouth a thin line, his eyes huge with fear. "I hadn't expected her to be this far along, or I would never have agreed to—"

The voices became louder in Jenine's head, drowning out Richard and Bree and making her ears buzz.

"Find her. Find her."

"Strip her flesh. Shut out her light."

The bulbs fizzled again, and in the flickering shadows, the ghosts shivered into sight. Six nondescript shapes appeared near the far wall, then two vanished, only to be replaced by another dozen on the next light flicker.

Richard pushed Jenine and Bree into a corner, then placed himself in front of them as he turned back to the room. He raised his voice above the roar of the rain and the screaming voices. "Leave her be!" he yelled, arms outstretched. "She is not yours. She does not belong with you! You can take the camera, but you cannot have her!"

The clearest ghost, the woman with blood-streaked arms, lurched forward in response to Richard's voice. Her mouth opened. The lower jaw distended far past where it should have, and blood pooled over her tongue and dripped over her lips.

"Leave her!" Richard yelled a final time, right as the ghost reached for him.

# SEVEN

Jenine covered her mouth to muffle a scream as the ghost and Richard made contact.

The impact forced Richard against the wall, and he let out a gasp of shock and pain as the woman's nails dug into his chest. Her head tilted, the blood pouring out one side of her mouth, as she sought Richard's neck with her teeth.

Lightning washed through the curtained window. In that second of intense brightness, Jenine saw that the room was full of the otherworldly beings. Tall, thin, and decaying, they crowded around Richard, their mouths open in hungry howls.

A drop of blood hit Jenine's cheek, and she thought her legs were going to collapse.

*This is happening because I'm here.* The realization hit her like an electric shock. *I'm attracting them. I'm the drop of water, merging two worlds and letting them touch him.*

She grabbed Bree's arm and began dragging her toward the door. Bree was in shock, staring at Richard, her mouth open. She wasn't moving, and Jenine had no choice but to let her go, and then bolt for the exit alone.

Her legs didn't want to carry her. She got through the door to the foyer and stumbled, catching herself on the table. The faint light was just sufficient for her to see the paintings, which had changed again.

The puppies could no longer be mistaken as asleep. Their flesh sagged off their skeletons, splitting in places to allow maggots and bone to peek through. Their empty eye sockets stared at each other.

The picnicking family had moved, as well. The mother and father were crouched over their child, holding his head under the stream's flow, their mouths splitting open into twisted smiles.

"No," Jenine whispered. As she backed away from them, the puppies raised their heads to look at her, slivers of mangy skin falling off their skulls.

A hand clapped Jenine's shoulder. She spun, nearly slipping on the marble floor, to find Bree panting behind her.

"What's happening?" she gasped, her eyes bulging. "He's—he's—"

"I need to get out of here." Jenine turned toward the front door. "Can…can I borrow your car?"

"Borrow? I'll drive you." Bree grabbed her hand and ran with her. Lightning flashed, and suddenly, the wild-haired woman blocked their path.

Bree didn't—or couldn't—see the specter, and she kept running. Jenine yanked on her friend's arm to pull her back and managed to twist them out of the way just before impact.

She hadn't anticipated how quickly the ghost would move. It flickered to the side and was on top of her before she could dodge. Long fingernails dug into Jenine's forearm, and she screamed. Bree turned, shocked, and Jenine threw her weight at her, pushing them both out the door. The ghost held her grip and opened her maw to expose bloody teeth, which she plunged into Jenine's arm. Jenine felt the blinding, icy pain. Then they stumbled out of the house and tripped down the front steps, landing in a puddle of water on the lawn. Lightning flashed and the ghost was gone.

"Car," Jenine gasped, clawing her way to her feet.

Bree grabbed her elbow and ran with her through the pounding rain. She threw Jenine into the passenger seat, then climbed into the driver's side and slammed her door.

Jenine looked out the window. Thunder crackled, and she could see the ghost through the thick sheets of rain, still on the porch, crouched on all fours like an animal. She was searching for them, her teeth exposed in a snarl.

"What the hell?" Bree gasped, fumbling to get her key into the ignition. "What the hell happened there?"

Jenine opened her mouth but didn't answer. The ghost's eyes had locked onto their car, and it was scuttling toward them like a malformed insectile abomination. "Drive," she hissed, watching the ghost eat up the distance between them.

Bree turned the key in the ignition, but the engine stalled. The ghost hit the vehicle like a charging bull. The car rocked wildly, and Jenine gripped her armrests while Bree swore. The woman reared up to press her hands and face against the passenger window, opening her mouth in a silent scream as her empty eyes bored into Jenine.

Bree turned the key again, and this time, the car roared to life. She floored the accelerator, skidding down the street and kicking up spray as the tires shot through puddles. Jenine glanced into the rearview mirror and saw the woman scuttling after them but losing ground. She closed her eyes and tried to slow her breathing.

"What was that?" Bree asked as they rocketed down the road, narrowly missing parked cars. "Can you…see them?"

"Yeah." Jenine wanted to explain more, but she felt drained. Her arm ached; she glanced at it, and shock washed through her. The spirit's teeth had broken the skin and hot red blood was mixing with rainwater and dripping off her elbow.

Bree looked at the rivers of red and exhaled through her nose. "I'm getting you to a hospital."

Jenine leaned back in her seat and swallowed, trying to clear her head. "Do you have your phone?"

"Yeah, in my bag."

Jenine reached down with her good hand and fished out the phone. She dialed the emergency hotline, gave them Richard's address, said "Send an ambulance," and then hung up.

She wished she could do more, but going back would only

make the situation worse. She fervently hoped the ghosts had disappeared once she was away from his house.

The rain wasn't easing. They passed a few people hurrying through the storm, some struggling to keep umbrellas right side up, others just making a dash for their destination. The clouds were thick enough that the streetlamps had turned on, but their light didn't extend far through the downpour.

Jenine turned to look out the window. Her vision was blurry, and maybe she really was hallucinating, but they seemed to be passing strange shapes. "Bree?"

"Yeah?"

"Can you pull over a minute?"

Bree did as requested and parked the car by the side of the road. They were still in a residential area, where tidy suburban houses lined the street. A man was rushing through the rain, a suitcase in one hand, holding his suit jacket over his head with the other. Calmly walking past him was a ghost.

"Do you see that?" Jenine pointed at the spirit.

Bree squinted through the window. "The man?"

"No, behind him."

The ghost had stopped and turned to look at Bree's parked car. He began walking toward them, lengthening his strides as he got closer. He had more definition than the ghosts in Richard's home.

"Keep driving," Jenine whispered. The man broke into a jog and his face twisted in rage. Another ghost came out from under the awning of the house across the street. A third, an elderly man, moved toward them from the opposite direction.

"Drive!"

Bree pushed the car into gear and sped down the road. A teen's ghost ran to block their path, and the car screeched past him just in time.

"Okay," Jenine whispered, closing her eyes. She didn't know what would have happened if the ghost had been in the way of the car. She didn't *want* to know. They seemed to interact with physical objects like regular humans when they were around her.

Sickness welled up inside her, and she clamped a hand over her mouth as she retched.

"There's a bag in the back if you need it," Bree offered. "Hang on. We're almost there."

A voice in the back of Jenine's head objected to the idea of a hospital, but she couldn't understand why. A pounding headache had started, and her stomach muscles were convulsing from chills. "Can we turn the heater up?" she asked through numb lips.

Bree flicked the switch up as high as it would go, but the hot air did nothing to warm Jenine. Her vision swam as Bree skidded into the parking lot of the hospital, and her anxious feelings were suddenly validated.

What place has a greater concentration of suffering and death than a hospital?

As the car turned toward the emergency entrance, Jenine reached out her good hand to grasp Bree's wrist and stop her. "No, no, no, no."

Ghosts wandered aimlessly through the parking lot, stopping to stare at Jenine as the car passed. She looked at the hospital's automatic glass doors and saw a concentration of them inside, turning to track her movements with blank eyes as she neared. "No, Bree, we have to get out of here."

"What?" Bree's voice shook with fear and anxiety. "Jenny, you need help—"

"They're everywhere." She forced the words through her rapidly closing throat. "They're coming for me."

"Dammit," Bree muttered. "You better not be hallucinating, babe." She swiveled the wheel and began to pull away as an orderly exited the hospital's front doors.

The open doors released a spectral tide. Dozens upon dozens of spirits poured through the opening as soon as it was wide enough, weaving around the oblivious orderly and racing for the car.

"Go!" Jenine screamed, her voice high and tight.

Bree put her foot on the accelerator and the car skidded, wheels spinning. Jenine saw shapes falling and looked up in horror. Ghosts were jumping from the upper levels of the hospital, exiting through open windows, and leaping off the roof. They swarmed toward the car and dozens of hands pressed against the windows and hood. Jenine screamed and covered her face with her hands as they began to tip the car.

Bree felt it too, and floored the accelerator. The car jerked sharply as the ghosts blocked their exit. Jenine instinctively pulled her feet off the ground as the spirits disappeared under the wheels, and she immediately wished she hadn't. Nausea and tremors washed over her.

The car broke through the wall of ghosts and shot out of the hospital parking lot, attracting stares from the patients getting into their cars and prompting a wave of ghosts to clamber over each other in single-minded pursuit. Jenine buckled forward as her vision swam.

"Jenny. Jenny, can you hear me?" Bree's hand was on Jenine's shoulder, squeezing to get her attention.

Jenine forced her eyes open to look at her friend. Bree's face was as white as a sheet, and her eyes were round with terror. "I need you to help me help you. What do you need? Where do you want to go? Do you want to try another hospital?"

"No," Jenine managed. "No hospitals. Go somewhere—no people. Try the mountains."

"The mountains?"

"No ghosts there," Jenine said. "I hope."

Bree obediently turned the car toward the forests to the north. The mountains were sparsely populated, and only a few roads ran through them, connecting the two cities on either side. Jenine hoped a smaller population would mean fewer spirits as well.

She closed her eyes and tried to brace against the bumps and turns of the car. She was shivering uncontrollably and the pounding in her head had been replaced with a strange emptiness, as though the contents had been sucked out.

"You don't look good," Bree said, glancing at Jenine out of the corner of her eye.

"I'm fine," Jenine muttered. Sweat poured down her face and soaked her already-wet clothes. Her legs had started twitching. "Just need somewhere quiet. Rest."

Jenine lost consciousness shortly after they left the town. One moment, she was squinting, checking that the road was clear. The next, Bree was shaking her awake. For a second, the movement felt exactly the same as driving over the ghosts in the hospital's parking lot. The car had bounced across them as if they were real people. *Did they feel pain? Fear? Is it possible to kill a ghost?*

Then Bree's voice, panicked and desperate, filtered through the fog. "Please, wake up. You've got to stay with me. C'mon, Jenny. Wake up."

Jenine tried to say "I'm awake," but it came out as a mumble. She heard a strange whistling noise, and a second later, she realized Bree was hyperventilating.

"I should take you back," Bree muttered. "You're sick. You need a doctor."

"No, not back," Jenine said. She opened her eyes properly and saw they were in the mountains, weaving through the narrow, bendy roads. Bree was driving too quickly to be safe in the heavy rain.

"I'm so sorry, Jenny." Bree slowed and turned the car into a driveway—the first she'd seen for miles, probably—to reverse direction. "Even…even if we stay at the outskirts of town and call an ambulance, maybe—"

"No," Jenine said. She tried to move, but her body felt leaden. She twisted her head to look at Bree, and the movement took far more energy than it should have. "No."

Bree's face was drawn. Jenine could see the conflict in it. Fear about what would happen if she went back to the city vied with fear about what would happen if she didn't.

Jenine felt like she was dying. If she was, she wanted to do it peacefully and quietly in the woods, not among the grasping ghost hands in the city, not to be overwhelmed and drowned in them. If she was going to die, it would be on her own terms.

"No, Bree," she mumbled.

Bree let out a choked sob through clenched teeth. Tears were running down her cheeks, and she turned the car back toward the city. "I'm sorry. I want to help, Jenny. Let me help."

The car was moving too quickly. The narrow road was full of sharp bends, and only a thin railing protected them from the drop-off to one side. Jenine tried to reach over to tell Bree to slow down.

Something moved into the road.

Jenine's eyes widened as she saw the ghost—an elderly woman with long hair frothing about her face as her lips twisted into a snarl—plant her feet firmly in the center of the street and extend her hands to stop the car.

Bree didn't see. Couldn't see. Kept driving.

"No," Jenine choked. "Stop!"

If anything, Bree pressed harder on the accelerator.

Jenine felt as if the seconds were playing in slow motion. The car got closer to the woman, then closer—too close for Bree to stop even if she had wanted to—and at the last second, Bree saw her. She sucked in a strangled gasp, applied the brake, and swerved.

The car clipped the ghost. The woman snapped away under the impact, jarring off the hood and pavement in a way that made Jenine recoil as though she had been a real person. Then the car hit the railing and barreled through it, and they were falling down the side of the mountain.

The next moments were all motion, noise, blinding pain, and the harsh glare of their headlights reflected back at them. Bree screamed but was abruptly cut off. Jenine tried to lift her hands to protect her face but found she could barely move them. Her seat belt locked and jerked her body back with it, whipping her head forward and sending bright light shooting across her vision. Pain sliced into her face and arms as the windshield shattered. Tree branches, dirt, and underbrush poured into the car.

After a final, agonizing jolt, the motion stopped. Jenine forced herself to look.

The car was tipped at an angle, nearly on its side, wheels stuck in the scrub that ran down the side of the mountain. Jenine's door was jammed against the tree that had stopped the car's descent.

Jenine gasped, trying to draw breath into her burning lungs. Tears mingled with the sweat coursing down her face.

"Bree," she whispered, trying to turn her head against the strain of gravity. "Bree?"

No answer. She managed to twist her head around far enough to see Bree slumped in her seat, as loose as a rag doll, held in place only by her seat belt. Blood dripped from the tip of her nose and landed on the gearshift.

"Bree!"

She didn't respond. Jenine tried to unhook her own seat belt or reach across to feel for her friend's pulse, but her muscles had stopped obeying her commands. Slowly, gruelingly, against her will, her head flopped back down to rest against the broken passenger window. Each inhale felt like lifting a weight, and the more she did it, the weaker her muscles became.

Then she saw the camera. Bree had put it back in the car, after all. She'd probably hidden it in the back seat somewhere, and it had been thrown forward during the crash. It balanced precariously on the dash beside the crushed windshield. Outside, something moved.

A pale, ghostly being was picking its way through the underbrush, coming toward her. She tried, and failed, to close her eyes. She didn't want to watch it as it came for her, but her muscles refused her bidding. Her eyelids stayed open, her body stayed still, and for a moment she thought she wasn't going to be able to breathe, but then she managed a thin drag of air.

The ghost stretched its hand through the windshield, reaching toward her. Even through her blurred vision, she recognized him. It was the little boy who'd owned the camera. He extended a long and slender finger but stopped just short of grazing her skin.

Her pain was fading as darkness began to creep into the edge of her sight. The boy looked down at the camera. He picked it up, examining it like a child inspecting a lost toy. Then he looked back at Jenine. He placed his fingers into the crevices around the lens and strained. There was a pop and a crackle, and the camera broke into three pieces.

Jenine felt as if a heavy weight had been lifted from her body. She suddenly had energy again—not much, but enough to draw in a deep, long, hungry gasp of air. The motion jarred her body, and pain returned in waves, washing over her and making her writhe. It wasn't the sluggish, cold pain, though; it was sharp and bright and told her she was very much alive.

The boy only glanced at her briefly before returning to his work on the camera. Bit by bit, he picked it apart, pulling out the blank film, smashing the lenses, pulling chips of plastic off the case, and emptying the insides. With each snap and break he became fainter, until he faded to just a pale outline, a hint of a person. Then he dropped the last remnants of the camera and was gone.

Jenine lay in shock. Pain roared through her, jarring her neck, head, and ribs, making her whimper. Then distant voices reached her. They floated down from the road far above, and after a moment they were joined by a siren. She blacked out just as the first rescue worker reached Bree's car.

# EIGHT

CARRYING A BOUQUET OF VIVID-RED TULIPS, JENINE ENTERED the hospital room and approached Bree's bed. It was a quiet Tuesday afternoon, just after lunch, and warm sunlight dripped through the window. Travis was sleeping in a chair next to Bree, snoring quietly. Jenine stepped closer and cleared her throat.

"Did you bring me chocolates?" Bree asked, not even bothering to look up from her laptop.

Jenine shuffled her feet. "Um. No. Flowers."

"Dammit, Jenny." Bree rolled her eyes in an exaggerated fashion. "Honestly, I don't know what goes through your head sometimes. I'm a florist. Bringing me flowers is like giving an Antarctic researcher a snow cone."

Jenine flushed bright red. "Sorry."

Bree flashed a wicked smile. "I'm kidding with you, babe. I love them. Put 'em in a vase somewhere and pull up a seat."

Stepping around Travis, careful not to wake him, Jenine found a vase in one of the cupboards and filled it with water from the sink. "How are you feeling?"

"Looking forward to getting this thing off." Bree tapped her neck brace. "Doubly so for the leg cast. But everyone tells me it could have been worse, so I probably shouldn't complain. How about you?"

Jenine sat down, fidgeting with the edge of a bandage on her arm. "The cuts are healing okay. They say I'll have some scars, but nothing major."

Bree closed her laptop with a click. It was the first time they'd been able to talk privately since the accident, so Bree's next question wasn't a surprise to Jenine. "What happened? I'm guessing that, since you're still here, things are...okay?"

"Seem to be." Jenine glanced at her arm, where the marks from the ghost's teeth were still fading. She briefly explained what had happened after the car crashed, ending with, "And he just disappeared. I haven't seen or heard any ghosts since, so whatever he did, it must have broken the curse."

Bree chewed her lip. "Richard Holt said he'd tried breaking one of the other cameras, though, and that woman still died."

"I think it worked this time because a ghost did it," Jenine said. "Like he could break parts of it—the parts that belonged to the ghosts' realm—that we couldn't."

"That makes about as much sense as the rest of it. But why'd he break it? Every other ghost was focused on you."

"That's the part I can't stop thinking about," Jenine said,

staring down at her hands. "I'm pretty sure he owned the camera when he was alive. He was chased, or pushed, from the top of the lighthouse by the ghosts that were following him. I think he was afraid of the other spirits, or he didn't like them. That's why he hid all the time. But he followed us and broke the camera… maybe because he didn't want to see the same thing happen to you and me."

Bree looked away to gaze out the window. "Huh."

"I wish I could thank him," Jenine said. "He saved us."

"Wish he could have saved us a bit sooner," Bree grumbled. Then she sat up a fraction straighter. "Oh, damn, I completely forgot. How's Richard? Any news?"

"Yeah, he got out of ICU this morning. I went to visit him. He asked you to stop sending flowers. He says he's in danger of drowning in them."

Bree grinned. "Oh, good. I asked Nina to send everything we could spare. We owe him big-time."

Jenine nodded in agreement. He'd been a reluctant participant, but he'd still done everything he could to protect them when they were cornered in his house. She wouldn't forget that.

Travis snorted and shifted in his sleep.

Jenine nodded in his direction. "What about—"

"Jerkface? We're back together." Bree had a smug, self-congratulatory tone in her voice. "You should have heard him. Couldn't stop apologizing. I've got him wrapped around my finger, poor dove."

Jenine couldn't repress a chuckle. "I'm happy."

"Yeah, so am I. I'm not a fan of the bed rest, but damn if I haven't had a chance to sort my inventory out."

Jenine leaned on the edge of the bed to talk and joke with Bree. Travis's snoring created a gentle backdrop as they discussed ribbons, make-up exams, and sleepovers.

———

Unseen by the women, a small boy stood at the back of the room, bronze hair drifting about his head as his vacant eyes watched the scene. His slack lips twitched into something that resembled a smile, then he closed his eyes, allowing himself to evaporate like dust in the wind.

**THE END**

# PAYMENT FOR
# THE DEAD

---

THE NIGHT WAS COLD AND CLOSE AND SECRETIVE. A QUARTER-moon lit Pieter's back as he walked ahead, forging a path through the bracken. We did not carry any lantern or candles. The light would draw too many eyes and raise too many questions. Instead, we moved through a world that was dark in the way it only could be in the youngest hours of the morning. I pushed a cracked and worn barrow. Pieter carried two shovels.

Frost snapped under our feet but, mercifully, there was no snow. It had been unseasonably warm for a December. That had been a blessing for us; once the ground froze, the gravediggers would give up their work and the bodies would be stored inside the under-taker's vault until spring. People notice when bodies go missing from the vault. No one checks on them once they're in the ground.

Pieter cast a look at me over his shoulder. His face was washed of color in the moonlight. Deep creases ran from his forehead and down into the hollow points in his cheeks, then spilled out again to circle around his jaw. His eyes were sunk so deeply into his skull that I could not see the lids or lashes, just a gleam of cold light on their glassy surfaces.

It was the kind of face that had seen a lot of things. Bad things. Dark things. I had repeatedly tried to tell myself that Pieter and I were not the same, that we walked different roads, but the truth was, our paths led us to the same destination that night, just as on nights before.

We all have our morals. The ethical lines that we hold sacred, that we weave into the fibers of our identities. We rarely ask what it would take to make us step across those lines.

It was three mouths for me. Three small, hungry mouths at home, in a year when blight had set into the crops, and the corn and wheat dropped to the ground, covered in black rot. Those mouths superseded any imagined morals. They *became* my morals. And they propelled me then, like an engine beneath my feet, driving me toward the cemetery and the coins that would be palmed to me once my job was done.

Sparse trails of fog washed across dirt and through the dying plants like a painter's careless brushstrokes. They hung on still air, not quite thick enough to hide us, but enough to help disguise us. I didn't see the graveyard's boundary until we were nearly upon it.

A metal fence grew out of the dead weeds and rocky ground. The bars were thin and rusted, but they ended in sharp points just above our heads. A barrier to segregate the dead and the living. To keep the graverobbers out. To keep *us* out.

Pieter approached our secret entrance and tugged on two of the bars. They pulled away from the ground, a scream of pained metal lingering around us as they formed a narrow gap to slip through.

I left the barrow outside the fence. It would make the journey back to town easier but couldn't come inside with us.

Pieter held the bars up for me and watched the leafless trees and unmoving mist as I slipped inside. He was wiry and angular, and his neck stretched long as he played sentry. At that moment, he looked like an extension of the sharply cutting metal fence.

Flecks of rust clung to my coat and hands as I crept through the hole. Pieter passed me the shovels, then crawled in himself. His breaths whistled between his teeth. That was the only sound I could detect. I clutched the shovels against my chest as I waited.

Pieter turned left. I followed. I didn't know which grave we would be turning to, or who might be inside. I preferred it that way. Pieter handled the details. I just dug. It made me feel…less dirty. Less guilty. At least, I pretended it did.

I didn't know where the body was destined to end up, either, though I could make a guess. Medical students in the city wanted to study anatomy in a way that their books couldn't meet. They needed to feel the give of the skin under their scalpel. To clutch the weighty organs in their fingers. To peel and scrape and carve until they were down to the bones' marrow.

They paid good money for corpses to practice on. Pieter never told me explicitly that was where our quarry was headed, but there were few other buyers when it came to the dead.

We passed the Catholic quarters, and then the Baptists, before entering the Protestant section. We'd been in all areas of the graveyard before. Religion made little difference once the body was exhumed. Pieter wove through the rows, mouthing silently as he traced our path. At last, he stopped beside a headstone, his bony shoulders tensing and relaxing as he tried to warm up his muscles. "This one," he said.

The gravestone was small and square. I could have read the name if I crouched, but I avoided looking at it. It was easier that way. I plunged my shovel through the frost and into the ground.

The soil was harder than the previous graves. More compact. The burial wasn't as recent as I was used to. Normally, we only retrieved bodies that had been interred that morning. This one must have been from at least the day before.

That was strange. The medical students wanted fresh bodies only, and they were willing to wait for them. Any corpse older than a day would begin to lose elasticity from its skin and plumpness from its organs. It would mottle and swell and leak—and be near useless to practice on.

It wasn't the only odd thing about this trip.

Normally, I would have warning when a job was approaching. Pieter would learn when a funeral was being held and then slip me a note in the marketplace or under my door to tell me when to meet him at the graveyard fence.

This night was different, though. Pieter had woken me by flicking gravel at my window. I'd tried not to disturb my wife as I slipped out of bed, only to see the glint of her eyes watching as

I hurriedly dressed. She didn't try to interrupt or ask where I was going. Just like she never asked where the extra coins came from. She understood the urgency of those three hungry mouths just as well as I did.

I'd gone to the door on silent feet, afraid to wake the children. Pieter didn't waste time on greetings. "Double pay," he'd said as I opened the door. "But it has to be tonight."

I hadn't questioned it. The end of the year was nearly upon us, and the weather was turning cold. We would have precious few opportunities until the following spring.

A hole formed beneath my shovel. The exposed earth was dark and moist and heavy. Even though the grave was older than I was used to, I worked quickly. It was vital we were gone before dawn arrived.

Pieter dug his own shovel in near the head of the grave. He worked in bursts, letting me take the brunt of the labor. I was younger, and my chest didn't ache with every breath like his did. In between digging, he acted as a watchman. The graveyard was outside the town's boundary, and we were careful not to leave any trace once we were done, but the constant fear of a night sentry left us wary of every snapping twig.

I dug deeper, until I stood in a depression of my own making and the dirt formed a pile at the pit's side. Tomorrow would be Christmas Eve. With the year as lean as it had been, the little ones were not expecting any gifts. But after tonight, and with double pay...I could sleep for a few hours when I got home. Then there would be just enough time to get them something from the market. Oranges, maybe. Their faces would light up. They would show me the gaps in their teeth as they smiled.

It would be worth it.

Pieter stepped out of the hole we had formed. He stabbed his shovel into the dirt and then leaned on it, panting. His dark eyes slid toward me, quietly scrutinizing me.

I didn't know much about Pieter. I never asked. He never shared. Just in the same way that I never asked where the bodies were to go once we dragged them out of the earth. I liked not knowing. And Pieter liked to work in silence.

Something felt different about that night, though, in a way I found hard to describe. It was in the mist, fragile and damp and lingering in unmoving clumps. It was in the loamy scent that rose from the earth, cloying and bitter.

And it was in Pieter's cautious glances. He'd never looked at me that way before: as though I was a skittish horse that might bolt at any moment. As though there were dangerous words lingering on the tip of his tongue and he didn't know whether to let them out or not.

But he did not speak, and I did not ask.

*Double pay. No warning. This is not a standard job.*

A sound came from behind us. I froze, gritty hands clutching the shovel that was half buried in the grave, as Pieter's head craned. The noise whirred, growing louder and then passing over us. An owl.

An omen, my wife would have said. And not a good one.

Pieter turned his head and spat onto the grass. I shoved my

foot into the shovel, digging it deeper, then lifted the burden
of dirt and dropped it outside the cavity we'd formed. When I
turned back to the hole, I saw its base was alive and writhing.
Worms had risen from the deeper realms of the soil. They flicked
and squirmed as though struggling to escape. As though the earth
itself was poison to them.

I reminded myself of my new morals: the three little ones
waiting at home. The pantry that was so dangerously close to
empty. Then I plunged my shovel through the worms as I continued to dig.

Pieter joined me in the hole again. It was gradually growing
deeper, dropping us further into the dirt with every shovelful
expelled. Beetles peeled out of the sides, their glistening bodies
tumbling to the ground, their spindly legs writhing frantically.

Standing inside the grave, my head was nearly level with the
stone. It was modest. Most of them were. The wealthiest families
could buy monuments that stood above the others, covered in
elaborate carvings or topped with angelic figures. This stone
belonged to a common person. No less loved, but simply with
less means. It was the sort of stone I would have once I died.

I looked away before I could see the name. None of my friends
or relatives had passed recently, but I still feared the day I might
be asked to dig up someone I knew.

Pieter lifted himself up to sit on the grave's edge and dropped
his shovel at his side. Tracks of sweat ran down the creases over his
face. They weren't all age lines. Some of them were scars. I'd never
asked him where he'd gotten them from. He rubbed his sleeve

across his face, trying to dry the skin, but fresh perspiration dewed there within seconds. He glanced toward me again, strangely wary.

Something felt wrong. Dangerously so. Most of the time when I dug, I kept my back to the gravestone. But I turned to it then and let my eyes glance across it for just a second.

I didn't read the name. Nor the date of birth. But my eyes touched on the date of death, and my heart turned cold.

"Pieter." I let my shovel fall still. Dirt caked beneath my fingertips, itchy and gritty. I couldn't quite look at my companion, and I knew it was not my place to ask questions, but the sense of wrongness—the sense of *danger*—was growing worse with each second, and I could not hold my tongue. "This body was buried more than two weeks ago."

"Aye."

He didn't offer any answer beyond that. My gaze became fixated on one of the shiny black beetles that had fallen into the hole. It lay on its back, its legs clawing the air frantically. Terrified.

A body that was two weeks old would be useless for the medical students in the city. And it was too fresh for anyone who wanted bones for an anatomical display. I tried to think of who might want a corpse so far gone and came up with nothing.

"It's been two weeks," I repeated, in case he hadn't understood me the first time.

"I know." His features were emotionless. The cold blue moonlight splashed over his weathered lines and his scars, carving shadows across them all. "But orders are orders."

"Who *gave* our orders?"

"Thought you didn't want to know," Pieter said. There was something like a warning in his words. As though he wasn't sure I truly wanted the answer.

And maybe I didn't. I'd always kept as much distance from the work as I could while waist-deep in it.

The beetle continued to writhe, desperately trying to flip itself over but unable to. I tore my eyes from it to stare up at Pieter instead.

"All right," he said, and turned, his long neck craned as he searched the low-lying fog. "Keep digging. We don't have many hours left."

My back was sore, but I lifted the shovel again, plunged it back into the earth, and felt the reverberations run up it as it grazed loose rocks.

Pieter's dark eyes were nearly invisible in the shadows of his face, but I could feel them on my back. He was quiet for so long that I was half convinced he would simply sit in silence for the remainder of the dig. Then he said, "You know Magdalen?"

"Yes."

Everyone knew the woman in the shack at the edge of town. She'd been born into it, just like her mother, and had lived there her whole life, also like her mother. The house seemed to crumble and crack around her, but she never repaired it, even though, according to the rumors, she had more money than most in town.

The rumors didn't stop there. They said she took part in unnatural things. That she stood in the moonlight unclothed. That she painted symbols in blood across her flagstone floor.

That she made mixtures of roots and mud and strange plants and whispered arcane words into them.

People said that, for a price, she could heal your ailing sow or bring an untimely end to a cruel relative or fill a woman's womb with child.

Those whispers were quiet—passed discreetly between neighbors, never loud enough to be overheard—but they spread fast. Some of those whispers ended with warnings to stay away from the shack and the woman who lived inside. Others came with a more discreet implication that she would help in your most desperate times, when no one else could.

Just like Pieter with his grave robbing, Magdalen had not wanted for income this past year. It seemed the secretive parts of society thrived when times turned lean.

"What does Magdalen want with a corpse?" I asked.

"It's not for her." Pieter's fingers, long and thin and with bulging knuckles, tapped uncomfortably across the ground by his knee. "The boy's parents paid for it."

"The boy?" I straightened. Sweat soaked through my clothes, and although the night wasn't yet freezing, I felt deathly cold. I turned toward the stone I had avoided looking at all night. As deep as I was, it stood almost precisely ahead of my face.

The death date was written as fifteen days ago. The birth date was eight years before that.

I hadn't realized we were exhuming a child. I'd been so intent on finishing the work that I hadn't noticed the hole we were digging was perhaps a foot shorter than the others.

A sour taste rose in the back of my throat. It was not from the nausea I felt, though. I stared down, toward where the tip of my shovel pierced the soil. Shadows wove around it.

No, more than shadows.

Tendrils of smoke rose from the earth, as fine as the fog around us. They smelled of rot and acid and the grit of wet, decaying leaves. I pressed my sleeve across my face so that I would not gag.

Above me, still perched on the edge of the grave, Pieter stared into the traces of smoke with unfeeling eyes. "The parents couldn't pay Magdalen's price when their son died. They chose to bury him, saying it was as God intended. But then they changed their minds. After two weeks of grief and an empty seat at their table, they found the money they swore they didn't have and crept up to Magdalen's door. She should have turned them away. Two weeks is too long."

Feverish heat ran through my core, warring with the icy pall that had dropped across my flesh. I lifted the shovel and continued to dig, half with fear, half with a morbid, horrid curiosity. I wanted this job to be over. I wanted to return home. The edges of a shroud became visible. Only the rich were buried in coffins in our town. I knew to be careful once I reached the shroud, lest I damage the precious remains.

"Two weeks is too long," Pieter repeated, and swiped the back of his hand across his mouth, as though the words were poison. "I knew that. Magdalen knew that. But the parents begged, and so she took their money, and she made her promises."

I used the edge of the shovel to drag dirt away from the discolored cloth. Its folds were soft and damp. "What promises?"

In the icy light, Pieter's eyes were cold enough and dead enough to be carved from stone. "That they could have their son back."

Something moved under the shroud.

I leaped backward, my shovel raised. The gray cloth appeared to undulate like a living creature. A sound came from beneath. Wet, dragging. Like air pulled into collapsed lungs.

Clumps of dirt fell away from the cloth as a face-like shape strained against it. The sound came again, followed by an inhuman groan. The cloth's tight wrap was coming undone as the body beneath squirmed. It wasn't fighting. Not like the beetle had, and not like the worms as they twitched their way out of the earth. Its movements were slow. Uncertain.

I'd pressed myself against the wall of the hole we'd dug. The body's movements inched it closer. I jammed my shovel against the shroud to push it away. It flinched in response, pulsing, twisting, and a cry caught in my throat as one thin, spindly arm pierced out of the cloth's folds.

Its skin was the awful mottled white of death, both sunken and bulging, pocked with rot. The nails were coming loose from the fingertips.

The skin on the forearm bubbled and moved as an insect crawled a path beneath. The grasping hand reached out and dug into the soil wall above it, as though looking for something to hold.

The shroud began to slip away from the head. I saw hair—the most lifelike thing about the corpse inside—and then a sliver of one eye. Bleached white, sunken into its socket, it still swiveled to fixate on me.

"Two weeks is too long," Pieter said, and pulled his feet out of the grave so he could stand. "But Magdalen promised their son would be returned to them come morning. We've been paid, no matter what they decide to do with it. Bring him up. We need to get him to town before dawn."

I stared into the sliver of dead eye. My heart had risen into my throat, choking me with each rapid thud, as I looked at the child that had been too loved to be left to the earth.

And I remembered the three of my own at home. My moral code. The thought of them had driven me to this graveyard again and again, and the thought of them prompted me to move once more. I reached down and took the corner of the shroud, then pulled it back across the melted eye so it could not watch me any longer.

Cold mist traced across my limbs, mixing with the acidic scent of something unnatural. I had made my choice when I answered Pieter's summons. Come dawn, the grave would be filled in once more, I would have money in my hand, and I would be able to slink home and scrub my skin until it was raw and red and then crawl back into bed and try to think of anything other than what I had just done.

Come dawn, this not-alive thing from the grave would be its family's responsibility. Their miracle. Their curse. And they would have to decide what to do with it, just as Pieter said.

**THE END**

# DEATH BIRDS

---

RYAN LEANS OVER THE NURSES' STATION, FIGHTING TO CONCENtrate on his patient's chart. Three feet away stands a death bird.

It's not looking at him, and that's meant to be a good thing, but it sways slightly as it waits, its head grazing the ceiling, and Ryan's concentration is shot.

He hears Trace approaching before he sees her. Once, over beers, she admitted that she moves fast to disguise her limp, so people won't think she's weak because of it. It gives the tap-tap-tap of her footsteps an uneven lilt. Ryan would never say it out loud, but he always feels a bit safer when he hears that sound coming toward him. No one thinks faster in a crisis than Trace.

She wears the same deep-blue scrubs as Ryan. The nurses in general care get to wear pink—meant to feel warm and nurturing, he's told—but in emergency, they wear blue. It hides the blood better, neutralizing it into a shade of gray that's less likely to upset patients.

Trace barely looks at the death bird as she stops beside Ryan and pulls the chart at an angle so she can read it as well. "You notice something you don't like?"

"Nah, the chart looks fine. Just…" He gestures.

Trace pulls a face at the bird. It doesn't react. They never do. "I still don't get why you work here if you have a phobia of those things. Transfer to general. Or radiology."

"And escape your invigorating presence? Never."

Trace crinkles her nose as she grins, and Ryan almost manages to match the expression. He knows she's right. The birds only care about one thing, and that one thing is something the ER has in abundance.

But he'll deal with the birds for one reason: ER is about saving lives. It lets him pull people out of burning buildings. Metaphorically.

He could try to explain it to Trace. Out of everyone in his unit, he thinks she would understand the best. But there are some things you don't talk about, even with your closest friends. Just like Trace has never told him the full story behind her limp.

He glances up at the monster and forces it to blur into a haze. The bird doesn't seem to care that he's watching it. They have very little interest in the healthy and the living.

The creatures are tall. At least seven feet, and some of the older ones can get up to twelve. Long arms hang at their sides, the fingertips trailing nearly to the floor. If you can call them fingertips. The death birds aren't exactly a part of this world. You can't touch them. You can't even see them clearly.

They're easiest to make out when they're just in your periphery. If you try to look at them directly, they fade into a hazy black shimmer, like a mirage. A lot of artists have tried to draw the creatures, but they never come out quite right.

People like to describe their heads as crow-like, probably because their forms have the same inky blackness as the corvids. But their beaks aren't straight like a crow's. They curve at the end, the tip hooked like a bird of prey. Designed for tearing, not pecking.

And they're drawn to death like flies.

At least flies can be killed. There's no known way to get rid of death birds. And, for the most part, researchers have given up trying.

When the creatures first appeared two decades before, the world panicked. Depending on who you listened to, it was the end times, or demons had risen from hell, or aliens had come to eliminate humanity, or, or, or…

Very little was known about the otherworldly creatures in those first days. The only confirmed information was shocking: when they appeared, people died.

Television reporters spoke as though it was their last day on air. Highways became choked as people tried to flee cities for the perceived safety of the countryside. Looters and protesters burned buildings and terrified citizens fired guns at any shadow that moved.

Most world leaders vanished into an enclave reportedly somewhere in the Pacific Ocean, and there was a massive financial collapse. The chaos lasted for weeks. But then…life simply continued. The sun kept rising. Most people kept living. The politicians slunk back into their offices over the following months, and eventually the economy began to recover.

Gradually, more accurate information about the death birds began to trickle out. Except for the panicked blip following the birds' initial appearance, death rates had remained largely steady.

Twenty years on, it's widely accepted that the birds don't cause death. They just predict it, like the ugliest omen imaginable.

For a period in Ryan's teenage years, new theories on the birds would make headlines every week. Did they come from a different dimension? Were they proof of the supernatural? A lot of scientists supported the idea that the death birds have been with us for all of human history, and only our ability to see them is new.

Over time, the reports grew further apart, and Ryan stopped reading them entirely. The only conclusion that's ever been reached is that *no one knows for certain*.

That, and there's nothing we can do to influence them.

They make noise, sometimes—the ruffle of feathers, the click of a beak—but they can't be felt. Ryan could wave his arm through a bird and cause the smoky form to blur but leave no lasting impact on it.

There's no way to contain them. No way to kill them. No way to communicate…at least, not in any way they'll respond to.

They're a part of life now, lurking wherever death is going to be found, and humans have just had to adapt.

Not that anyone except for the edgy teenagers really *likes* having the death birds about. Ryan hates watching them stalk the halls of the emergency department, their heads swiveling slowly to peer into the trauma ward and ICU as they wait for their next meal. All the dark-blue scrubs in the world can't soothe a patient when there's a death bird looming over their hospital bed.

A second one steps into view at the end of the hallway. Patients and staff part around it like water. People have adapted to their presence, but there's still plenty of superstition hovering around—like the belief that touching a death bird will hasten your own demise (studies say no) or that looking a death bird in its face will bring bad luck (an urban legend, no statistics to back it up).

Ryan's supposed to be above that kind of paranoia. He cohabitates with the creatures on a daily basis and his luck's no worse than the average person's, but they still make his stomach turn. Having two of the creatures in sight means someone is going to die that night.

An alarm beeps, and Ryan flinches so hard that his clipboard slaps into the desk. A level 1 patient has arrived: someone critical. Ryan thinks, *There you go, you buzzard, there's your meal,* but the death bird doesn't react to the noise, and it doesn't try to follow Ryan as he and Trace join the other staff converging on the crisis.

The birds are drawn to death. But they don't cause it. They're more like omens, and omens can be wrong.

If he's good enough and fast enough, he might be able to drag another body out of a burning building.

The man on the stretcher is a mess. Blood streaks across his body and a breathing tube is being forced through a swollen jaw and down his throat. He's unconscious. Another nurse works to cut open his shirt, but there's something wrong with his legs. They don't sit right in their sockets.

*Had his feet on the dashboard during a car crash*, Ryan hears someone say, but he tunes it out as he pulls on his PPE. He doesn't need a cause. He just needs to know what to do to stem the life dripping away.

A death bird has entered the room behind them. He hears a soft shuffle, a muted exhale. Out of the corner of his eye, he sees it tilt its head, passively examining the body on the bed.

He does his best to ignore it as their team works over the patient.

---

There are two additional death birds waiting in the hallway as Ryan leaves the room. The man's still alive and is being transferred to the ICU. It's a fifty-fifty split whether he makes it through the night. Ryan wants to believe he will. He wants to believe it for every patient he works on.

He doesn't like the sight of the death birds, though.

They don't mean death is a certainty. He had a high-school teacher who kept reminding him of that. They're a warning, not a guarantee.

Ryan's seen that countless times before, as they saved someone they thought was unsavable and watched the shadowy creatures slink back to wherever they live. It's cathartic in a way he can't put into words, a victorious high he's always chasing, even if it's rare.

The death birds don't vanish this time, though. The man going to ICU wasn't their main focus. Ryan turns and sees another bird crossing the hall as it vanishes into a room. His mood turns sour as he begins to tally up the birds.

He's not the only one who'll be counting them. The hospital tracks death bird activity, and since the creatures show up on camera, they can do it through CCTV. It's a useful metric to predict staffing requirements and for preventive care.

On an average night, the emergency department might see two or three death birds hovering in the halls. On a bad night, it might rise as high as ten.

Those bad nights are usually during heat waves or on long weekends. But this is a Tuesday, the ER is about as calm as it ever seems to get, and Ryan counts no fewer than twelve death birds as he loops through the halls.

Trace was supposed to have clocked out, but he finds her in the ER waiting room, her satchel hung over her shoulder and her car keys in one hand, silently staring at the rows of seats. Two death birds stand in the aisles, swaying slightly. The automatic doors slide open, but the intended patient, a man with a kitchen towel wrapped around one hand, stops on the threshold. He looks between the two birds, then licks his lips and backs out of the waiting room.

"I don't think I'm going home tonight," Trace says simply.

As the automatic doors creep closed, Ryan catches sight of one more death bird pacing through the parking lot.

The waiting room only holds four people.

Not enough to justify this many death birds.

Something's coming.

---

Ryan moves fast as he tends to his patients. He metes out medication and fluids slightly ahead of schedule, knowing he might not get another chance later.

By the time the clock ticks past nine that night, whispers say the emergency department holds at least thirty death birds.

The last time Ryan saw that number was minutes before a catastrophic train derailment. Body after body was funneled through the ambulance entrance, strapped to gurneys, spitting up blood. Ryan had worked in a feverish state, his scrubs doing little to disguise the shades of red as he pretended he hadn't seen a death bird feasting on what was supposed to be his next patient.

Today he can still hear the screams. Still hear voices begging for help as the birds converged around them.

It's coming again. Maybe not a train derailment, but *something*.

The hospital administrators are scrambling. Staff who were meant to be off duty are called back on, including Trace. The excess staff linger in the hallways or help Ryan and the other nurses with their work, but there isn't much for them to do until the inevitable event arrives.

The seismology institute has been asked to report any risk of an earthquake—minimal to none. Requests are put out for any reports of gathering death birds within a twenty-mile radius of the hospital. Airports, sporting venues, and theaters are contacted. There are a couple of birds scattered around a nearby intersection, and social media posts identify another bird just down the road from the hospital, but so far, they have no real clue about where their catastrophe is going to come from.

Ryan's pulse runs hot and fast as he files paperwork to keep busy. Two death birds linger behind the counter, their beaks flexing open and closed again. They're growing impatient.

Trace's uneven footsteps announce her arrival before she appears around the corner. She rests one hand on the counter, her voice low and hurried. "Current count's up to fifty. Admin's called in backup from other hospitals."

Fifty death birds. More than Ryan has ever seen in one location before. The screams and gasps of blood-choked lungs echo in the back of his mind. Trace is waiting for a response, and he thinks he says something, but he can't hear his own words under the soft *rasp rasp* of the creatures' shuffling feathers.

---

Their hospital makes the eleven o'clock news. Ryan watches it on the waiting room television until a triage nurse switches the channel. The news anchor advises patients with non-life-threatening concerns to go to different hospitals instead, to leave beds free for whatever is about to happen. Ambulances slip in and out of the hospital's bay, transferring patients away or simply circling close by.

Promises of support are already flowing in from the district officials. Extra blood transfusions are being rushed into the hospital. Extra surgeons, extra nurses, extra bandages and oxygen and coagulants and portable X-ray machines.

Their preparations do nothing to stop the death birds. Sixty, then seventy, and by the time the clock moves past midnight, the official count is close to a hundred.

The waiting room chairs are empty. With so many staff, any new arrivals are assessed and treated immediately, and then either transferred to another hospital or discharged to go home.

But, considering how slow the night is, the halls are packed. Not just with staff, but with the ghastly carrion creatures. They dip their heads and lurch from side to side and shuffle long pinion feathers. They pace and pant. One bird stares Ryan directly in the face, and he has to stagger into a bathroom to be sick.

He's just emerged back into the hall when his arm is clasped in a tight, slightly clammy hand.

"*There* you are," Finn says, and pulls him back toward the desk. "I'm trying to get the team together to go over a plan. We can't keep wandering all over the place like this, not with as many *Mortuus carrinae* as we've got."

He's the only person Ryan has ever met who religiously uses the death birds' scientific name.

Trace is already at the desk, two of the birds hovering just behind her, and she drums her pen against the palm of her hand, a tic that barely hides her frustration. As their charge nurse, Finn is in control of the department, but he's a nitpicky blur of anxiety even on a calm day.

Technically, Ryan can't complain about the impromptu meeting. He's cleared his plate of work. He cleared it hours ago. Every fiber of his being is braced for the inevitable impact that's about to arrive, and as Finn begins to talk about the importance of maintaining handwashing procedures in an emergency, he feels like he's going to scream.

He looks to Trace for an empathetic eye roll, and that's when he sees it. The two death birds that stand behind her aren't just *lingering*. They're watching Trace, their blurred and distorted beaks clicking open and closed with anticipation.

He glances toward Finn. Three more birds are converging toward the charge nurse in shuffling, impatient movements.

*We were wrong. Survivors from the disaster aren't going to be brought here.* Ryan's heart turns leaden, and a whining pitch rises in his ears. *We* are *the disaster.*

Death birds might linger nearby in the last hours of life, but they only really start staring when there are just minutes left. Trace drums the pen on her palm, her jaw working, the lines around her eyes etched with tension and frustration, and she has no idea that two of the creatures are prophesying her last seconds on earth.

Ryan reaches for her, his mouth open, right as the pristine tiles beneath his feet began to shake.

Finn's monologue breaks off midsentence as his eyes turn toward the ceiling.

One heartbeat, the world is clean and ordered and predictable. Then Ryan's heart pulses one more time, and the world he knows is gone.

The ceiling bulges downward. Lightning-bolt shaped scars spread across the edges of the floor, peeling the vinyl tiles away from the walls. The ground shudders under them, and every bone in Ryan's body vibrates with it.

Chunks of the ceiling shatter free and crumple toward them. Trace stares at Ryan through the showering plaster and concrete dust. She's frozen, shocked into uncharacteristic stillness, and the death birds lean toward her.

Ryan staggers forward as the buckling floor threatens to tip him. He catches Trace's arm. And he pulls, just as the entire hospital collapses.

---

Ryan was ten years old, and the house was burning around him.

His mother fought to breathe through a throat torn open. She dragged herself across the floor using one forearm, the other trailing limply behind her as vicious red embers singed the back of her shoulders.

A death bird followed her, pacing through the line of red she'd painted in her wake.

The death birds had appeared a week before, and the world had been gripped in a frenzy of terror. On Monday evening, the rarely used television in Ryan's living room was turned on to the news station and then stayed on around the clock as reporters with loud, ragged voices talked about the monsters roaming through suburbia. On Tuesday, Ryan's parents kept him home, even though it was a school day. On Wednesday, his father made a final emergency trip to the grocery store and came back with bags bulging with whatever food he'd been able to find in the nearly-gutted shelves. From that point on, no one was allowed to leave the house.

The TV finally turned off on Thursday, when rolling blackouts cut the power. Ryan's mother paced the house, checking that every door and window was sealed and making sure no one could see through any gaps in the curtains.

For that entire week, Ryan barely spoke. He was scared that if he opened his mouth, he might let slip how amazing he thought the death birds were. He stayed up late, hunched behind the kitchen counter where his parents wouldn't see him, to watch the blurry photos and scrambling eyewitness accounts on the TV.

The feathered beings were as close to magic as anything he'd seen before. He was at the age where he'd begun to realize that none of the fantasies his storybooks promised were real: there were no talking tigers, no magical worlds hidden in the back of wardrobes. No Santa Claus.

And then the death birds appeared and reversed that aging in a heartbeat.

They were genuine monsters. Everyone said it. You couldn't touch them; you couldn't kill them.

But they could kill *you*. Like the grim reaper brought to life, like Hades stepping out of his underworld domain. Death, personified.

He wanted to see one. Badly. When his parents told him to stay in his room, he'd hunch by his window, the curtain's corner pushed back, and watch the street below. Sometimes he'd see people who were bolder than his family, people who had stepped out of the perceived safety of their homes. No matter how many hours he spent watching, he never saw one of the birds.

Behind closed doors and when they thought he wouldn't hear, his parents talked about a news segment that had been aired repeatedly. In it, a man said the death birds were demons. That anyone whose body had been defiled by the monsters would be damned for an eternity.

By Friday, the news reported rumors that the water mains would be shut off. Ryan's parents filled their bathtub and every saucepan and bucket they owned, just so they would have something to drink. Gunshots rang through the night and the power cut out three more times.

By the early hours of Saturday, Ryan's parents seemed to have come to a decision. Their faces looked different to Ryan now, like a decade of their life had been drained out of them overnight. They told Ryan to put on comfortable clothes and collect his favorite toy, and then they left the house together for the first time in five days.

They drove for hours. Ryan begged to stop for food, but his mother just passed him a packet of dried fruit and a bottle of water.

It was dark when they finally stopped, but Ryan still recognized where they were. It was the lakeside cabin they'd visited last spring. It was a rental, and this time there was no one to give them a key. Ryan's father had to break one of the glass panes on the door and reach inside to unlock it.

Ryan's parents spent the next hour making their son comfortable. They brought blankets into the main room and turned them into a puffy, sagging tent for Ryan to sit inside. He was given more dried fruit and chocolate and bottles of water.

While they worked, his parents talked, but only in fragments of ideas. *Far enough out, I'd say*. Or *It should be fine. It won't take more than ten minutes.*

They were excited. Frightened, too, but their eyes shone with the kind of eagerness Ryan only saw with other children on the playground, like when a game of pirates versus skeletons got really exciting. When the world felt extra sharp and extra powerful, and you could taste the salty air in your lungs when you breathed in.

His parents didn't seem to be playing a game, though. His mother gave him four tablets and told him to swallow them, but Ryan was getting scared, and when she looked away, he hid the tablets in the piles of blankets. She told him to lie down, and he did.

His father carried in a huge carton that smelled like the gas station and spilled the slick liquid into each room. The cabin started to stink, and Ryan didn't want to be inside his collapsing blanket fort anymore, but he also didn't want his mother to stop stroking his hair and talking soft nonsense to him.

"They won't get us," she kept saying to Ryan, all tenderness and comfort, as though this was what he wanted to hear. "Our bodies will be gone before they do. It's going to be okay."

Ryan knew she was talking about the death birds, and he didn't want to tell her that he'd finally seen one. A huge shape, not much more than a blur that resembled a curved beak and rustling feathers, had moved past the window minutes before.

"Is he ready?" Ryan's father asked.

"I think so," his mother replied.

They both kissed Ryan's forehead. They told him they loved him. They said he should close his eyes. And then they moved to the opposite side of the cabin and faced away from him, and Ryan knew something very bad was about to happen. But he didn't know how to make it stop so he just lay still like he'd been told to.

Something dark moved in the room's corner, and a death bird, nearly ten feet tall, passed by Ryan's hiding place and stalked toward his parents.

They each held something in their hands. They glanced toward one another—a final, unspoken look—then raised the jagged shapes. Too late, Ryan saw they were holding knives. Too late, he opened his mouth.

Both of their arms moved in tandem, pulling back in a sharp, sawing motion. In tandem, they fell.

Two more death birds passed Ryan's tent. They were focused on Ryan's father.

He closed his eyes so hard that he saw stars and dragged the blankets up over his head.

The gas station stink was fading, but it was being replaced by the burn of smoke. Ryan didn't dare move. He was crying and he couldn't stop. The blankets blocked out the sights, but he could still hear the sounds. The rustle of feathers. The clatter of eager beaks. The *thump, thump, thump* of his mother struggling against the floor.

The smoke was growing worse, and with it came heat. Ryan pulled the blanket away from his face. Dancing flames raced across the floor and licked up walls.

The three death birds tore at Ryan's father.

And his mother…

Red blood sprayed from her severed artery. Her lips were parted as she gasped for air that wasn't reaching her lungs. Her eyes were wide and bulging with terror as embers spiraled around her, but it wasn't the terror of death. She'd seen the birds. One arm stretched ahead of her, dragging her away from them an inch at a time.

Ryan choked on the building smoke. It was growing hard to see. To his right was the door. Flames were licking close to it, but not yet there.

*Thump, drag, thump.* Her twitching hand grasped toward him, but she no longer looked like his mother, and it was a week since she'd really felt like it, and her bulging, bloodshot eyes and gaping, drenched flesh horrified him, and he ran.

Through the burning smoke. Past flames that were so hot he thought his shirt was going to melt into his skin. Out the door.

Ryan spat clumps of black phlegm as he collapsed into the dirt outside the cabin. Already, the roof was entirely ablaze. Trees nearby began to catch fire.

The door stood open, but he could no longer see his parents through the flames and smoke. Just the rise and fall of three feasting death birds.

He wanted to crawl back in through the smoldering doorway and drag his mother and father out. He wanted to be a superhero.

More than anything, he wanted his parents to come back for him, to snatch him up from the dirt and carry him back to the car and drive back to the world as it had existed before the *Mortuus carrinae* had appeared and made everything go bad.

But his parents never left the cabin again. The smoke rose like a languid river into the sky, toxic black and feeling as permanent as the stars.

There was no one around. The drive into the mountains had taken hours, and the cabin had no neighbors. Ryan felt sicker than he ever had in his life. Too sick to even cry.

Finally, as the house began to collapse in on itself, the death birds came outside.

The three creatures felt impossibly enormous as their smudged forms stopped ahead of him. They didn't move, and they made no noise. He looked up at their unreadable faces, at the dark holes that were their eyes, and he knew they were waiting for him now.

And he understood. He was going to die there in front of the cabin.

The abrupt fear gave him strength. Enough to get to his feet. He thought the death birds would try to stop him—shove him back to the earth, stand over him until his time was up—but they didn't.

And so he started walking.

They followed, their feathers scraping with each swaying step, their heads tilting as they watched him.

He knew if he stopped, they would come for him. And so he coughed cold air through damaged lungs and rubbed grit out of his eyes and kept moving.

He walked through the night and most of the next day. His feet were covered in blisters and his head felt like it was on fire by the time he reached the main road.

Ryan stood there, staring at the cracked, painted lines on the asphalt, and the death birds stood behind him. They stayed like that until a car's headlights appeared in the distance, and then they simply vanished back into the shadows.

---

For a second, Ryan believes he's back in the cabin again. Smoke burns his lungs and blinds his eyes. Only it's not smoke—it's dust. Tons of it, filling every inch of breathable air, coating every surface in a fine powder of cement.

He can't see. He fumbles his cell phone out of his pocket. Taps the flashlight button. His fingers are already so coated that it takes a few attempts for the phone to register his touch. Then the light comes on and he holds it up.

He's no longer in a hallway, but a hellish crisscross of rebar and slabs of what used to be the walls and ceiling. It's a cramped cave, a tight little nook with tunnels burrowing in every conceivable direction. He's in a pocket with barely enough room to sit upright, and tidal waves of pain run down his neck and his right arm. In the distance, bare electric cables spark.

Something warm shifts against his thigh. There's a sound: a choke, a gurgle. He turns his light. Trace is there, collapsed against him. Blood trails from a gash in her cheek, spills into her open mouth. She's not entirely conscious. Panic stabs through him even as muscle memory kicks in.

*Stabilize her neck. Don't move her without assistance. Watch her breathing—*

But she's not breathing. Not properly. Blood gluts over her lips as she chokes on it, and Ryan has to press himself sideways and jam a bruised hip against metal in order to get his arms around Trace. He turns her as tenderly as he can, fighting to keep her neck straight and supported, to let the fluids drain out of her airways.

There's a shuffle of feathers nearby, and Ryan doesn't even need his light to know a death bird is watching.

It couldn't have been an earthquake. Something strong enough to drop the entire emergency department would have impacted the rest of the city; there would have been a death bird on every street corner. No. Whatever happened was localized.

*Something to do with the gas pipes beneath the building, maybe. A fault in them. An explosion.*

It's the only explanation that makes any kind of sense. The death bird's feathers ruffle again, and the sound could have been snatched right out of the recurring nightmares of the night he lost his parents. Ryan finally forces himself to look up.

There's no bird standing over them, like he'd thought. Of course not. They don't need to wait for the injured and trapped to die when the rubble already contains a feast.

Tentatively, Ryan raises his phone. Rapid movement comes from behind a slab of concrete. A crouched bird's feathers flick upward every time its body jerks. It's feeding.

Ryan needs to know. He keeps one hand on Trace's shoulder as he stretches himself up, his head pressing against the jagged ceiling of their cave, in order to see what the creature's fixated on.

Finn lies behind the concrete slab. Even without the death birds there, Ryan would have known he was dead. His body's twisted, one leg pinned beneath him. The crumbling building stabbed two lengths of rebar through his chest and stomach and held him partially suspended in the air. A pool of red drips down the metal and turns a pallid gray as the settling dust coats it.

Two death birds eat at him. Their beaks stab into his chest, between the pieces of rebar, and tear backward. Finn's body doesn't move—doesn't so much as shiver as the crooked beaks carve into it—but it's clear they're consuming something from inside him.

That was what fueled most of the terror in the early days. No one knew what the birds ate, or why they could only get it from the dead. Weighing the bodies pre- and postmortem revealed no difference. Photographs of the process only showed the blur of ravenous beaks. But the birds were eating, there was no mistaking that. And now they eat at Finn eagerly, decadently, and will continue for several more minutes.

Ryan drops back, coughing as the dust clogs his lungs. Trace is alive. At least for the moment. But that came at the cost of letting Finn die.

He'd seen the birds at his supervisor's back. And he'd focused on Trace instead.

He tries to ignore the sounds coming from the feasting birds as he looks down at her. The rise and fall of her chest is a jagged, pained movement.

He's an ER nurse. This is his bread and butter. And yet he's sitting stupidly, staring at a bleeding woman, and not doing anything about it. He could slap himself.

Instead, he spits, clearing grit from his mouth, and then begins to triage his friend.

Airways first: you can't support life if there's no oxygen. Trace is breathing, and he doesn't like the way it sounds, but it's better than silence. He fights to keep her neck stable as he parts her lips and checks inside her mouth, just to be sure there's no obstruction. There's still blood rolling over her tongue, but he thinks it's come from the gash in her cheek. Something—a piece of metal?—has cut through the skin, allowing blood to pool in her mouth. He'll have to be careful she doesn't choke on it.

Ryan tastes salt through the dust. He's started crying and doesn't know how to stop.

He feels around her throat to take a pulse. This would normally be done by machines, as well as an immediate CT scan to assess for potential bleeds in her cranial cavity. She's not responsive, and that frightens him.

Ryan's fingers shake too much to get a good read on her pulse. He lifts his phone with his other hand as he tries to scan the rest of her body. The space is too cramped; he can't see her properly, and there's no room to work alongside her.

But there's a lot of blood. It spreads out from beneath her in a sluggish wave.

*You were only a child*, the counselors told him. *You couldn't stop it.*

He's not a child anymore. He's no longer powerless.

Ryan holds his phone between his teeth as he reaches around Trace, trying to examine her in the narrow cave they're trapped in. He pulls her shirt up first. Discoloration blooms across half of her chest. Multiple displaced fractures to the ribs. Potentially punctured lungs or punctures to the pleural sac. It would explain the pained breathing if her lung was collapsing.

But it doesn't explain the bleeding. There's already more of it. Too much.

Nerve pain sparks down Ryan's arm as he stretches further. The lower half of her scrubs are saturated, but this time it's the poor light and not the blue color that disguises the blood. His fingers run down her thigh and then plunge through a tear in the cotton and into a gap in her skin. He's found the cause. A major injury to her right quadriceps, about halfway down. A chunk of her leg is missing. Her femoral artery has been ripped open.

She'll bleed out if he can't stop it.

His mind goes blank, like a thousand fireworks are crackling just behind his eyes, blinding and deafening him. Trace needs a medical trauma team working over her. She needs a blood transfusion, intubation, a neck brace. Her vitals should be displayed on a screen. Ryan would be there, just one pair of hands out of a half dozen, following the instructions of the lead surgeon.

Instead, it's just him, alone in a cave with no supplies and no support, trying to save his friend's life.

His shaking hands fumble through the darkness. His uniform doesn't have any kind of belt or drawstring. The ER had tourniquets—extras were even brought in for the expected emergency—but they're lost in the rubble, along with everything else that might help him.

Feathers shuffle at Ryan's back. Even further behind them, there's the hiss of electrical cables sparking together.

He leaves Trace tilted to one side to keep her airways open, then begins crawling. Phone jammed between his teeth, the metal hurting his jaw with every movement, he creeps through the narrow passageways and over the remains of his workplace.

Finn comes into view, partially suspended by the lengths of rebar. Blood has stopped flowing from him. Just one death bird is crouched at his side now, picking at whatever it found to eat inside his chest. The others have left for fresher meals.

Ryan tries not to stare as he passes his old supervisor. He and Trace used to laugh about Finn when they got drinks together, imitating the man's nasally voice as they barked increasingly pedantic orders at one another. He feels sick and ashamed for it now.

Past Finn's body, the underground world is lit up by the hissing, sparking wires. He knows he's going to be clumsy as shock, fear, and nerve damage dull his reactions. He approaches the wires carefully, lying on his stomach, phone jittering between his molars, one hand stretched forward.

The sparking wires hold enough voltage to kill a man. But there's a loop of unmoving cord within reach. Ryan grips one part of it, careful not to touch the exposed end, and pulls as hard as he can.

It jams, and for a second he fears he won't be able to get it out, but then the unseen end snaps free and Ryan drags the length toward himself. It's longer than he wants, but it will still work, so he loops it around his shoulders.

Familiar shapes rise through the gloom and dust. A bed, overturned, its rails twisted at strange angles and its mattress collapsed on the floor. Ryan creeps toward it and snags one corner of the sheets. He begins to pull, then falls still.

Behind the bed is another body. They're wearing scrubs, but he can't recognize who the form belongs to. The top half of their torso has been sheared clear away. A death bird eats at it, the sunken sockets of its eyes closed in ecstasy.

Ryan averts his gaze and pulls on the sheet, dragging it free from the fallen bed in painful increments. He bundles it tight against his chest, tucking it beneath the cable, and then turns back toward Trace.

The ground shifts again. Ryan clamps both hands over his head. The surface he's on drops several inches. It's enough to jar the phone out of his mouth and send fresh pain blooming through his spine. He keeps his head low, spit dripping from between his clenched teeth as he forces himself to inhale the dust. The tremors fade.

A shard of light breaks through the darkness. It comes from above—not sunlight, but something harsh and artificial. A street-light, maybe. Ryan passes through it as he retrieves his phone and creeps back to his friend's side.

Trace is still breathing, but the sound confirms his fear that one of her lungs has collapsed. The pool of blood has spread. There's no helping it. He has to move her to reach her leg. Ryan can only hope she hasn't sustained spinal trauma as he hooks his arms beneath her shoulders and drags her closer.

There's almost no room to move between the jagged blocks of concrete. Ryan has to hover over her body as he loops the torn cable around her upper thigh and cinches it tight. It's a poor tourniquet. He still has his pens in his pocket and takes one out to write the time on her scrubs, right next to the cable.

He thinks he sees her pupils move beneath lids that hang half-open. Ryan calls her name and snaps his fingers next to her face, but there's no reaction. He swallows, his throat clotted with the taste of metal and bitter powder, as he turns to look back at the shard of artificial light cutting into their pocket of air.

He's supposed to wait for rescuers to come to him. Struggling against the rubble only risks further collapsing it. But Trace needs more help than he can give, and she needs it urgently.

*You were a child then.*

*You're not a child anymore.*

*You can save her.*

He pants and chokes as he maneuvers Trace onto the sheet, then wads the loose corners around her neck to help support it. He grips the cotton in his cracked and bleeding hands and begins to pull.

There's no such thing as flat ground in the hospital's wreckage. Ryan wishes he could do better for Trace—wishes he could make her a stretcher, or somehow carry her over the shards of broken structure—but he can barely manage to drag her an inch at a time.

As he gets closer to the light, he sees something shift through the rolling dust. A death bird, so enormously tall that it has to bend double to fit in the cavern, stalks toward him. Its form blurs and smudges when he looks at it, but he can feel its eyes lingering on Trace, hungry and impatient.

There were more than a hundred death birds at the last count before the collapse. They've already eaten through the first wave of casualties. Now they're stalking the sick and dying, waiting for those who are close but not quite ready yet.

*They're a warning, not a prophecy. You can change this.*

The hole in the rubble is narrow and leads upward at a nearly ninety-degree angle. Ryan is forced to abandon the sheet and instead hooks his arms under Trace's shoulders to drag her up. Every muscle in his body hurts. His lungs ache from the airborne particles. His arm turns hot and numb as damaged nerve endings misfire.

The death bird creeps up the tunnel after him, moving on all fours, nearly hovering over Trace's body as it stalks them.

He can hear voices at his back. Screaming. Crying. Panicked words being exchanged as feet pound across the ground.

They're all sounds he's heard before. All sounds he dreaded hearing that night. They're made worse, though, because they're coming from his family. Not the original one—not the one that he let burn in a cabin in the woods—but the family he built. Work friends. Supervisors and colleagues and the interns he mentored, crying out in pain, calling out for help.

He fixes his eyes on Trace's face, gray under the coating of dust and streaked dark brown from the blood she's shed, and pulls harder.

They burst out from the rubble, and Ryan staggers as he gets them into the open air. He doesn't stop pulling until they're ten feet from the wreckage and then he drops down to cradle Trace's head in his lap.

They're in the parking bay outside the emergency unit's entrance. The ground is strewn with debris: glass, metal, a stray roll of gauze soaking in an inky black liquid. Ahead, the familiar glass doors and tiled waiting room have been transformed into an alien landscape. Shards of metal jut upward, disturbing the sky. The chairs have vanished into the pit carved into the earth. It's all sharp angles and terrible rolling hills of pain.

People run toward Ryan. Hands press his shoulders. Voices ask urgent questions: Is he hurt? Does he need help? The ambulances are already carrying the first batch of injured toward the next closest hospital, but they'll be back soon.

Ryan doesn't answer.

Trace left a trail of blood on the asphalt, just like the streak of red Ryan's mother painted over the cabin's floor. Her eyes no longer flutter.

The death bird followed them out of the cave. It bends over Trace, its curved beak stabbing into her chest as it feasts.

Ryan drops his head until his face is buried in Trace's hair. He cradles her softly, carefully, and lets the bird devour what remains of his friend.

**THE END**

# THE HOUSE ON BOXWOOD LANE

"HAS THAT HOUSE ALWAYS BEEN THERE?"

That was the question we asked about the two-story brick building on Boxwood Lane.

It *looked* as though it had been there a long time. Rosebushes grew against the walls, and the paint on the windowsills was peeling. We thought it might be abandoned; tiles were missing from the roof and water stains darkened the bricks where a gutter had broken.

But there were a few strange things about it.

First, no one could remember seeing it there, on the outskirts of town, before.

Second, it seemed to have a lot of doors. At least six I could count on the three sides visible from the road and possibly more around the back.

Third, all the doors were open. Some hung wide; others were

open barely a crack. The house had a built-in garage and the door was rolled half up. Even the windows—rectangular, painted white to contrast against the red bricks, large enough for a person to climb through—were left ajar.

Sebastian was the first one to mention the house. He was the odd kid in my class: a little too intense, and a little too interested in catching beetles and pinning them inside framed boxes. When he started asking, "Does anyone know that house on Boxwood Lane? Has it *always* been there?" we thought it was just a new angle to his oddities.

But then other classmates started mentioning it. They said things like "I've never seen it before" and "It must have been there, right? We just didn't notice it" and "My parents told me to stay away from it."

And so I went along Boxwood Lane too, and I stopped in front of the only house down that stretch of road and stared up at the cracking paint and the door that tilted on its hinges and the dirty bricks and the overgrown shrubs clinging to it.

It looked like it must have been there since long before I was born. And yet, I would have sworn on my life that section of the road had been empty.

We began to call it the Mystery House. It was outside my route to school, but not by much. I started a habit of looping around to it each day on my way home. Sometimes I just biked past and watched it for the few seconds it stayed in view. Sometimes I stopped and stared.

Most houses in my town seemed to repel curiosity. Windows

that faced the main roads had curtains over them so you couldn't see inside. Garages stayed closed; doors were always locked.

The Mystery House was the opposite of that. Each door seemed to invite me inside with glimpses of items beyond.

Photographs hung in the hallway, just slightly too far away to make out the faces in them. A board game was set up on a table visible through one of the windows. The garage was full of open boxes; we could barely see the contents, even when we craned our necks, but they were brightly colored and shiny. Black marker had been used to write on the boxes. *GAMES*, one said. *COLLECTIBLES*, claimed another.

And, most strangely, a Christmas tree still stood in the living room, its lights glittering and piles of wrapped presents spilling over one another around its base, even though everyone else in town had thrown out their trees months before.

"It's *obviously* been here for ages," Angus said. He was coming home with me to play on my new console. We'd taken the looping route past the house again, and this time we'd stopped to look at it.

"There's no path to the door," I said. The Mystery House stood in a field of tall grass. Even though it had a garage, there was no driveway. Not even a dirt trail leading to the open entryway.

"Because it's abandoned," Angus said. "No one uses the path, so the grass grew over it. Mystery solved."

He wanted to leave, so I didn't argue. But, as we climbed back onto our bikes, I couldn't stop a question from bubbling into my mind: If the house was abandoned, why were the lights on?

Weeks passed, and people still talked about the house. A

divide cut through my friends: those who were convinced it had always been there and had just gone unnoticed and those who said they'd walked down Boxwood Lane twice a week for years and it had never been there before.

I didn't know who to believe, but the mystery gnawed at me like an insect bite that wouldn't stop itching.

And then, one afternoon, something snapped in us. During lunch, a group from my class decided we were going to look inside the house.

The thought was infectiously exciting. The doors were all open and no one seemed to live there. Why not peek inside? We could see if the shiny jars in the kitchen really held candy. Or fully open the closet that seemed to have elaborate costumes peeking out of it. Or peel back the wrapping on the presents under the Christmas tree. We might even figure out who owned the building.

I didn't feel any misgivings until the house came into view.

The long grass shifted in the wind. One of the loose shutters creaked. I climbed off my bike but didn't drop it onto the grass as the others had.

"Maybe we shouldn't," I said.

"What?" Angus was already stepping off the road. A group of eight other children—some friends, some stragglers who had overheard us talking about it—were already leading the way toward the Mystery House.

The sun was getting low. The house's lights were still on, its many doors and windows still open, but I suddenly wasn't sure that it was actually abandoned.

"Someone owns it," I said, hoping they wouldn't hear the fear in my voice. "We'll get in trouble."

"You can stand lookout, if you want," June said. She jogged after the others. None of them were listening to me.

They were too excited to see inside.

Most of them stopped by the windows first. They rose up onto their toes and cupped their hands around their faces as they looked through. I could hear quiet chatter but couldn't make out what they were saying.

Despite all my misgivings, I took a step nearer.

Three of them approached the front door. One at a time, they stepped over the welcome mat and into the lit entryway.

Others approached different doors, trying to find their way to the parts of the house they were most curious about. June walked into a living room that was crammed with shelves full of colorful books. Perry climbed the stairs toward the second floor. Angus ducked under the open garage door and pulled back the flaps on the nearest box.

Eager chatter rose from different parts of the house. I kept moving forward, approaching the open front door, but I stopped before stepping over the threshold.

The house's insides didn't seem right. It was hard to describe, but it almost felt like peering into a dollhouse. All the pieces for a home were there—the wallpaper, the rugs, the dinner tables and chairs—but none of it seemed *real*. It was like looking into a very good imitation of a house.

A gust of air slowly rolled out of the hallway and across me. It felt strangely cool and damp. The hairs on the back of my neck rose as my heart began beating painfully fast. I backed away and didn't stop backing away until I reached the street.

I could see my friends through the windows—darting up and down the stairs to reach different rooms, rushing past the lit windows, crowding around the Christmas tree as they picked out brightly colored parcels. Angus was working his way deeper into the garage, tipping over boxes that were full of strange baubles and trinkets I couldn't name.

And then the house shifted.

It was very slight. Like a shudder had run through the building. I would have thought it was an earthquake, except the ground under my feet didn't move. The doors did, though. Just a small twitch. There were so many of them, each open like an invitation inside.

I looked up at the house, and in that second, I could have sworn it was looking back at me.

It happened in a heartbeat. Every door and every window snapped shut with enough force to shake the glass panes. The rolling garage doors rushed down to meet the ground. The lights inside the house all vanished, and the windows turned as dark and as empty as a mirror. I could no longer see my friends. But I could hear them.

At first there were screams, and then doorknobs rattling, and then fists slamming against unyielding glass.

The house shifted again. It shuddered, and then it rose up. The brick foundation slid out of the raw earth. The rosebushes and shrubs I'd thought were growing against the walls were *attached* to them and rained clumps of dirt as they were carried into the air.

I staggered backward and tripped over one of the bikes. I barely felt the ground as I landed. The screams were growing louder, no longer coming from shock but from pure terror.

Eight spindly legs extended from beneath the home. They were thin and glossy dark, like a beetle's, and stretched as they shook themselves out. Clawed tips planted themselves in the ground, sinking into the dirt.

The screams rose in pitch, louder and louder. And then, all at once, they cut off.

Perfect, terrible silence came from the house.

I watched in sickened horror as drops of dark liquid began to ooze from under each of the multitude of doors and windowsills. Fresh blood, shockingly dark, trickled down, dripping over the roots hanging beneath the house's foundation and falling onto the earth below.

The house's spindly legs stretched out, lifting the building higher before beginning to carry it away toward the hills. Where it had once sat was a rectangle of dark earth in an overgrown field.

All I could do was sit hunched and shaking as I watched the Mystery House walk away to digest my friends.

It wasn't hard to guess where it was going.

To settle down and set its trap at the edge of some other unfortunate town.

**THE END**

# THE RUN TO BROKEN RIDGE LIGHTHOUSE

AMON AND JOSH HAD THEIR HEADS TOGETHER, AND THAT MEANT trouble.

They sat on the other side of the bonfire, their skin lit by its glow as dusk thickened into night. Josh had his shirt unbuttoned. Amon wore no shirt at all. Their bare feet dug into the sand, and grains clung to their soles and thighs from where they'd gone wading into the waves an hour before.

"What do you think they're talking about?" I asked Brin. She lounged at my side, her sundress tied around her knees so her legs could feel the cool breeze. She kept herself neatly contained inside the footprint of her beach towel to escape the sand.

"Knowing them, something awful," she said, and I would have laughed if it didn't strike so close to the truth.

On their own, Josh and Amon were smart. Sensible. They'd both passed the semester's classes, even though they'd both sworn they were going to fail.

Something happened when they were together, though. Like a volatile chemical reaction with unpredictable consequences. They became risk-takers. Goofy. Just a month before, Josh had gotten a tattoo of a bear on his bicep after going out drinking with Amon. He said he was going to get a whole sleeve of them. I told him I'd divorce him before he even had a chance to marry me.

I didn't mind the way they acted, not really. Not as much as Brin did. But when I saw them leaning close to each other, both of their faces scrunched up with laughter, I knew something awful was coming and I'd likely be pulled into it.

"I bet they're talking about the legend."

Drew sat to my left, slightly apart from the rest of the group, with Reese leaning her head against his shoulder, near dozing. His toes flexed as he dug them into the still-warm sand. The firelight didn't fall on him quite as well as the rest of us, and I struggled to make out his expression.

"What legend?" Brin asked, and on the other side of the fire, Josh and Amon both broke into uncontrollable laughter. I tried to count the beer bottles dug into the sand around them.

"Well, the lighthouse is up there," Drew said, and his long, pale finger flicked toward a concrete pillar rising out of the jagged rocks near the horizon. "That means this is Broken Ridge Beach. Where Cami Alan died."

I shuffled around and felt my heated flesh chill as it turned away from the fire. "You're not joking, are you?"

I didn't need to ask. Drew didn't really do jokes. His laughter was always a few seconds delayed, like humor was a medium he didn't completely understand. I felt bad for him. And I felt ashamed for feeling bad for him, because if he knew, he would hate it. No one wanted to be pitied.

Sometimes Amon and Josh planned things for the group, and I'd have to prompt them to invite Drew. They weren't excluding him maliciously. At least, I don't *think* they were. But it was like he was easily forgotten. Never a core member of the crew, no matter how many years he'd been hanging out with us. He was like a comet trapped by a planet's gravity, its arc widening with each day, on the verge of falling out of orbit but somehow clinging on.

Amon was the planet in the center. He was the gravity that kept its moons—Josh and Brin and Reese and me—glued together. At least for now.

And Amon had picked this beach. We were in the middle of the summer holidays, the month had been broiling, and the popular beaches were all crowded to bursting.

But beaches were something Australia had in abundance. You just needed to know where to go to avoid the citysiders and the tourists. Find the shorelines without any parking lots or barbecues or bathrooms. Sometimes that meant walking through scrubland for half an hour, as we had that night. But pick the right stretch of coast, far enough away from the usual spots, and you could have as much room to lay your towel as you wanted.

Amon's choice had been almost too effective. The beach was barren except for us. There had been enough driftwood to pile up for a bonfire, and an abundance of shells, and we'd even found the long-ago rotted remains of a seal some distance away.

The closest sign of life was the lighthouse that stood on the horizon, and its lack of light suggested it was as abandoned as the beach.

"Someone died here?" Brin still sounded incredulous, even though Drew's narrow, drawn face showed no sign of deception.

"It was a while ago," he said. "Like thirty years back. It's one of the area's biggest unsolved crimes."

"Yeah, I heard that one," Reese mumbled from her place on Drew's shoulder. "Cami Alan. She came out here one afternoon and a maniac killed her. No one even found her body for days."

"My dad told me about it," Drew said. "Apparently hundreds of police were involved. The investigation went on for years. There were suspects but no convictions."

"That's not why it's famous, though." Reese lifted her head, blond hair spilling over her face as she scratched the back of her skull. Her nose crinkled as she tried to pull herself awake. "She's a local urban legend."

"Yeah?"

Reese gave me a weary, grim smile, her eyes squinted against the fire's light. "Some people say you can see her along the beach around dusk."

I glanced back at Amon and Josh. They were still talking in hushed tones, nudging each other, all bright eyes and muffled laughter. They'd taken their wallets out. Some kind of bet.

"Nice," I muttered. This was the sort of thing they'd love. I didn't doubt that Amon had chosen Broken Ridge Beach because of the legend. The only thing that did surprise me was that they hadn't told the story themselves. Ghost tales and jump scares around a bonfire were exactly the kind of thing they'd think was funny.

As though sensing the conversation had fallen into a lull, Amon shuffled around to face us. "Hey," he said, his skin shining gold in the firelight. "Let's do something fun."

"I'm already having plenty of fun," I said, plucking my near-empty beer bottle from the sand and raising it as proof.

"We can have more fun than *that*," he insisted. "Let's have a race to the lighthouse."

"No," Brin said, and leaned back on her elbows, stretching her neck backward to flex stiff muscles. "It's too hot."

"You won't be doing any running, baby." He began crawling around the fireside to reach her. "We'll do it as a piggyback ride. I'll carry you the whole way."

"I honestly cannot think of anything I want to do less."

"C'mon," he wheedled, creeping onto her beach towel and dragging sand with him. "It'll be fu-u-un."

I wanted to ask Amon if he knew how close he was to losing her. But I also knew there was nothing he could do at that point to keep her.

Amon didn't seem to realize it, but their relationship had been winding toward its end for months. Brin liked him. But she was going to transfer in the new year to continue working on her political science degree, and she didn't plan on dating long-distance. And Amon was completely ignoring that looming deadline.

That was the crux of the problem, I knew. Amon took each

day as it came, basking in the warm glow of the present. Brin had a five-year plan, a ten-year plan, and a twenty-year plan. She liked Amon, but not enough to rewrite her life for him.

I was fairly sure she was only still dating him so she wouldn't break up the friend group before she left. I was grateful for that. We were slowly fracturing apart. I don't know if the others felt it as acutely as I did, but it was there. I looked at Josh, but he wasn't looking back at me. Hadn't the whole night. Our relationship had always been casual, but he was only growing less interested, not more.

The six of us had been friends since high school. And I was fairly sure this would be our last summer together.

"Come on," Amon whined, not noticing as Brin tried to brush the sand off her towel. "It'll be fun. I'll carry you, and Josh will carry Sarah, and Drew with Reese—"

"I'm game," I said. Maybe it was the beer. Maybe it was the painfully close knowledge that Amon's gravity was weakening, and that we would all be drifting into the cosmos sooner or later. Maybe it was a desire to make one more lasting memory while I could. I clasped my hands over my knees. "Let's do it."

Brin sighed, glowering at me as though I was letting her down. "Fine," she said, though her tone made it very clear that it wasn't fine.

"All right." Amon's face was alight with eagerness again, and I wasn't sure how a simple race could make him that excited. "We'll go to the lighthouse. Right up to the highest room. Loser pays for late-night takeout."

"I don't want to go," Drew said. The fire was growing lower, and his face was becoming more shadowed. He refused to meet our eyes but focused on the spitting wood. "It doesn't sound fun."

I didn't blame him. He was thin, with perpetual dark circles clinging around his eyes. He'd never done well in athletics. Amon, on the other hand, thrived when he was moving. He surfed. He ran. He played football. And he excelled at all of them. I wasn't sure why Josh was so willing to agree to the race, considering his chances of winning were close to none.

"Don't flake on us," Amon said, turning to Drew. "Come on. One race. I won't even make you pay if you lose, okay?"

Drew just shook his head. Reese, still hanging close to his side, nudged him lightly. "It kind of sounds fun," she whispered.

"No" was all he said.

They'd always been an odd match. Beautiful, sunshine Reese. Shy, awkward Drew. When they'd first started going out, it had felt almost by obligation. I was dating Josh; Amon was dating Brin. They were the only two singles left in our group.

But, while both Brin and I were on the edge of ending our relationships, Reese and Drew seemed to be growing closer. I never would have guessed it when they first came out as a couple, but if any of us had a chance of really making it, it was them.

"Come on, don't be such a wet rag," Amon said. He'd crawled around to Drew's side, laughter in his face. "Everyone else is going."

"Cut it out," I said. "Drew doesn't want to race. Keep pushing him and I won't want to either."

"Sarah," he said, and his voice held the thinnest strain of a whine.

"I'm serious."

He dropped back, sighing. "Fine. Drew can stay and watch our stuff. The rest of us are going to go see the lighthouse."

"I'll stay too," Reese said, and leaned her head back on Drew's shoulder. "Have fun."

"You're both the biggest killjoys." Amon grinned to show there wasn't any bite behind his words, then rose. "Come on, Brin. Hop up."

"Hold still, first." Brin shook out her towel as she stood, then rubbed it over Amon's bare back, cleaning grit from his skin.

I took my time standing and brushing sand off myself. Josh bounced beside me, unusually energetic as he waited for me to be ready. I eyed the distance to the lighthouse. At a walk, it might have been twenty minutes or half an hour. Running? With another human clinging to their backs? They were setting themselves up for heatstroke.

The sun was in the last stages of setting. Once we stepped away from the bonfire, we would be relying only on moonlight to guide us to the craggy rocks.

"It's too dark," Brin said, as though guessing my thoughts. "Can't we just stay by the fire and enjoy another beer?"

"No," Amon said, and he crouched, arms reached behind himself, ready for Brin to climb on.

Josh mimicked the motion, bending, preparing. He was smiling at me more than he had all day. *Last chance to make some memories*, I reminded myself, then jumped to get onto his back. My arms went around his neck and crossed over his chest. My legs hooked around his waist, just over his hips, and he brought his arms up from behind my knees to hold me there. He was warm and solid and staggered slightly under my weight. I heard a grunt behind us as Brin climbed onto her partner.

"To the top floor of the lighthouse," Amon said, sharing a look with Josh.

"You're on," Josh said.

Together they chanted: "One," then leaped forward, feet digging into the sand as they began the race toward the rocks at the end of the beach.

*One?* I tightened my arms around Josh's shoulders. His gait was unsteady, and the jostling motion made it hard to think. I'd never heard just *one* used as a countdown before.

Josh was fit. Not quite as fit as Amon, but he was a regular at a gym and had participated in two marathons. Still, my weight and the soft sand were working against him. Within twenty paces, he was panting. He was running too hard, trying to keep up with the faster Amon. He'd be spent before he was halfway to the lighthouse if he didn't slow down.

I turned my head slightly to see our competitors. Amon was already a pace ahead of us. His body was bent forward to hold Brin on his back. She clung to him, loose folds of her sundress whipping behind her, her face scrunched up to shield against the wind.

The motion was jarring, bordering on painful. I tried to adjust my grip around Josh's neck and felt my hands slip over sweaty skin. I was too hot…and heating up faster as I pressed into Josh's back.

Amon had promised fun. I don't know if any of us were having it.

Then Josh said something. The word had vanished into the air before I could catch it. Through the pounding motion, I tried to catch enough breath to call to him, "What?"

He just shook his head slightly. To my left, Amon said something—a single word—and even through the ragged breathing and drumming feet I was fairly certain it was the same word Josh had spoken.

*Something about this is wrong.* Amon loved competitions. He liked to show off, even though he made theater out of being a good sport after winning. But this race was just unusual enough, and just out of character enough, that I felt like I'd underestimated what was happening. I pictured the scene at the bonfire again: Amon and Josh, heads together, laughing as they formed a plan I couldn't hear.

Josh called out again, and this time the word was unmistakable: "One."

It was echoed from my side as Amon repeated it. "One."

And then both of them began chanting it, the word spat from open mouths and fueled by breathless lungs: "One, one, one, one."

Flecks of sand stung my face. The wind was changing; what had been a light, warm breeze was turning sour as it funneled cold, salty air toward us.

"What are you doing?" I tried to ask Josh, but he didn't answer. He was laughing through his breathlessness, and his expression held such a wildly reckless aura that I couldn't help but think he'd done something truly dangerous. "What did you *do*?"

"One, one, one," he chanted, and although I could no longer hear Amon under the footsteps and the gasps and the crashing waves, his mouth was still moving in sync.

"Let me down. I don't want to do this anymore." Brin was struggling, leaning back, but Amon kept his grip on her legs, refusing to release her.

The wind was harsher. It shot sharp flecks of sand across our exposed skin. I squinted, putting my head down, trying to shield myself behind Josh's coarse hair. The ocean, which had held a gentle swell until that point, was growing stormy. The wind was shockingly cold compared to the heat of the day. It was loud too. So loud that I almost didn't hear the footsteps behind us.

Someone else had joined the race. *Drew?* Even as the idea crossed my mind, I knew it couldn't be him. We'd left him behind at the bonfire, and our pace had been fast enough that he couldn't possibly have caught up.

The beach had been empty, though. We'd been there for hours and hadn't seen or heard another soul.

The laughter had faded from Josh's face. We were nearly halfway to the lighthouse and his pace should have been flagging, but if anything, he seemed to be moving faster. Each breath was ragged and raw as it snagged through his throat.

I tried to tilt to the side, to look behind us, but Josh yanked me forward again. The footsteps were gaining. I tightened my hold around Josh's chest as I tried to hear them through the whistling wind and the waves at our side.

They were uneven but fast. Desperate, almost.

Ahead, the rocks marking the beach's end rose up like a black wall. At the top was the abandoned lighthouse—tall, narrowing into a point that grazed the moon.

Amon had pulled ahead of us. He was nearly at the rocks. Josh hadn't slowed down, though, and it hit me that this hadn't actually been a race, and that Amon had been deliberately holding pace with Josh and me until that point.

He threw a look over his shoulder as he reached the dark stones. "Come on!"

Josh didn't respond, but his gasps were like a ragged saw in my ear. We were still a good twenty paces behind. The jarring motion left my skin chafed, and nausea pooled in my stomach. I wanted to get down, but Josh's grip only tightened further when he felt mine loosen. The footsteps were still in our wake, pounding, frenzied, and I turned just enough to glimpse the beach behind us.

In the distance was the bonfire. The howling wind had brought up so much sand, it was scarcely more than a hazy light. At our side, moonlight reflected off the heaving, crashing waves as they collided against the break.

And behind us was a woman.

Her arms were spread out to her sides, her bare feet thundering against the sand. Long black hair whipped across her face, hiding it, and it might have been my imagination, but I thought

I glimpsed one of her eyes, except it wasn't an eye, not really. It was a pit of pure black, and in its center was a small, cold light, shining as it fixed on me.

When we reached the first of the rocks, I was forced to face forward again as our path lurched upward. Josh was barefoot, and I'd expected him to slow once he crossed onto the jagged, treacherous basalt but he didn't. He hurled himself onto the rocks, bending forward to help the climb. His breathing sounded painful and phlegmy.

"Let me down," I called, but he either didn't hear me or pretended he hadn't.

Ahead, the lighthouse door was open. Amon paused in the opening. He was shivering. Brin struggled, trying to pull off him, but he had gripped both of her wrists and held her pinned to his back. There was something uncomfortably raw in his eyes, and I had less than a second to recognize it as terror before he turned and disappeared into the stairwell.

Josh stumbled over an uneven rock and dropped to his knees. I grunted as the impact drove his shoulder into my chest.

The footsteps were still behind us, and they were drawing nearer. I tried to speak, to ask Josh if he was okay, but he lurched back to his feet, and it was all I could do to cling on. We were nearly at the lighthouse. Its white paint had taken on a sickly blue haze under the moonlight. The door stood wide open like a screaming mouth, and all I could see inside was darkness.

I squeezed my eyes closed as we crossed the threshold. The sounds changed. Josh was no longer running on sand or basalt but on stone steps, worn in the center, where thousands of feet had passed before.

*This will kill him.* He shook. His gasps were broken. He'd crossed the beach in a frenzy, as though his life had depended on it, and yet he still didn't slow.

He clutched at me, refusing to let me off his back. I no longer fought. As much as I feared for Josh, I feared what was coming behind us more.

"Hurry!" Amon yelled. He was above us, out of sight, and his voice reverberated in strange ways as it bounced down the winding stairwell.

My head throbbed. Josh lurched and my arm grazed cold, rough stone. I squinted my eyes open, but the tower was almost pitch black. I could barely see the stone walls encircling us and the achingly steep steps leading ever higher.

The footsteps were closing in. Maybe only a few steps below us. Maybe less.

I had to look. I tilted my head, bending so far that my neck ached.

Through the dark, I saw a rush of movement. Black hair, flowing like smoke. A flash of a face, as white as the crumbling paint on the lighthouse's exterior. A hand, streaked in red, reached out from the folds of a pale dress, stretching up toward me.

I bit my tongue and tasted blood.

And then the stairs ended. An open door stretched ahead of us, and a pale light bobbed inside of it. Amon yelled, "In, quick," and then we were over the threshold, and Amon slammed the door behind us.

Josh crumpled to his knees, and then to his side. I rolled off his back, breathless even though I hadn't been running. Josh was shaking, each gasp of air seeming to rock him.

A light shone in my face, and I raised a hand to shield my eyes. The beam lowered, and I realized Brin had turned on the LED that hung from her key chain.

We were in the lighthouse's highest room. The old light still hung in the room's center, suspended above us, so enormous that I could have crawled inside and sat comfortably.

Brin stood closest to the light, one arm holding her own bulb, the other tucked tightly around her chest. She had that pinched shape around her lips that I knew meant she was frustrated but trying to keep it hidden. Amon stood against a wall near the door, both hands braced on his knees. He was grinning, his eyes alight with the kind of excitement I hadn't seen in years.

"That was crazy," he said, and Josh, still on the floor, began to laugh weakly.

As I looked around at our small group, a slow, seeping certainty formed in the base of my stomach. *This was some kind of prank.* Amon and Josh had wanted to scare us, and they'd gotten a fair way toward their goal.

But…who was the woman I'd seen?

I remembered her hand, reaching toward me. Streaked with red. With blood.

"There was someone behind us," I said, and Amon nodded eagerly.

"Okay, so, get this." He made a placating gesture. His fingers were shaking. "This beach has a legend, right? A girl called Cami Alan died here years ago."

"Yeah, Drew told us." I folded my arms to hide just how rattled I was.

"Well, I bet he didn't tell you the full story. Come on. Sit down a moment." He lowered himself to the floor, beckoning for both Brin and me to do the same.

I glanced at Brin. Her expression was steely, and for a second, I thought this would be it—the moment her tranquility broke, the moment she severed ties with Amon. But then she sat on the floor beside him and let him take her hand as he leaned against her.

Amon was still breathing heavily, but not quite as desperately as Josh was. Josh had rolled onto his back, arms spread wide, eyes closed, and I felt a drop in my stomach. He wouldn't have pushed himself so hard for a prank. He wouldn't have cut his feet for a prank, either, but beads of red were welling on his bare soles where he'd run across the rocks. I lowered myself to a crouch, arms wrapped around my knees as I listened.

"Cami Alan was attacked on Broken Ridge Beach, the place we made our bonfire," Amon continued. "She tried to run. And she tried to call the emergency helpline, right? Triple zero. But as she ran from her attacker, her hand slipped and she mistyped the number as zero-zero-one."

Brin pulled her hand from Amon's. She hunched forward, her light still aimed at the floor between us, as she tucked her sundress tightly around her legs. The lighthouse was cold. I could feel its chill seeping into me already.

"So Cami Alan ran for the lighthouse," Amon continued. "People think she was trying to get up here, to the highest floor, where she could lock the door. But she didn't make it in time. She ran as fast as she could, but it just wasn't enough."

"So now people claim to see her on the beach," I finished for him. My irritability was rising up through my chest, hot and prickling.

"Not if they're not looking for her." Amon leaned forward, and the LED light painted wan shadows over his face. "But you can call her. That's what the legend says, anyway. You're supposed to run along the beach, toward the lighthouse, just like she did. And you're supposed to count *one, one, one*. That's the number she mistyped. Got it? The story says you run, and you say the number, and she'll appear behind you, and she'll start chasing you, just like her killer chased her. And she'll try to catch you, just like her killer did. And if she's faster than you—if she catches you—then she'll kill you in the same way she was killed."

Goose bumps rose across my arms. It was just the cold, I told myself as I tried to rub them away.

Josh had pulled himself up onto his elbows, his legs akimbo, as he beamed at me. There was genuine delight in his expression. He was *proud*, I realized.

"We made it," he said, and his voice was raw and raspy. "I kept you safe. We *made* it."

"You guys are idiots." Brin had started to shiver. "Can we go back to the bonfire now?"

"No, no way." Amon grabbed her shoulder, smiling and apologetic in the same moment. "We have to stay here until dawn. That's part of the legend. If she chases you, the only way you'll survive is if you get to the highest room of the lighthouse and stay there until dawn."

She rolled her shoulder to shake him off. "Not a chance. I have work in the morning."

"No, hey. Slow down." Amon caught her wrist when she tried to stand. "I'm sorry. I'm sorry. I really didn't think it would actually work. We have to stay, though, okay?"

"I *know* you're not this superstitious." Brin shook his hand off again, and I realized with a jolt that she hadn't heard the footsteps behind us.

Amon turned to me, desperation in his eyes. "Sarah. Tell her she has to stay. She'll listen to you. Please."

My mouth opened, but no words came out. Brin's light swung on the key chain, and it sent leaping, grasping shadows across the walls. I felt very small and very lost. One thought surfaced, and I ran my tongue across dry lips. "What about Drew and Reese?"

"They'll be fine. They stayed by the fire. She only comes if you try to race her." The smile was fading from Amon's face, leaving just the sheepish apology in its place. "I didn't think it would actually work."

Brin stepped over Amon's legs as she crossed to the door. Josh looked at me, then staggered to his feet. "Hey, Brin—"

"I don't want to hear it." She reached for the door. Amon went after her, his voice sweetly pleading as he tried to cajole her to stay.

My head was buzzing. My eyes tracked the trail of red that Josh's feet made as he limped across the floor. "Brin," I started, but she ignored me. Her hands fastened around the latch. Its hinges groaned as she heaved it open, and a gust of chilled air coursed around us.

The landing was empty.

"You can be such a selfish jerk sometimes," she said to Amon, then stepped into the stairwell.

A scream ripped through the cold night air. It was sharp and animalistic and desperately frightened. Brin froze on the top step, her eyes wide, her lips barely parted. She glanced back at us, and I saw a flickering fear in her eyes.

The scream came again, followed by a man yelling.

*I know that voice.*

I shoved past Brin. The steps were achingly cold on the soles of my feet as I flew toward the ground. The stairs seemed to last for an eternity, winding and winding until I felt sick from the motion.

Then the narrow stairwell opened into a wash of moonlight. I burst outside, breathless, my heart throbbing in my throat. The wind funneled sand across my skin and dragged my hair back, and I raised an arm to shield my face.

There. Near the base of the black rocks. A form was crouched in the sand, its back heaving as it struggled to breathe.

"Drew?" My toes curled over the black stones as I climbed down to the sand. Josh was somewhere behind me, calling my name, but I didn't turn. I only had eyes for the hunched figure ahead of me, and the tracks of footprints leading to him.

"She wanted to do it." Drew's fingers dug into the sand, clawing at it, as he lifted his head to look at me. His eyes were red, wide, pleading, even as his gasps cut through his breathless words. "She wanted to try the legend. But I wasn't—I wasn't—"

"Where's Reese?" The words tasted like chalk in my mouth.

"I wasn't *fast* enough—"

A sound cut through the air, blending with the crash of breaking waves and the low, mournful howl of the wind. A scream. It came from somewhere further down the beach, in among the dunes and the stringy grass that grew there.

A hand touched my shoulder. Brin. "What happened?" she asked.

"Give me your light."

"Sarah—"

I found her hand and pulled the key chain from it, then broke into a run, following the dying notes of the scream. Josh called my name again, but he was still inside the lighthouse, clutching the edges of the open doorway. Amon stood just behind him, as still as a statue, his face unrecognizable without the familiar smile.

Plumes of sand kicked up behind me as I ran. My eyes burned, even though I'd narrowed them against the cutting wind. The light flicked across a chunk of driftwood. Long tufts of grass. A large stone, washed smooth by years in the water.

"Reese!" My voice choked. I swallowed, tried again. "Reese, answer me!"

There was no reply. Just the wind, the ocean, and my own thundering heart.

I thought I was moving in the right direction, but the moonlight made it impossible to see clearly. It had transformed the world, turning it alien; each crest of dune teased my eyes, each new shadowed dip confusing me.

"Reese!"

Something dark appeared through the endless field of sand and grass. I turned toward it. My lungs hurt from the pace, but I didn't slow, not until I was nearly on top of her.

Reese lay on her back. Her eyes were open but stared blindly, not even flickering as the wind drove sand into them. Her arms were outstretched to her sides. Her blond hair flowed like a halo around her head.

I dropped to my knees as something like a moan struggled out of my throat. Sweet, sunshine Reese. As warm as summer. It was rare to see her without a smile.

She wasn't smiling now. Her lower lip was missing.

My hand shook as I pressed it across my own mouth, as though that might smother the choked sobs that were rising through me. I tasted the grit of sand and the brine of ocean, along with something more metallic. The scent of blood had flooded my nostrils, and once it was in, I couldn't get it out again.

Bites scored Reese's body. I could see the clear outline of teeth marks, welled with blood. The sharp incisors. The pointed canines. The blocky indents of the molars. Dozens of them, across her arms, her legs, her face. Someone had bit her, and then bit her again, and not stopped until she was dead.

They'd bitten off her lower lip. Her nose. Part of her left ear. Her throat.

The sobs were building in me, turning into something nearer

to a scream. I lifted my head, afraid that if I looked at my friend for even a moment longer, I would lose everything that remained of myself.

A silhouette stood no more than thirty paces away. A sundress dress whipped about her form as the wind tugged at it. Her hair flowed across her face, obscuring her. But I was certain, if the curtain of hair were to pass, I would see identical bite marks marring her own bloodless face.

Cami Alan, come for justice. To pass on her death to anyone foolish enough to race her across that stretch of sand.

I rocked back onto my feet. The lighthouse was supposed to keep me safe. But I'd left the lighthouse far behind. My limbs were already shaking from the effort it had taken to search for Reese. I didn't know if I could be faster than Cami Alan. I didn't know if I could reach the lighthouse's highest room in time.

But that was the bet I'd unwillingly placed. I'd started a race with the dead woman of Broken Ridge Beach. And now, if I wanted to live, I would have to finish it.

And so I ran.

**THE END**

# REMAINS

---

Douglas Bridges died in his room at age sixty-three.

His remains were discovered by his wife of forty years, Helene, at two-thirty in the morning. It didn't dawn on her until the following day that she'd heard him die.

She slept in the room next to him and had done so for close to twenty years—a result of his insomnia and her being easily woken. That night, Douglas had seemed unusually restless, and not even a foot of brick walls and insulation had been enough to shield Helene from the creaks and shuffling footsteps. She'd gotten up at two-thirty to check on him. By the time she entered his room, he was already dead.

Helene blamed herself. If she'd gotten up earlier, if she'd registered the noises for what they were and not dismissed them as symptoms of his insomnia, maybe she could have done something for him.

But she blamed Douglas too. He'd known she loved him more than life itself. And he'd still left her.

That same night, Helene closed every window in their home. Wiry hair stuck to her sweat-and-tear-streaked cheeks as she brought her hammer down, again and again, on the nails she lined across the wooden casings.

Then she pulled the curtains closed across the dirty glass. A needle and spool of black thread came out of her sewing kit, and she set to stitching the curtains together until her feet were numb and her fingers cramped.

Helene was one of eight siblings who had been raised on a rural farm, where there was frequently not enough food for the hungry mouths. Hospitals weren't ever mentioned. If you were hurt, you either got over it, or you didn't.

She, along with her seven siblings, had been present at her grandfather's death. The family had gathered around his bed as late-stage throat cancer strangled him. Each day tightened his esophagus slightly more, until the sleep deprivation and physical toll overwhelmed his body's survival instincts, and he simply stopped breathing.

As his skeletal body fell still for the first time in weeks, Helene's mother had pushed the narrow farm window as wide as it would go. "We open the windows so the spirit can find its way out," she'd murmured to the row of quiet, pale children. It was the closest thing to comfort she gave them that day.

Now, Helene had not only nailed the windows closed but had

sewn the curtains over them as well. She thought she'd gotten to them in time. Douglas's body was still warm.

Her breathing was labored as she placed the near-empty spool of thread into her robe pocket and shuffled to the bathroom. Her bare feet smarted on the cold tiles, and her knees cracked as she crouched to sort through the clutter she had accumulated over a lifetime in the two-bedroom, single-floor home.

Inside the mildewed cupboards were spare mirrors. Some cracked. Some narrow hand mirrors that had become so smudged through use, they barely reflected. Helene took them all. And she moved, with painstaking care, through the house, either nailing or taping a mirror to each door.

The largest mirror—the one that belonged over the sink, oval and with a wooden frame that made Helene stagger from the weight—went onto the front door. It took forty-five nails, hammered around the mirror's edges and bent over the wood, to hold it in place.

When Helene's grandfather had died, after opening the windows, her mother had placed cloths across the two mirrors they owned, lest the reflections confuse the spirit.

Douglas had never been a smart man, and she thought his spirit must be slow too. Helene didn't count that against him. She knew she wasn't intelligent, either, and clever men could talk circles around her until her mind buzzed and her stomach ached. She always knew where she stood with Douglas. And he always knew where he stood with her.

She loved him. Always. Even when he had confessed to his

first affair and she had wept hot tears for days, she had loved him enough to keep him. Even when he had confessed to his second affair—with their neighbor, this time—and asked for a divorce, she had loved him too much to give it to him.

Helene knew that was selfish. But then, he'd promised her, hadn't he? In their vows. They'd said they would belong to each other until death do them part.

Now, even death seemed too soon.

She went back to his room. Dawn slipped around the edges of her sewn curtain barrier, but it still wasn't enough to light the space. Helene didn't reach for the switch to the single bulb hanging above them, but instead closed the door firmly behind her. The dark might help confuse his spirit too, and she needed every ounce of assistance she could get.

Helene found his hand. Large, weathered, wrinkled. As familiar to her as her own. She massaged the skin, feeling slippery tendons and wormlike veins underneath. It was still supple. Still warm. She cried again, this time howls of gratitude as much as relief. He was still there, she was sure. Maybe not in the same way he'd always been, but…in some form, in some way, he was still with her.

She'd loved him more than he'd loved her. They both knew it. Helene rejoiced in that. It was good to love. And she didn't need the same devotion in return. For her, it was enough to be near him. To be *allowed* to love him.

Helene touched his hand to her cheek like a caress.

Her love hadn't just kept them together, it had *brought* them together. On their wedding day, as he gave her the vow that he would be at her side until death divided them, she'd seen the quiet panic dancing in his eyes. It had been there for weeks, intensifying as every day drew them closer to the wedding.

But he had to marry her, he'd decided. He wasn't much. He had no real prospects, no money to his name, no family inheritance. He wasn't handsome. He wasn't smart. He had a high-school education and a trade—bricklaying—and that was it.

And she'd loved him for how little he had. How could he turn down a woman who saw the good in him when he couldn't even see it in himself? Wasn't love the thing that was supposed to make you happy?

He'd asked her that question on their twentieth anniversary. She'd planned an outing for them: a trip to the ocean with a picnic basket full of his favorite foods. He'd bought her a box of dollar-store chocolates, and along with it came that question.

As they sat on the beach overlooking the briny water, she'd pulled him close, nestled against the crook of his neck, and kissed the skin that was already starting to wrinkle.

And he'd repeated, over her shoulder, in that dull, resigned tone, "Isn't love supposed to make you happy?"

That was shortly before his third, and final, affair. She didn't think he even liked the last woman very much. She was older than Helene and even plainer. There had been something akin to desperation in Douglas's voice when he'd confessed to the fling unprompted.

Helene stayed with his body until well after midday. Her

joints ached from standing for so long, but the curtains were still tightly closed and the hand she held was still warm.

She walked through the house, moving through each door carefully—opening it just wide enough to slide through sideways, then snapping it shut behind her so he couldn't follow. When the front door was closed, she stopped on their worn welcome mat and simply breathed. The sun was pallid, smudged over with streaky clouds. Helene didn't drive, always relying on Douglas to ease their rusted car in and out of the garage, but the corner store was only a fifteen-minute walk away. She was still in her robe, she realized, as she shuffled along the sidewalk.

The neighbor's dog raced along the fence line, nails scraping the compacted dirt run it had formed there, as it snarled at her. That house had once belonged to the woman who had an affair with Douglas. That woman had moved away decades before, but Helene still disliked the home…and anyone who moved into it.

She liked the corner store, though. It was more expensive than the larger shopping mall, but she knew every face in it.

Not everyone met her gaze with a smile, though, as she moved through the aisles. Rumors had been circulating about her and Douglas for as long as they'd lived there. Everyone had heard the story about how Douglas held a gun to her head one night and tried to shoot her. They just didn't know—or remember—the details. Helene did. She remembered the rough cotton pillow pressed to her face. The glimpse of the gun behind it. Sweat dripping from Douglas's jaw. The noise the revolver made as it misfired.

Helene took it for what it was: a miracle. A sign from heaven that they were supposed to be together. Not everyone held that night in the same reverential light.

The store carried eight small mirrors between the soaps and the hairbrushes. All the same black, rectangular design. Helene took them all. The weathered store owner raised one questioning eyebrow as she pushed rumpled money from her robe pocket across the counter, but he loaded the mirrors into a bag without prying.

Back home, those mirrors were placed across the walls and doors of Helene's small house. From then onward, every weekend she returned to the corner store, and if the store owner had restocked his stash of mirrors, she purchased them all.

No one asked after Douglas. He had never come with Helene when she went shopping, and she'd gently pushed him to drop out of his social groups after he retired. She hadn't liked his friends. They'd always talked badly about their wives, and Helene feared what Douglas might say about her. It had been a relief when they'd stopped visiting.

If he needed company, he had as much as he could want and more in Helene. After everything they'd been through together, he knew, with unwavering certainly, that she would never abandon him.

Her love had seen them through every rocky ocean. How could he leave her at the altar when she loved him so? How could he divorce her when she was a perfectly devoted wife? He'd tried to split them apart that night with the gun, but even then, the universe had agreed that they belonged together.

And now, Helene held them together after what was meant to be the final severing of ties: death. The four walls of Douglas's room were reflected in endless layers, having been plated with mirrors.

He'd begun to decay. With every window in the home permanently closed, no fresh air flowed, but Helene found herself adjusting to the odor. She spent most of the day in his room with him. He was still there, she was sure; if she held his spongy hand for a few minutes, it began to feel warm. She talked to him about everything, telling stories from their life together, repeating the same anecdotes a dozen times in a day.

And Douglas, suspended from the light fixture by the rope he had fashioned as his final attempt to escape the unyielding love, watched his wife with dull, helpless eyes.

### THE END

# UNTAMED THINGS

---

TEN MINUTES BEFORE TOTAL ENGINE FAILURE, I WAS TRYING TO focus on anything except the turbulence.

The plane shuddered against walls of icy winds. Sometimes it dropped so suddenly that my heart filled my throat. The *Fasten Seat Belt* lights shone above us, and they'd been on for nearly forty minutes. Thousands of feet below, disguised by the ice and darkness, jagged mountain peaks jutted out of the earth like teeth.

I glanced at the woman across the aisle from me. She sat by herself, her clothes loose and casual, her jaw-length brown hair forming loose waves against the side of her face. She looked calm and composed, a perfect juxtaposition against my clenched muscles, faint nausea, and sweaty skin.

I had a habit, sometimes, of being captivated by people. Most of the time I couldn't even explain why. But she'd captivated me from the moment she'd boarded the plane.

Her face wouldn't have been called conventionally beautiful, but it was *captivating*, made up of sloping angles and a defined jaw and deep, bright eyes framed by faint creases. She seemed like everything I'd ever wanted to be: lively, fascinating, unpretentious, unconcerned about how people saw her and almost radiant from it.

And I couldn't stop watching her as our plane rattled through the sky twenty thousand feet above the snow-coated mountains. The flight attendant had vanished into the cockpit. No one was telling us anything. But as long as the woman across the aisle looked so calm, I felt like I could still breathe.

Just before the engines failed, the woman looked back toward me. She smiled, revealing canine teeth that were slightly too large but perfectly rounded out her face. *It's all okay*, that smile said. *Just hold tight.*

And I knew I should feel embarrassed—embarrassed for staring, embarrassed for being so shriveled and sweaty and for holding the armrests like they were the only thing anchoring me in the plane—but I didn't feel it in that moment.

Then a loud *bang* came from outside the windows, on the plane's right-hand side, not far from where I sat. The other passengers had already been anxious, but the hushed whispers suddenly dampened into silence as everyone strained, looking through the narrow oval portholes and into the vicious loops of white snow outside.

"There's smoke," someone said, and I thought I was going to be sick.

The whispers started up again, and this time they held a sting of panic.

*Planes are built to survive damage*, I told myself over and over again, as though repeating the words fast enough might save us. *Planes are designed to keep flying, even if an engine breaks.*

There was a second bang, and the plane lurched so hard that I choked on air. The lights above us went out, plunging the cabin into darkness; I could barely see anything except the oval windows and the static-like snow outside.

*Planes are built to survive—*

I didn't finish that thought. Something was very wrong. We all felt it now. The plane was dropping dangerously fast. Staccato voices rose in the cockpit, punctuated by swear words. There was a clatter above, and the pockets over our seats opened to release the oxygen masks.

The clear bags and orange cups looked unearthly as they bobbed in the darkness. I clutched for one, already feeling like I couldn't breathe. The whispers had transformed into indistinguishable yells as panic took over. I'd paid attention when the flight attendant showed us how to put the masks on during the safety briefing. He'd made it seem like the easiest thing in the world, but in reality, it was nearly impossible. The plane shook so badly, I couldn't get a good grip on the cup or even find the strap.

I looked at the woman across the aisle. She looped her own mask on in one fluid motion, calm and in control. I tried to mimic her as my heart thundered.

There was another horrendous *bang*, and this time it sounded like it came from right behind my shoulder. Bright orange lights sizzled across the nearest windows. *Fire.*

The plane lurched so violently that my seat belt bit into my lap. A passenger two rows ahead couldn't have been buckled in; he jolted out of his seat and slammed into the plane's ceiling. The impact broke his nose. He left an arc of blood in his wake as he plunged to the floor.

The screams were so loud, they almost drowned out the sound of the plane tearing itself apart.

Freezing air rushed into the cabin, stinging my face and snatching my breath away. I still didn't have my oxygen mask on. The strap was lost, somehow, so I pressed the orange cup against my mouth and held it there for dear life.

A seam opened up in the plane, tearing through metal and carpet as the sheer force of the fall pulled the plane in half. The line ran between my seat and the chairs ahead, right beneath my feet. I tried to draw myself up into a ball, but the plane's momentum was so overwhelming that movement was impossible.

Objects flew past as they were sucked out. Spectacles, magazines, water bottles, shoes. The gap between me and the seat ahead widened. The plane was barely holding together.

I looked at the woman across the aisle.

In that moment, the woman looked back. Her loose hair flew about her face as our eyes locked.

A piece of the crumbling plane crashed down and sheared through the woman's right arm, just below her elbow.

The limb passed me as it was sucked out of the plane. Tears

stung my eyes as I screamed into the oxygen mask. And then the plane shuddered again, and the entire front half pulled away, ripping free with a screech of tearing metal, pulling the face mask out of my hands and sending it spiraling away into the dark and the snow.

I felt myself tip forward. My seat, right on the precipice of the plane's broken body, was pulling free. The wind snatched at me, trying to suck me out. There was nothing I could reach for except the raw, jagged edge of metal at my side. Nothing to kick against except the dark sky sprawling out ahead. No one trying to pull me back.

My seat broke free, and the plane vanished from around me. The belt became a painful cinch across my hips. I was shaken, wildly, horribly. My mouth gaped open, but I couldn't hear my own screams. A whirlwind of darkness and snow and the tooth-like mountain peaks flashed across my vision.

I pressed my hands to either side of my head in a futile attempt to protect it. My knees pulled up close to my chest.

Everything bled together. There was the harsh slap of branches crashing against my sides and face. I spun so hard that I thought my head was going to be pulled off my neck.

And then, all at once…

…it was over.

The vertigo had been so overwhelming, it took a moment to realize the world had stopped moving. Snow pressed into my right-hand side. It was difficult to breathe. Carefully, I took my hands away from my head.

I was alive. Against all odds, the seat must have protected me during the fall.

All the bones in my body hurt, as though they had been pulled out and then replaced wrong. I thought I might throw up if I tried to move. But I was alive. A choked sound, something between a gasp and a scream of relief, escaped me.

The snow was pressed against my face, threatening to smother me, and I tried to roll over. The seat was still at my back and the seat belt kept me locked in place. Carefully, I reached down to find the buckle and I released it. Fresh pain rattled through me as I flopped free, into the piles of snow, and rolled onto my back.

Pine trees stretched above. Their branches created a lattice over the sky, with broken branches marking the place I'd fallen through. It had been night through most of the flight, but early morning light bloomed in the distance and worked on erasing the stars.

My head throbbed. Grazes ran like red rashes across one arm where I'd hit the pine trees. The snow helped numb the pain, though. There weren't any of the vicious gale-like winds at ground level. The world felt strangely peaceful, almost comfortable.

I wanted to stay there and let the softly falling snow cover me like a blanket. Instead, I rolled onto my knees. Every movement hurt. My legs felt as fragile as toothpicks, but I was able to stand, at least.

A trail of smoke cut through the pale sky. I followed it as I staggered through the patchy trees, trying not to fall into any of the snow pockets that formed around their trunks. I wasn't dressed for the outdoors, and plumes of icy mist rose with every exhale.

The trees ended, and I stepped into a field of sloping snow. Just ten feet ahead was a piece of jagged metal, half buried. Past that was a neck pillow that had been charred on one side. My gaze moved slowly, following the trail of debris as it led to one horrendous, inevitable conclusion.

The plane's wreckage pressed against a rising mountainside. It looked nearly a mile away. Smoke rose from it, and it was almost nothing like the plane I'd boarded six hours before.

The tail was shattered into a hundred pieces and scattered out behind it like dark flags across the brutal white landscape. The front half of the plane was missing entirely. The only part that seemed even partially intact was the back portion of the carriage I'd had been sitting it. It was twisted and stained by ash. Both the front and back gaped open like dark, yawning mouths, exposing loose cables and knives of twisted metal.

I couldn't see anyone moving, either near it or inside it.

I broke into a staggering run, wading through the snow to reach the wreck. I had to keep my head down as I moved, but every few minutes I'd glance up. As I drew closer and closer to the broken cabin, the horrific details became clear.

What had once been a cylinder was now squashed on one side into an oval. The wreck didn't seem to be on fire anymore, but some kind of flame—from the engines?—had scorched its outer wall, blackening it.

Large shards of the plane were scattered along the landscape.

Between them were pieces of luggage: carry-on suitcases, stowed luggage, and cartons of mail from the cargo hold.

Two hundred feet from the plane, I passed the first body.

It looked like the man who'd been thrown from his seat a moment before my own chair tore free. I'd caught a glimpse of his face as he tumbled through the cabin. It was contorted in sheer terror.

He lay face down now, each limb flung out at a strange angle, as though he was trying to imitate the shape of a chalk outline in a cartoon murder scene. I stopped by his side, breathing heavily. I needed to know if there was any chance he was alive, but then I saw his face. His eyes were open and bloodshot. The pupils were dilated, the lids unmoving. His head was turned at such an extreme angle that his neck must have been broken.

I hunched, arms wrapped around my aching rib cage, as I focused on getting to the wreck ahead.

There was a flutter of movement near where the plane had been sheared in half. I ran toward it, but it was only a coat, snagged on the torn metal and flapping limply in the breeze. That's when I became aware of how eerily quiet the wreck was. No sobbing, no voices, none of the screams I'd heard in the plane's last moments. There was a whistle of air moving against the ragged rock face and the distant, repeating groan of some compartment door being tugged open and closed again by the wind, but nothing human.

My mouth was bone dry. I was nearly at the plane's side now, close enough to see the frost around the edges of the windows and the individual scorch marks where the fire had licked.

More than a hundred people had been on board the plane. I couldn't be the only survivor.

I stepped toward the section of the plane that had been torn open, right where my seat had once been. I could still see the stubs of the bolts, now little more than twists of discolored metal.

Slowly, I raised my eyes to look inside the cabin.

Light streamed in from the back of the plane, where the tail had been torn off, turning it into something like a tunnel. It created a backlight that made it nearly impossible to see the inside's details clearly.

The plane listed at an angle, its carpeted floor slanted. The damage had been obvious from the outside, but it was even more undeniable on the inside. The walls and windows I'd spent my flight staring at were distorted or shaved away entirely. One half of the plane buckled inward from where it had hit the jagged rock slope, compressing seats and buckling them up from the floor. The ceiling had come down in another area, like a tin can being crushed.

My body turned numb as I stared into the wreck—at the bodies that had been my fellow passengers.

I knew some of them. I was one of the guests invited to a wedding in a snowbound chalet high in the mountains. A bridesmaid, brought in to help with the preparations. The bride's parents had been on board this flight, along with two of the groomsmen. I'd waved to them in the lounge before boarding, but I hadn't seen where they were sitting. They might have been in the front half of the plane, the part lost further into the mountains.

I waited. For what, I wasn't sure. A voice. Some rustle of movement. Anything.

A magazine flapped on the tilted floor; its pages were covered in spots of blood. Many of the overhead luggage compartments had sprung open during the crash, and cases and laptop bags filled the aisle like rubble.

*I can't be the only one.*

My legs were unsteady as I pulled myself up and stepped into the wreck. The metal creaked under my weight. I took a shuffling step deeper into the tube, past the place where my chair had once been. Almost out of habit, I glanced at the space across the aisle, where the woman with curling, jaw-length hair had sat, but that part of the plane had been shorn away entirely against the mountain's side.

I swallowed, then spoke, and my voice came out strange and echoey. "Hello?"

The magazine continued to rustle. The lost coat flapped. Not a single body moved.

I took another step into the tunnel. Details started to emerge from the gloom. Faces, painted with vivid-red streaks of blood, eyes open and staring vacantly, mouths hanging loose.

My focus darted from body to body, searching for any sign of life. The forms hung limp in their seats. Some were crumpled forward, heads hanging between their knees. Bodies drooped across the center aisle, their fingers barely touching the carpet.

A gust of wind moved through the plane's body. It brought the harsh copper smell of blood and the acrid tang of urine and something deeper and more cloying: death. Hair ruffled, and it almost looked like the rows of corpses were slowly raising their heads to stare at me. And then the wind faded, and they fell still again, and I was so excruciatingly alone, I felt like I was going to suffocate from it.

I reached toward the nearest body: a man about my father's age. He wore a tidy suit that he'd unbuttoned. He might have even been another early guest for the wedding. I gingerly touched the side of his neck, feeling for a pulse. His skin was pliable and warm, but it was different from the warmth of any person I'd felt before. It was the warmth of a seat recently occupied. The kind of warmth that said life had been there moments ago but was now gone.

I pulled my hand back and held it close to my chest, as though I'd been burned. That small touch had stolen the last scraps of hope. These people were all dead.

I staggered out of the plane and dropped to my knees in the snow outside. From that angle, the freshly churned snow marking the plane's path to the crash site was clear. The debris scattered out in a broad line, almost like a shadow of the smoke trail above.

*They're dead. They're all dead. I'm alone on a mountain, and everyone I came here with is dead.*

I felt dizzy, like not enough oxygen was getting into me, even though I was gasping. My mind scrambled. There was no kind of human settlement for hundreds of miles in any direction. Nowhere I could walk to. I was going to die in the barren mountains, and it would be slow and painful, and I almost wished my chair had stayed inside the plane so that my death was as sudden as everyone else's.

Then I clutched fistfuls of snow in my numbing hands and pressed them to my face. It worked. The panic bled out in response to the sudden shock of cold. I counted out the seconds as I slowed my breathing, then let the snow drop away from my stinging skin.

*I'm not going to die. There will be a rescue effort. The pilots would have put in a Mayday call, and even if they didn't, people will notice when the plane doesn't arrive. They'll come looking for us.*

Above, light spread across the sky.

The plane was due to touch down in about an hour. The tower would try to get in touch with the pilots. When no one answered, they'd begin to trace the plane's route, searching for it. The smoke and the wreckage would be hard to miss.

I'd been lucky enough to land within walking distance of the broken plane. Now I had ten hours of daylight ahead of me. I just had to wait by the wreck until someone arrived.

The world was almost unearthly quiet. The wind created a strained, strange note as it floated across the landscape. In the plane, the loose door creaked, but even that sound seemed muffled.

And then I heard something else entirely.

The crunch of boots on snow.

I swung around. A form stood behind me, silhouetted against the rising sun so all I could see were the wisps of curling hair billowing around its head. Then a woman's voice spoke, shockingly clear: "Hey there. Looks like you survived."

I choked on my words as the woman crouched to my level. It

seemed impossible. But I was staring at the woman from across the aisle, the woman with the striking angles about her face and the too-large canine teeth. She smiled at me, her head tilted slightly as she took in my reaction.

"You—" I glanced down, toward her right arm. It was missing below the elbow. She'd wrapped a jacket around the stump, and the fabric was stained red.

"It doesn't hurt as bad as you'd think," she said, following my gaze. "The shock's probably helping."

I belatedly noticed faint marks where mascara had bled across her face. But her eyes were sharp and bright and her lips expressive as she spoke. "But what about you? Any injuries I should know about?"

Every inch of me ached, but it felt almost insulting to say that when I hadn't lost anything as vital as a limb. "I'm okay."

"Good. I'm glad." The woman's smile shifted wide again, exposing full rows of teeth. "I'm glad you made it."

"Ah...yeah." There was a flutter of fabric behind us, and I instinctively looked back toward the plane, but it was only the loose jacket in the wind.

"I'm sorry," the woman said. "I already checked. There are no other survivors."

"Y-yeah. That's... I'm glad you..." I couldn't stop stammering. Or staring. I forced myself to look away again, back toward the debris scattered through the snowy field, only for my eyes to flow straight back to the woman's face. "Ana," I said, to break the stillness.

"Hmm?"

"My name's Ana."

"Oh!" She actually chuckled, and somehow it felt full and warm and natural. "Of course. I'm Chloe."

"Are...are you sure you..." My eyes trailed to the crudely bandaged stump.

Chloe rolled her shoulders in a shrug. "I'll survive this, don't worry. What I care about more right now is making sure we're found. What do you remember about our route?"

"The...the flight route?" I stared at my hands, which were turning a chapped red from contact with the snow. "Ah—landing in Camden Regional. We left from Holbrook."

Chloe squinted at the distant sun. "Yeah. I wanted to make sure I had that right because we're way off course. By at least an hour. The pilot was probably trying to avoid the storm but ended up being sucked into it instead."

"You can tell where we are?"

"Sure. This is a regular route for me. I know these mountains pretty well." Her eyes flicked back toward me. "This is going to be hard, Ana, but I don't think they'll find us here. At least, not as fast as we need them to. As far off course as we were, the search could take days or even weeks."

A drop of crimson fell from the end of her stump.

Chloe shifted her arm back so I couldn't stare at it anymore. "That's unless we get a message to them. Do you understand?"

"Yes. Uh...a cell phone, or..."

"We won't get any signal out here; it's too wild. We need

to use the communication set the plane has. That's in the cockpit."

The metal hull next to us was only half of the plane. I stared at it, then tilted my head back to watch the fading smoke drift into the sky. I turned, and the sun seemed painfully bright as I squinted into the fog-blurred horizon, in the direction the plane had been traveling.

In the distance, along the mountain's ridgeline, a tinge of dark smoke stood out like a thumbprint in the haze.

"Over there." I pointed. "That has to be the other half."

"Mm." Chloe's hair danced in the cold air. "Looks like it's within walking distance."

Barely. I tried to gauge the rocky, mountainous terrain between us and the crash site, and I knew the trip would take at least half a day. And most of it would be uphill.

If Chloe was right—if we needed to signal for help in order to be found—then we had no choice except to make the trip.

And yet...

I clenched my hands. If a rescue crew somehow did find the wreck and we weren't with it, the rescuers wouldn't know they needed to search for us. At least, not for a few days, until they counted the bodies and saw they were two short.

We couldn't risk being missed. One of us would have to stay with the smoking hull. And, with Chloe's severed arm, it wasn't hard to know who should stay, and who would have to fight their way to the front half of the plane.

"We're going together," Chloe said, almost as though she'd

heard my thoughts. I opened my mouth to disagree, but Chloe spoke first. "We'll leave a message in case anyone comes here. But I don't want us splitting up. Not in these mountains."

"It's a long way to walk." I fought to keep my eyes from turning to her partially hidden arm.

"That's fine. I know the region; I can guide us. But I'll need you by my side. I won't be able to do much that's actually useful." Chloe held up her other hand. She'd managed to wrap a handkerchief around it, but even with the cloth softening their edges, I could tell at least two of the fingers were broken. I'd been so focused on her other arm, I hadn't even noticed. "You'll have to be the hands for both of us. Do you think you're up for it?"

"Of course." We didn't really have a choice. Not if we wanted to survive. "I can do whatever we need."

"Good. First, let's get you a jacket. You're freezing." Chloe nodded to the luggage scattered across the snowfield. "It shouldn't be hard to find. People would have packed for the weather."

The owners were dead, but it was still a strange and uncomfortable experience to unzip bags that didn't belong to me. The first suitcase I opened was overflowing with clothes, and at the top, a thick winter parka. I held it out to Chloe. "I'll help you put it on."

"Sorry, love, it won't fit over my arm."

She was right. The makeshift bandage was large and bulbous; the only way we could get it down the sleeve was by removing the wrappings, and that came with a frightening chance of reigniting the bleeding.

I must have looked devastated, because Chloe chuckled. "I've spent enough of my life in the snow that I've adjusted to the temps. I'm comfortable, I promise."

"But—you've lost blood—"

"Not enough to kill me. Not yet. And I'll be plenty warm once we start walking. Put that on, though. You need it."

Reluctantly, I shuffled into the parka and zipped it up. It must have belonged to someone with broad shoulders; it hung off me and puffed high around my throat.

"There are gloves tucked down the side there," Chloe said, standing over the case, her head tilted as she examined the contents. "And a scarf. There's a water bottle lying in the snow close to the plane too. Take them all."

The gloves were too big, but at least they were warm. I took the scarf, but instead of wearing it, I looped it around Chloe's neck. She raised an eyebrow but didn't argue.

"We...we'll need something to leave a message." I was grateful the jacket was at least shielding me from the brisk wind as I fit the half-frozen water bottle underneath, where my body heat would keep it melted. "We could write in the snow, but the wind might erase it."

"And whatever we leave, it has to be clear enough it can't be missed," Chloe added.

"Maybe..." I glanced through the fallen luggage. There was a purse nearby. I opened it and sifted through the contents. Tangled in with earbuds and credit cards and loose receipts was a tube of lipstick.

We approached the plane's scorched side. Chloe nodded, and so I took the cap off the tube and wrote a single word in large, ragged letters:

SURVIVORS
—>

The oily red lipstick smeared through the ash. It looked a mess, but the color contrasted against the grays. The implication would be clear enough, I hoped; the arrow pointed toward the plane's other half. At the very least, if someone found the wreck, they'd know to keep looking.

"That's very good," Chloe said. She paused, staring into the distance, and something in her expression turned dark. "We should go."

I tried to follow Chloe's eyeline, but all I could see were faraway rows of dark tree trunks crusted in frost. "What is it?"

"Nothing." There was a second of hesitation, and then Chloe was smiling again. "Absolutely nothing, except for the daylight we're burning. Let's head out, yeah?"

I followed as Chloe led us away from the site of the crash. The snow was pristine and came up to our mid-shins, forcing us to wade more than walk. Chloe seemed to have our path picked out because she led us up a sheltered incline without hesitation, toward one of the many rocky outcroppings dotting the region.

As we reached the peak, I turned, glancing back down at the

area we'd left behind. The wreck stood out against the white landscape, a line of char and debris fanning out in its wake. The sun was at just the right angle to shine inside the open barrel. It lit up row after row of bloody faces, all staring out—staring up—toward me. Their hair ruffled in the wind, and although their bodies were as limp as rag dolls, they seemed almost alive.

I hunched, pulling the jacket tighter around my throat. My eyes drifted toward the plane's side, where I'd left our message. The writing still stood out clearly, except for one part. The arrow was smudged.

My heart missed a beat. Even from that distance, I could see four distinct lines running through the red. As though someone had pressed a hand there and dragged their fingertips through the arrow, smearing it.

*How did…*

I looked down at my hands. The glove tips were stained an oily red. I'd been fumbling to hold on to the small tube with numb hands; had I smeared it then?

Or had I accidentally leaned against the plane's side? Had I dragged my hand over the message without meaning to?

Chloe had stopped at the crest and turned to watch me. The sun hit her back, illuminating her like something mythical, and glazing her hair in a syrupy golden glow.

"Chloe?" I dabbed my tongue over cracking lips. I was suddenly very afraid to ask her my question, and even more afraid to hear its answer. "Are you sure no one else survived the crash?"

"Yes." The light's angle obscured Chloe's features. "I searched for a long time. I'd given up when I found you." Her head tilted a fraction, curious. "Why do you ask?"

I looked back at the red tips on my gloves. "No reason."

There was faint concern in Chloe's eyes as she watched me climb up to meet her, then she tilted her head toward our destination, the distant wreck. "We'll try to stay on high ground, when possible. Less snow to wade through."

It was my first clear look at the path ahead. My stomach dropped. The terrain was jagged and unfriendly; dark stone stuck out of the dense white. Strands of pine trees huddled where they found shelter, but they were the only signs of life as far as I could see.

*Maybe there were survivors on the front half of the plane.* It felt like a pitiful hope, but it was all I had to cling to. Already, the distant smoke marking our destination was starting to fade. I captured a mental snapshot of it, triangulating it against the nearest peaks so that we wouldn't lose it.

Chloe set a quick pace. She moved fluidly, even as I staggered to hold my balance. I had the distinct impression that, even with one arm missing and the other hand crushed, Chloe could have easily outpaced me in a race. She never let us grow more than ten feet apart, though. At least once or twice a minute she glanced back to check that I was still there. Sometimes, her gaze would flick to an area over my shoulder, but anytime I turned to look, the fields behind us were empty.

The rising sun warmed me despite the snow. I breathed heavily, my throat cut raw by the cold and the exertion. We skirted past a band of trees, near a steep drop, where the snow was shallower. Chloe seemed to have a knack for finding paths, even where it looked like there weren't any. A suspicion had begun to grow, and I couldn't ignore it any longer. "If it's not rude to ask, why were you on the plane?"

One of Chloe's eyebrows rose as amusement picked at the corners of her mouth. "Why would that be rude?"

"Sorry—I just—you said you know the area. But I don't want to pry if you don't want to talk about it."

"Ha!" The crooked teeth flashed into sight, and I loved them. "We're stranded in an untamed, unsafe mountain range together. A little prying is probably the least we're entitled to. And you're right, I know these mountains. I know them very well."

She lightly stepped over a fallen branch, and I felt like a newborn deer scrambling to keep up with its graceful yet patient mother.

"I'm a researcher," Chloe continued. "And this region has a special interest for me. I've been here many times before, though usually with more…" One shoulder rolled in a shrug. "Backup. And what about you? Since we've opened the door to prying."

I tried to chuckle, but it came out strained. "I was a bridesmaid. There…there's a chalet about an hour outside the airport, and my friend's getting married in a week. I was flying in early to help prepare."

Chloe's expression softened, empathy and grief creeping in around the edges. "I'm so sorry."

I hadn't let myself think too much about it yet. I wasn't the only early guest on the plane. Even if, by some miracle, the others had survived, it was hard to imagine the wedding going ahead when—

My mind shorted out, the train of thought abruptly stilled. Ahead, the black-and-white landscape was interrupted by a subtle splash of color. One of the cracked tree trunks bore four distinct red spots, about the size of fingerprints.

I glanced down at my glove, then back at the trunk ahead.

The marks looked exactly as though someone had rested a lipstick-stained hand against the bark without thinking. Only, the mark wasn't at shoulder height. It wasn't even at head height. I reached one arm up to gauge the distance; it had to be at least eight feet off the ground.

"Chloe?" My voice came out as a whisper.

Chloe was already at my side, gazing up at the marks. Her expression was flat and unreadable, but I caught a flicker of something in her eyes I hadn't seen before. Panic?

"We should keep walking" was all she said. "Stay close to me."

"Chloe, wait." I reached for her damaged arm before catching myself and pulling back. "What—what is this?"

Chloe's eyes were sharp and intense as they searched mine. She didn't speak for a beat, and when she did, the comforting tone didn't quite match her expression. "It's nothing to worry about, I promise. We're making great time. Stay with me."

She was lying. I was as certain of that as I'd been of anything. But she was also my only companion, and she was being friendly, and I didn't want to ruin it. I looked back at the fingerprint marks a final time, then pulled my jacket tight around myself.

We reentered the fields of white. The silence hung over us like a shadow. Twice, Chloe glanced back toward the trees as they faded into the white mist. Each time, I looked with her. I never saw anything.

"I've spent a lot of time out here," Chloe said suddenly, and I had the sense that she was trying to make amends for her earlier lie by sharing more of herself. "Usually with other researchers, but I've gone on solo day trips as well. There are…rules we all kept to. Things designed to keep us safe."

"What kind of rules?"

"Get indoors after dark. Don't travel alone unless necessary." Chloe paused after each sentence, punctuating them. "Don't lose sight of your end goal."

"Is that why you want us to keep walking?"

"If we falter, we create gaps for other things to creep in." Chloe's eyes were so bright they seemed glassy. "It's always safer to have something to aim for. Something to focus on."

My tongue felt like lead. I wanted to press—*What things? What are the things that can creep into the gaps?*—but fear had coiled around my heart, and giving it a voice felt like giving up a part of myself to it.

I'd been frightened before—frightened and so full of shock and pain and sickness that I felt like I might burst from it—but now a new emotion joined the mix. Dread.

Chloe seemed to be pushing us faster. Her movements were still fluid and easy, but there was more of a lurch to her gait as she climbed the rocks and crept down slopes. We both breathed heavily.

And then I heard it.

A low, subtle chattering noise. It almost sounded like a voice, speaking a complex sentence in a short burst. Except it came a little too fast and too guttural, like a recording that had been deepened and then increased to double speed.

My first thought was that it had to be an animal call. Not a deer and not a wolf, but some other animal—a large bird, maybe—that had learned to survive in the barren icy world.

And yet...

I could have sworn there had been words mixed into the garbled sound. It was just too low and too far away to make them out.

I stole a glance at Chloe, as though that would help me know how to react. She looked so calm and unconcerned that I began to think she hadn't heard anything.

And then she parted her lips and spoke three words.

"Don't turn around."

Prickles ran though my limbs like a thousand needles. I didn't even think. I simply moved. I turned against my better judgment, almost against my own will, to see the field behind us.

Two pairs of tracks—Chloe's and mine—formed lines leading through the aching white, back toward the distant crop of trees. The dark trunks were already fading into the haze of white that blurred the landscape.

Something stood ahead of the trees, though. Something with arms and legs and a head. Something watching us.

"Face forward," Chloe said, and her voice was calm and gentle but gave no opening for argument. "Keep walking. Don't look at it."

I snapped back around. My tongue wouldn't work. Neither would my mind. The image—the distant figure, entirely naked, arms spread at its sides and legs braced—wavered in my mind, horrifying beyond description.

My legs kept moving, almost without me being aware of them, but I was staggering with each step. I pressed my tongue against the back of my teeth until I thought I had the strength to speak. "Chloe?" I swallowed, but my mouth remained deathly dry. "What is that?"

Chloe inhaled deeply as the slope began to draw us upward again, toward another peak. When she let her breath out, a cloud of condensation raced past her face, vanishing into the void behind us. "Something very old."

I wanted to laugh, but I wasn't sure I had the strength. Every nerve was alight. Every hair stood on end. I couldn't stop myself. I turned a second time to look back at the figure.

Its pose was identical to how I'd first seen it: legs braced, fingers splayed, back hunched to bring the head forward. Gusts of snow wrapped around its flesh. It wasn't moving, and yet I was certain it was closer than it had been before.

"Don't look at it," Chloe said again. "It moves faster if it thinks it's being watched."

My heart was hammering hard enough to bring nausea. My eyes burned. I faced forward, fighting to match Chloe's pace, to not be left behind.

The man's skin had been gray, mottled, uneven. Like progressing frostbite. But somehow even that was less unnerving than the way Chloe called the man *it*.

"That thing back there isn't human." I'd wanted it to be a question, but it turned into a statement as it broke out of me. And I knew it was true. Even before Chloe's slow, wary nod, I knew that the presence behind us wasn't truly a man.

"What is it?" I asked again. Chloe didn't respond. My voice rose as the shock began to billow into panic. "What is that thing?"

"Stay calm," Chloe said, not breaking pace. The angles in her face seemed harder than they had before. "I don't know its name. I don't think even *it* knows what to call itself. It's going to follow us, and we can't do anything that will stop it. We just need to keep walking."

I thought of the handprint on the tree, and how high it had been. Our follower—whoever or *whatever* it was—had been too far away to see clearly, but it had been tall. Taller than a human.

I thought I'd understood what true fear was before, when I looked inside the plane's open cavity filled with only death. This fear was worse. Sharper. It was the fear of prey that knew it was being stalked.

My shoes slipped in a snowbank and I scrambled, suddenly terrified of falling behind. Chloe paused to give me a chance to catch up. There was something like regret in her eyes. Almost like an apology for what was happening.

"You've been here before," I managed as we crossed over a rocky ridge. "You've seen that *thing* before. Tell me what it is."

She took a slow, heavy breath before speaking. "Humanity, over the time it's existed, has spread into every continent, every crevice. It has conquered the arctic and the deserts, claimed the skies and plunged into the deepest parts of the ocean, and settled in places that should, by every reckoning, be uninhabitable. With how much land humanity has covered, it's easy to think that there's nowhere left that hasn't been explored."

Our shoes crunched through the snow. I became convinced I could hear a third set, far in the distance, trailing behind us.

"But humanity *hasn't* covered every part of the earth," Chloe continued. "There are places that are still purely raw. Purely wild. And in those untamed places, untamed things live. This is one of those places."

I knew I wasn't supposed to look back, but the compulsion was like a constant weight in the back of my head. I clenched my hands hard enough to make the tendons ache, just to give myself something to focus on. "It's not dangerous, is it?"

Chloe didn't answer. That meant it was.

"You still haven't told me what it is."

"That's because I don't exactly know what to call it. This part of the mountains is dangerous, and no one has managed to stay here long enough to name it. It's old. It's hungry. It will follow, and if it feels your fear, it will grow bolder. Sometimes it looks like a human, or an approximation of one. But it's not. Not even close."

A flash of understanding snapped through me. "You said you were coming here to join a research expedition. You were going to research *it*, weren't you?"

"You're quick." Despite the fear, despite the panic that was beginning to eat me from the inside out, Chloe's words gave me a small rush of warmth. "All the paperwork says we're here for geological studies, mind you. But we were much more eager to learn about it, and the things like it. Not that we'd ever admit it to the folks who give us funding."

A sound came from behind us again. The same deep, guttural, chattering sound, like a human voice chopped up into garbled syllables.

"It wants you to turn around," Chloe said. Her head was high, her gaze fixed on the horizon. "Don't give in."

That was a hard ask. The sound was a lot closer than the first time I'd heard it.

A band of trees rose up ahead, running like a ribbon across our path. My stomach twisted. I didn't want to step into the forest, where the trunks would close in around us and rob us of our sight. But we didn't have a choice.

"You said something about *things like it*." My palms itched as our unrelenting pace carried us closer to the trees. "How many are there?"

"I'm not exactly sure." Her smile was soft. "But this might be a comfort: they're not all hungry. The earth seeks balance. That's one thing I've seen, again and again, throughout my life. For every vicious beast, there is a gentle one. For every creature that can be called *evil*, there is one that must be called *good*." She raised her eyebrows. "The good ones are hard to spot. They're shy. Most of the time they appear like snow hares: small, flighty.

But you'll know what they really are by looking at their eyes. Normal hares almost never blink."

The monster behind us called, its chattering voice cutting through the chilled air. I flinched, hunching my shoulders. Chloe's words felt horrifyingly close to delusional. The only thing that kept me from putting up a mental wall against them was the undeniable presence of the thing that followed.

I looked for little white hares in among the dark trees. There were none. A drop of scarlet fell from the end of Chloe's bandages as we stepped into the shadows of the trees.

The world felt altered inside. Each press of our shoes into the snow seemed louder, each breath a little more desperate, a little more ragged.

"Tell me about the wedding," Chloe said, and I knew she was trying to drag my focus away from the creature trailing us. To keep my eyes from flicking toward every twitching shadow. It was a distraction, but I still clung to it.

"I know the bride from work," I said. "We get along really well. One of her bridesmaids had to cancel at the last minute, so she invited me instead. She's always loved celebrations—birthday parties, Christmas; even Halloween becomes an excuse to invite people around to her house. So I guess the wedding was kind of like the ultimate celebration, to her. She wanted everyone to have a good time. And she paid for our plane tickets…"

My mind flickered back to the flight, just before the crash, our bodies wound tight and rattled loose all at once as the aircraft trembled around us.

"She wasn't on the plane, was she?" Chloe asked, her voice gentle.

"No. Thank goodness." I saw those last moments again. Glancing toward Chloe. Getting that tiny smile and nod in return.

I wanted to tell her about the small thought I'd had on the airplane, during boarding, when she took her seat in the aisle across from me. She'd tossed her bag into the overhead compartment as though it weighed nothing and then slipped into her seat with more grace than I've ever been able to muster. I'd longed to be friends with someone like her. To *be* someone like her. In that moment, I'd hoped she might be another early guest for the wedding. That maybe we could have spent time together, talked, gotten to know one another.

Just…not like this.

I thought I heard something move through the trees behind us. I fought to ignore it.

"Is she scared?" Chloe asked, masking the sounds echoing through the cold air. "Your friend, is she nervous about the wedding?"

"I…I guess?" I blinked as the trees ahead thinned, and we crossed back into open snow. "She was excited too. She really loves her fiancée. He's a good guy. I don't think she'll regret it. But she was still nervous. It's hard not to be."

"It's the unknown," Chloe said. "That's what we always fear the most: the things we can't see, and the things we don't yet understand."

The band of pines was fading behind us. I made it forty paces before succumbing to temptation and looking back.

The *thing* stood at the edge of the pines. Its mottled, gray skin blended into the shadowed trunks. Despite the camouflaging effects, that was the closest I'd seen it—and also the clearest.

Its mouth gaped open. Blackened, bleeding teeth jutted out of its gums, and they'd grown so long that they forced the mouth into a permanent scream. It had no eyes, just folds of cracked and blistered skin pulled over the concave spaces where eyes belonged.

As I watched, the stretched jaw moved, tearing already strained skin as it released its deep, rapid cry. The teeth chattered together, punctuating the not-quite-words. The call seemed directed straight at me.

I swiveled forward again, my heart in my throat. Chloe didn't say anything, even though I probably deserved to be scolded for turning around. Maybe Chloe understood just how hard a temptation it was to resist.

"What happens if it catches up to us?"

"I won't let it." Another drop of blood fell from the edge of Chloe's bandage, and I tried not to think about how much she'd already lost. Or about what would happen if she lost so much that she couldn't stay upright, couldn't walk.

Chloe must have heard the hitches in my breathing, because she moved closer.

"You're not alone. You're not going to die. We'll get through this, you hear?" There was something almost tender in her expression now. "I'm here. You're not alone."

The words were like a small, burning hot coal in my stomach. At the same time came a wash of self-loathing. Chloe had lost an arm. She had to be in enormous pain. It was a miracle she could even walk. To take comfort from a woman who had already lost so much seemed unbearably selfish.

A scent carried across the landscape. It was foul and damp, and I would have thought it came from the creature behind, except the wind was moving in the wrong direction.

"Try not to stare into the holes," Chloe said, right before we crested a ridge and I saw them.

Ahead of us, enormous cavities appeared in the ground. Each one was the width of a football field; jagged rocks ringed their edges, though the rocks were so worn down by wind and rain, I felt certain the holes had existed for as long as the mountains had.

Damp air floated out of them. It was full of ammonia and decay and something else, something almost like the queasy scent of rotting skin and stale breath.

"What are they?" I asked, unable to tear my eyes from the black pits. Our path was leading us right toward them.

"It's the place the untamed things crawl out of."

We'd been hiking through snow since the crash. Now, though, the ground turned to pure, dark stone, holding only small shreds of ice in its crevices. Air gusted out of the holes. It didn't feel warm, though—if anything, it felt colder than the ambient air. I pulled the zipper on my jacket all the way up and buried the lower half of my face in its collar to buy some respite.

It took a moment to realize the icy air didn't come in a constant stream. It rushed from the hole in a heavy flow for forty or forty-five seconds, then fell frighteningly still for just a few heartbeats—two, maybe three—before changing direction. As though something in the hole was sucking the air back down.

As though the mountain was breathing.

Chloe seemed untroubled. Her curling hair billowed around her face as the air rushed past her.

"Don't get too close," she said. "We can't risk you falling in. I'd have no way to get you back out if you did."

The ground was unstable; with no cushioning snow, each angled rock threatened to turn my ankle or send me sprawling. As we passed between two of the holes, the stretch of ground between the gaping mouths less than twenty feet wide, I clung to Chloe.

The air changed direction again, no longer sinking into the holes but rushing out of them, bringing the stink of death and oil and rancid mouths. And with it came a sound. Something familiar. Something that sounded like men and women calling up to me for help.

I turned to my companion, my heart squeezing. "Those are—"

"They're not speaking. Not really. Don't listen to them."

She was right. I was hearing refrains of the creature behind us: chattering, guttural, a staccato of looping syllables flowing over one another.

They sounded very much like someone begging to be saved. But the voices were vacant of any real words.

"Look," Chloe said. She raised her broken hand to indicate above us. "Keep your eyes ahead. Don't lose focus."

She was pointing to one of the peaks ahead of us. Something dark spattered across its surface, as though a painter had struck his brush across the canvas in anger. Snow was already building over it, helping to soften its jagged edges and cover the parts that had been smoking just hours before.

The plane.

One shattered wing lay fifty feet off to the side, torn free during impact. The other clung to the plane's body, a lattice of metal and wires. The body itself was crumpled and twisted, the plane's nose crushed and spilling open against the dark rock.

All remaining hope of finding other survivors vanished. The plane's front half was barely recognizable. It would have taken a miracle for anyone to get through that.

Which meant everyone I'd seen at the airport terminal...the best men, the bride's parents...

"Focus," Chloe repeated, and I tried to fight back the pain as gusts of icy air spiraled around us.

She was right. We weren't here just to look for the living. We were here for the radio. If it still worked.

I thought about what would happen if it didn't. I pictured Chloe and me, trailing over the barren landscape, trying to keep ahead of the creature at our backs as the hours ticked away and night fell.

The voices floated out of the holes. They still pleaded, but now the broken syllables were turning angry. I fought the impulse to look into the pits as tears burned at the edges of my eyes.

The thing behind us joined in the angry voices, louder, closer, demanding attention.

"Stay with me," Chloe said, and she repeated it again and again as we passed the holes. "Stay with me, Ana. Stay with me."

Blood dropped from her arm to freeze on the bare, icy stones.

And then we were past, and the snow began to thicken underfoot, and our path led directly upward to the broken plane.

Bodies lay in the stark field, partially covered by gusting snow. Sometimes whole bodies. Sometimes just parts. They were scattered between the luggage and shards of plane, burned in places, turning ghastly white in others as they froze. One head was turned to look up at me. Frost grew thick across its staring eyeballs, and I was almost convinced those eyes followed me as we trailed past. They couldn't, though; of course they couldn't. The head was connected to a neck and part of a shoulder, but nothing more.

The debris grew denser as we came up alongside the plane. In some places, there was no way to avoid them. I swallowed thickly as the shards of metal and scattered belongings crunched underfoot.

Gaping tears ran through the shattered plane body. I stared into them as we passed. The dead stared back out. I listened for any signs of a miracle inside: labored breathing or a whispering voice or the rattle of someone struggling against their seat belt. Wind whistled through the holes in the cabin, but it and the crunch of our shoes were the only sounds to disturb the eerie quiet.

My survival was the first miracle of the day. Chloe's was the second. I told myself it was foolish to long for a third.

"We're almost there," Chloe said. She looked different now that the light was falling. Sicker, paler. She smiled, and her teeth were as angular and wonderful as ever, but the folds of skin around her eyes seemed heavy and thick. She'd lost too much blood. "Look inside the cockpit. Find the radio. I can't use it myself, but I can tell you what to do."

The untamed thing behind us called out, loud, hungry. I blocked my ears to it and approached the very front of the plane. It had torn open on one side. I saw an arm hanging loose, scorched and nearly severed from the body. The badges on the sleeve told me it belonged to the captain.

"There," Chloe whispered. She'd come up behind me, so near that I should have felt the warmth from her body. She pointed with her broken hand. "Hold that switch there to speak."

The hole into the cockpit was narrow. I had to squirm, my stolen jacket snagging on metal and wires as I reached across the dead pilot's body. The dashboard looked like nothing to me: just a confusing jumble of dead panels drowning in shadow. But I followed Chloe's direction and pressed the switch she'd pointed to. The system crackled.

That call still remains a blur in my mind. I can't remember exactly what I said or even who I spoke to. I remember they had a quick voice, partially distorted by static, and they sounded stressed, but their words were kind.

Chloe stood behind me. She whispered the coordinates for both halves of the plane, and I relayed them through the radio.

The call couldn't have lasted more than five minutes. I would have stayed with that brisk, kind voice, but the angle I had to lean at made my back and thighs ache. My arm was braced across the dead pilot's chest, his staring, crushed face just inches from mine. Even though the voice on the other end of the radio asked me repeatedly to stay, I eventually let the switch go.

Shivers ran through me as I slumped back out of the hole and dropped into snow that had been churned up by the plane's impact. Chloe carefully sat beside me.

"You did amazingly," she said, and her voice was faintly slurred around the edges. I wondered how long she'd been falling apart like this. I'd been so focused on the untamed thing behind us, I hadn't been paying enough attention to my friend. "Help's coming. You're going to get out of here."

"*We're* going to get out of here," I said.

We stared at one another, and we both knew that was a lie. A beautiful lie. A soothing lie. Chloe smiled again, and I saw the soft agreement in her graying eyes. *Yes,* that smile said. *We can pretend. For a little while longer.*

Angry, staccato syllables rattled across the frozen world. I wasn't supposed to look, but I did anyway. The untamed thing was crossing the expanse toward us. Its body was humanoid, but the way it walked borrowed more from the wild creatures of the mountains. Great, swinging, loping steps carved away the ground six feet at a time.

"It's going to reach us before help does," I said, and averted my eyes from the monster.

"Rescue will take a few hours." Chloe seemed peaceful. "We

can loop this crash site, or we can travel back to our starting point. But we should keep moving."

In the distance, I could see the enormous holes burrowing into the earth. I thought I could still hear the chattering voices rising from them. I looked up at the sky. Night was still hours away, but the world was going to get darker and colder very soon as the sun fell behind the mountain peaks.

"I want to go back to the first crash site," I said. I clenched my gloved hands, felt the muscles strain. "Can you...are you..."

"Of course I'll be with you." Chloe lurched to her feet. Her movements had lost a lot of the lithe energy from that morning. She nodded toward the horizon. "Come on, Ana. We'll stick together."

Retracing our steps involved circling around the untamed thing. It had stopped, its broken face turning to follow our movements. Its emaciated, twisted body shivered in delight as we drew nearer. I fought to keep my eyes focused ahead, on one of the distant bands of trees, as the staccato, deep-pitched voice screamed at us.

Another creature, horribly like the first, emerged from behind a rock wall thirty yards in the distance. Snow crusted over the cracked and bleeding skin covering its face. Long and dexterous fingers, each containing three knuckles, flexed at its sides.

"Focus ahead," Chloe coached. "Don't let them know you're scared. Don't let them know you can see them."

I forced my face to hold a neutral expression. My breathing was heavy and my limbs felt numb, but I pushed myself to keep moving. I needed food. I needed rest. Neither were possible while the creatures followed.

We passed the holes again just as the sun fell behind the mountaintops. Shadows spread across our world, deepening the color of the rough, exposed earth.

The ground breathed, slowly, the air snagging our hair and clothes as it rushed past us.

This time, despite Chloe's earlier warning, I let myself drift closer to one of the holes and leaned over to look into it.

The chasm seemed to stretch downward for an eternity. Through the mountain's bulk, through the earth's crust. There was no sign of an end. I knew, if I dared to throw a rock into the chasm, I wouldn't hear it hit bottom.

I could see something inside it, though. Eyes. Yellow, lamplike eyes staring up from the chasm's walls to fix on me. The voices called up, pleading for help, the syllables so close to speech and yet falling so far short.

Chloe didn't say anything as I turned away from the hole. Her skin was sallow and graying, her lips losing color, her sharp eyes growing dull.

"The untamed things come from there," I said, repeating what she'd told me earlier.

"Yes." She kept close to me as we passed the holes. "Many kinds of them. The bad ones. The good ones. They're all a little different. Most won't come out until night sets fully."

*Most,* I thought, and tried not to let my feelings bleed onto my face.

As we passed the holes, I thought I heard some of the bodies inside scrambling up to the lip. Creeping out onto the rocks. Into the snow. Lured by our presence, like moths around a lantern.

I didn't look back to be sure.

The expanses seemed endless, but we both fought through it, pulled forward by the knowledge that rescue was close, and death even closer. Chloe began to stagger. I put my hand out, offering to help her, but she only shook her head, her smile lopsided as the muscles beneath began to fail.

We passed between the trees. I saw the red handprint, left so far above our heads. There were signs that others had passed through since our first trip. Claw marks dug deep into the pine trees, leaving rivers of beading sap in their wake. Seven-toed footprints dug deep into the snow, crisscrossing where our boots had marked our path. I imagined our pursuers pacing the space, like wolves sniffing out blood.

Back into the expanse. Our path carried us downhill, which was a mercy. I was exhausted. I'd finished the bottled water, and my throat was parched, but I didn't want to stop and refill the bottle with snow. Not when the end was so close.

Chloe's steps had grown uneven and stumbling. I wanted to say something to her. Maybe *I'm sorry*. Or maybe *thank you*. But I could barely spare the breath to stay upright.

A small chorus of rattling voices followed behind. They were so near now, I thought I could smell their stinking breath. The landscape was growing dimmer as twilight began to descend, and

I instinctually knew that not even Chloe could keep me safe once darkness fell.

We passed through another band of trees and then, as we stepped between the final row of trunks, I saw the wreckage we'd started at. The plane's back half, torn open and abandoned on the snowy mountainside like a child's toy forgotten when playtime ended.

It was no longer the only shape there, though. Two helicopters had touched down in the snowy expanse. Figures, distant but unmistakably human, crossed between the helicopters and the wreck. Lights shone across the glittering snow as they searched for signs of life.

I took a step forward, my heart hammering.

Chloe didn't follow.

She stood at the edge of the trees. Her shoulders seemed too angular. Her face was gray and pale and drooping; her lower lids sagged away from her eyes, showing the red insides. Her lips looked like putty as she pulled them into a toothy smile.

"You did amazingly, Ana," she said. "I'm so proud of you."

"Chloe." I didn't know what else to say. She looked like a skeleton wearing borrowed skin; nothing fit right, nothing hung right.

"Take the scarf," she said, bending forward so that I could pull it off. "It's not for me to keep."

My hands shook as I took it and looped it around my own neck.

"Chloe…" Words knotted themselves on my tongue. "Can't we…can't you…"

"Shh." A final flicker of those beautiful, uneven teeth, as the unnatural things closed in behind her. "We did it. You're a survivor. Go, now, and live."

I tried not to let her see me cry as I turned back toward the wreckage. Flashlights fell over me when I was halfway across the expanse. Voices called as the distant figures began to run toward me.

Something crunched under my shoe. I lifted my foot. It was part of the debris: a case for designer eyeglasses. The company's name was splashed on front in curling golden script: *Chloe Acarda*.

Not far away was a novel, half buried in the snow. Its title, *The Arctic Researcher*, was an embossed black against the white cover.

I kept walking.

"Are you hurt?" they asked as they caught up to me. I said I wasn't.

They asked if I'd been with any other survivors.

I looked back to the trees I'd emerged from. It was barely possible to see them through the fading light.

The monstrous things had vanished. Too many humans made them uncomfortable, I supposed. Chloe said they only existed in places that were utterly untamed and utterly alone.

Chloe no longer stood where I'd left her. Instead, a small, white snow hare was at the forest's edge. Its eyes blinked once, then twice.

"No," I said. "I'm alone."

They got me onto one of the helicopters. They handed me coffee from a bottle and wrapped me in thermal blankets. The last of daylight faded entirely as they closed the helicopter's doors.

They took me to the closest town's hospital. There were a lot of questions, both on the flight and after I'd been given a medical all-clear.

Was I sure I'd been alone out there? I'd written *SURVIVORS*, plural, on the plane's side.

Yes, I said. I'm not sure why I used the plural. Maybe because I hadn't *felt* alone.

How had I made the trip? It was common for survivors to walk in circles, or at least meander a little. They'd found my footprints and my path had been amazingly direct, almost as though I'd had a map of the region.

I told them that was all luck. I'd followed the smoke to the front half of the plane, hoping someone might be there. I guessed I was just good at finding my way.

They found some of Chloe's footprints. Not many, from what I could gather—she'd been good at covering them up. But a heel print here, a scrape there, running parallel to my own tracks. Again, they asked if I'd been with someone else. Again, I said no. The questions only stopped once they'd recovered all the bodies and checked them off against the manifest.

One of those bodies was Chloe's. The real Chloe, the one who'd sat across the aisle from me. Her chair had broken free during the crash, and she'd become crushed beneath the plane. It would have been an instant death, the reports said; she wouldn't have even known it was happening.

Her real name had been Susan. She wasn't a researcher. She'd been an event coordinator for the wedding, arriving early to help with the preparations. It was a strange fulfillment of the wish I'd made during the trip, that maybe, in another life, we could have gotten to know each other at the chateau.

Chloe had adopted her face because it was the face I'd had at the forefront of my mind. She knew nothing about the real Susan's identity; she just saw enough to scrape together her form.

A lot of things began to make sense when I realized that. Chloe had deftly gotten me to recite the plane's intended route, because she didn't actually know it. When I'd tried to introduce myself, Chloe had been surprised that we didn't already know each other's names.

She'd known the coordinates for both wreck sites, though. Of course she had. She understood the mountains better than anyone.

That crash was one of the deadliest in modern history. Out of a hundred and sixteen lives on board, I was the only survivor. The miracle. I've spent nearly four years trying to process it, to cope with it.

Friends and counselors have tried to help me. I've recounted my story multiple times, but it always rings false as soon as I talk about reaching the first crash site. Because I can't tell them what followed. The most important part.

I was the first miracle. But I only survived because there was a second miracle out there on the snow with me.

A special thing.

A wild and untamed thing.

### THE END

# CATHEDRAL

---

"Take a look over there," Keith said.

Tam lifted her head from the car's window, squinting against the sun hitting her eyes. "Is that…"

"A church, yeah."

They'd been driving for most of the day. Tam's legs were stiff and her neck sore, and the last town they'd passed through had faded from their rearview mirror more than an hour ago. They were surrounded by endless fields, so it wasn't hard to see what had caught Keith's notice. A spire rose in the distance, extending out of heavy stone walls.

"It looks big," she said.

Keith's grin betrayed how taken he was with the building. "Right out in the middle of nowhere too. Should we stop and take a look?"

"It's probably locked up."

"We might get lucky. It's Sunday. We'll hop out and stretch our legs and maybe get some photos, yeah?"

Tam eyed the sun. They were trying to get home before dark and still had a long way to travel. On the other hand… "Five minutes can't hurt, can it?"

They had to follow a narrow side road to reach the church, and it carried them deep into the fields of half-mature grain. The high stalks blocked most of their view, and it was only when the fields thinned enough to grant them access to the parking lot that Tam realized just how massive the building was. Buttresses surrounded high arched windows. What she'd first identified as a spire was one of many—great jutting metal and stone points rising out of the stone construct's immense length.

"It's a cathedral," she breathed.

"I can't believe it." Keith turned the car into the dirt parking lot. "Why'd they build it all the way out here? It's amazing anyone makes the trip, even on a Sunday."

The parking lot was far from empty, Tam saw. Trucks and sedans, their paint peeling in the harsh sun, had been arranged in informal rows.

Even though a congregation was present, Tam still felt squirming misgivings in the base of her stomach. With the car's engine off, she could hear noises from the outside world filtering into their car. Crickets, their songs overlapping. A distant bird's call. Even the click of their car's engine as it began to settle.

No sounds came from inside the cathedral.

She suddenly felt uncomfortable there, as though they were

intruding on something private. The cathedral's doors were open, but she couldn't see any further than the top step. The hot sun gleamed off the roofs of the cars surrounding her, and this detour no longer felt like a fun adventure, but like a mistake. "Hey, maybe we shouldn't—"

The driver's door snapped closed. Keith was already outside and halfway to the cathedral, his face eager with anticipation.

Tam muttered under her breath as she opened her door. She was wildly underdressed in her jeans and polo shirt, and neither of them looked like they belonged there. But Keith jogged up the stone steps ahead of her and paused on the landing, waiting just long enough to be sure she was coming, then disappeared inside.

Tam crossed her arms and put her head down. She dragged her feet as she paced along the dirt parking area, prolonging the seconds she spent outside, but before she was ready, she was at the steps.

The enormous wooden doors loomed above. They dwarfed her: tall enough for giants, tall enough to make her feel like nothing more than a morsel to be consumed as she climbed the steps and crossed the threshold.

Cold air rolled across her exposed skin. The day had been hot and humid, but entering the cathedral was like stepping into an icy tomb. The narrow windows let in less sun than she'd expected. Stained glass images of men and women, heads bowed, eyes downcast, filled them. The inside was dim enough that she could believe it was dusk.

Two dozen figures were spaced around the hall, sitting in rows of wooden pews, utterly dwarfed by the size of the space. It could easily fit two hundred.

The congregants were perfectly, unsettlingly silent. Tam's shoe hit a shard of broken stone just inside the opening, and the sound seemed to ricochet through the space. She hunched, waiting to feel eyes turn in her direction.

No one moved. Every single bowed head remained facing the stage at the cathedral's far end.

A cowled figure stood there. Its arms were held out at its sides, palms toward her, as though inviting her in. Layered gray material covered it so thoroughly that only its long, gray fingers were visible. The draped material hid its bowed head in a pool of perfect shadows.

Tam froze. She couldn't see the figure's face, but she could feel its gaze, staring directly at her. It didn't move or speak but held perfectly still. As though waiting for something.

Waiting for *her*.

Tam drew a quick, shuddering breath. It wasn't a human. The gray fingertips and the drapes of the material were a little too blocky, and a little too stiff, to be real.

It was only a statue.

Her mouth was dry. Even though the figure couldn't be real, she still felt as though its gaze was following her movements as she stepped past the open doors.

She couldn't see Keith. He'd come inside only a minute before she had, but she'd somehow lost him. Her eyes darted across the figures scattered through the pews, searching for movement or for the familiar blue of Keith's shirt.

He couldn't have just *disappeared.*

Her shoulder brushed against the cold stone walls. No matter how quiet she tried to be, the cathedral was quieter. Every breath, every thump of her heart, traveled.

But none of the figures moved. A sense of unreality pressed over Tam. They were as still as the statue they all faced.

And the cars outside—she'd been too distracted by her own discomfort at the time to really pay attention, but the cars had all been old models. Decades old. Paint peeled under the hot sun. Dust had gathered thick over the roofs and the windows.

The cathedral doors had been open, but Tam was struck by the idea that she and Keith were the first people to walk through them in a long time.

Her eyes fell to her feet. Dead insects gathered around her sneakers, smothered in dust and grime that had been allowed to gather, perhaps for decades. Spiderwebs had turned to cobwebs, growing fragile and thin. Their strands shivered in the cold air. And it *was* cold. Outside it was summer, but the hairs on her arms stood on end.

"Keith?"

Even her whisper sounded invasive in this still space.

She thought she saw him. He was as unmovable as the other bodies, but his dark hair and blue shirt were unmistakable. He sat in one of the pews near the front of the cathedral, facing the cowled figure, seemingly attentive.

"Keith!" Tam moved forward, her arms wrapped around her torso and her shoulders hunched as she passed between the pews. Keith didn't respond. It was as though he couldn't even hear her.

She had no choice except to walk between the motionless congregants. A stark paranoia filled Tam that she might have been mistaken. That they weren't all statues, after all. That the bodies around her—unmoving and as silent as death—were alive and breathing.

Her heart skipped uncomfortably. She was passing near a cluster of three figures. Every step, she dreaded seeing one of those still heads rise to stare at her. To ask what she was doing there, in this house of worship, during their time of silence.

But they didn't look.

And so, Tam looked instead.

She tilted her head just far enough to see the shadowed faces, using her peripherals at first, then staring openly to be sure she wasn't deluding herself.

The figures surrounding her truly were made of stone.

A man was nearest. The face was so realistic that it could have passed for a real person's except for the cold, stony gray shade. There were creases around his mouth and across his forehead, tiny lines underneath his eyes. The creator had even given him a mole on his jaw.

Beside him were a woman and a child. All three were dressed in clothes that might have come from the sixties or the seventies. The woman held a stone purse in her stone lap.

Tam moved faster, desperate to reach Keith and escape the deathly chilled building. Her footsteps rang out on the stone floor like gunshots, but Keith refused to turn away from the cloaked statue.

As she drew nearer, the cowled figure seemed to rise out of the gloom. It was an angel, she realized. Enormous wings were pinned to its back. They stretched from its head to its bare feet, the longest pinions grazing the floor. Its hood hung far over its bowed head, hiding its face.

"You're not going to scare me," Tam whispered to Keith. Her words were betrayed by her hushed voice. Even though she knew the two of them were alone in the cathedral, she couldn't bring herself to speak any louder.

Keith still didn't respond. Tam's shoes crunched over dead insects as she came to a halt at his side. She'd been so focused on the figure ahead that it took her a second to realize something was wrong.

The shape next to her had lost its color. Or maybe she'd only imagined it in the first place. Where she'd seen brown and blue was now just gray.

She'd approached one of the statues by mistake.

"Keith?" She turned, scanning the great hall. All around her were stone walls, rising into the sky until the dark, vaulted ceiling was hard to distinguish from the gloom.

And ahead were the congregation. Stone faces. Stone clothing. Stone eyes, staring without seeing. Staring toward her.

Tam hunched, feeling the heavy weight of those lifeless eyes.

She turned back to the statue she'd mistaken for Keith. The sense of discomfort that had clung to her since she'd first seen the cathedral intensified.

The stone was old. It was weathered to the point of staining, especially around the eyes. Lines of discoloration ran down the face, almost like tears.

But it was Keith. The nose was his. The lips were his. The eyes, crinkled around the edges, were unmistakably his.

Tam's lips parted, but no sound came out.

Behind and slightly above, stone cracked as it ground against itself. She turned, her heart racing.

The statue before the congregation lifted its head. Shiny black eyes fell on her. Piercing. Deeper than should be possible, deeper than she could endure. Tam staggered. Her legs wouldn't hold her. She collapsed, falling into the pew next to Keith's statue.

Every part of her felt heavy, all of a sudden. So heavy she couldn't stand. Couldn't breathe. Couldn't even turn her head away from that awful, immense statute that stared into her soul.

The day was hot outside. Hot enough that, with time, Keith's car would dust over and begin to peel, just like the others.

Inside, though…

Inside, the cathedral was as cold and as hungry as always.

**THE END**

# A BOX OF TAPES

---

WHY WAS A STRANGER'S SHOEBOX IN MY DAUGHTER'S CLOSET?

I'd been searching the shelves for a lost toy. The space seemed to manifest clutter. We'd only been living in our new home for six weeks; it seemed impossible that the modest packing boxes we unloaded could have ballooned to such a mess, and yet, they had.

Popsicle-stick crafts and picture books were stacked on top of pine cones from the forest behind out house. A knit cardigan from her great-aunt, worn once and then rejected for the crime of being itchy, lay like a morgue blanket over a plastic doll whose head had been pulled off and then replaced backward.

"Come on, Big Gray," I whispered, shuffling a make-your-own-bead-jewelry kit to one side as I searched for the missing chicken. Kayla was pacified with cartoons for the moment, but that was only a temporary fix. Getting her to go to bed without her favorite toy would be an ugly ordeal. I *needed* to find it.

I shoved a crate of building blocks aside and saw something that didn't belong. It was a shoebox. That itself was strange: Kayla was growing fast enough to need new shoes pretty often, but I always threw the boxes out when I got them home.

It wasn't even the right size. Children's shoes would rattle around in it; this box was designed for an adult's shoes. And it definitely wasn't mine.

I carefully dragged the box out. Something solid shifted inside. A line of duct tape had been stuck around the edge of the lid, sealing the box closed.

*Is it Kayla's? Something she wants to keep secret?*

It seemed too soon. Kayla was only four, edging toward five. I hadn't expected the private diaries and secret treasure boxes to pop up for another few years at least.

I thumbed along the edge of the tape and realized there was no way it had been placed there by my daughter. A ring of grime had formed at its sticky border. As I moved it into the light, I realized the box was very old. The tan cardboard was faded and discolored. The corners were turning ragged. It looked like it could have been living in a closet for decades.

But that wasn't possible. We'd moved into our home just six weeks ago, and the rooms had all been empty then.

Hadn't they?

But what was the alternative? How had this box ended up in my daughter's room? And why at the very back of her closet, as though it had been hidden there?

Ugly thoughts flashed through me: a stranger on the street

pressing the box into Kayla's hands. A child from preschool telling her she had to keep it a secret. The urge to tear the duct-taped lid off the box overwhelmed me, but I reeled myself back. My mother had searched through my belongings when I was a child. I'd never forgotten the feeling of shame and betrayal when I realized she'd been reading my diary. And I'd promised myself I would never do anything like that to my own daughter.

I held the box gingerly as I went downstairs to the den. Kayla sat on the floor, her blanket—not quite as good as Big Gray, but a close second—clutched against her chest. Her face was washed in the sickly light of the television as a cartoon dog learned a valuable lesson about honesty.

"Hey, Cookie," I murmured, not wanting to break her rapt attention but also desperately needing answers. I crouched and held the box out, showing her. "Where'd this come from?"

She stared at it blankly, then shrugged.

"Did…" I paused, picking my words carefully. "Did someone give this to you?"

She shrugged again. There was no flicker of recognition in her face.

"Do you know what this is, Cookie?"

This time, she shook her head. "Shoes?"

It wasn't hers, then. At least, nothing that she remembered adding to her closet. Her memory was about as good as any four-year-old's, but I didn't think she'd forget the box in the span of six weeks.

Her focus was already drifting back to the show. I let it absorb her as I took the box to the kitchen. Its unseen contents rattled again as I set it down.

My cell phone rested on the counter. Two messages flashed up on the screen as I tapped it.

Any luck finding the big guy?

Have you checked the laundry basket yet?

That was Jax. He was thin as a beanpole, tattooed down both arms, worked in the local thrift store, and had enough piercings to set off every metal detector in town. And he was my best friend. Losing Big Gray was a tiny drama in the scheme of things, but Jax gave even the littlest storm in a teacup his fullest attention.

Still looking, I texted back with one hand, my attention on the shoebox.

Was it possible it was actually mine? Maybe something I'd thrown in the packing boxes by accident, then forgotten? But the box's tatty edges made me think it had emotional value for whoever owned it. Someone had picked it up and put it down hundreds of times. And that certainly wasn't me.

And the fact that it had been sealed shut, like some kind of tomb...

I sifted through my kitchen drawer to find a pair of scissors, then ran their sharp edge along the duct tape. It made a soft tearing sound as it separated. Then, slowly, carefully, I peeled the lid back.

My heart caught as I looked inside. I knew what the items

inside were. I'd seen them often enough when I was a child. But I hadn't actually touched one—let alone watched one—in at least fifteen years.

VHS tapes.

Black, boxy, and with a clear panel on the side to show the tape spool so you could easily tell whether it needed to be rewound. Just looking at them flashed up memories of pixelated cartoons and the discolored streaks that appeared at the edges of the child-hood movies I'd replayed to death.

White labels were stuck to the tapes. They were old enough to have started peeling up at the edges, the tape curling in on itself. Although there was plenty of room for a detailed descrip-tion, only numbers had been written on them: 1, 2, 3, 4, 5, 6. Together, the six tapes completely filled the shoebox.

But that wasn't the strangest thing. A small, slim piece of paper rested on top of the tapes, fixed in place by a sliver of yellowed sticky tape. And it held a message.

DON'T WATCH. YOU'LL REGRET IT.

———————

I stared at that small note as I placed it on the countertop next to the shoebox.

It was written in a tight, controlled hand, but something about the way the lines ended in sharp tips, like scalpels, made my skin crawl.

In the background, Kayla's show played, but it seemed muted, like it came from a whole world away.

Slowly, I lifted the first tape out, the one labeled *1*.

*Don't watch.*

What was on them? I tilted the tape as though I might be able to see the contents just by staring at it hard enough.

*You'll regret it.*

What could possibly warrant a warning like that? Had the owner written it to themselves, in the same way that I wrote NEVER EVER CALL next to my college ex's name in my phone?

Maybe the tapes held painful memories. Film of a loved one's final moments. Some traumatic family event that warranted keeping but would cut like knives every time it was seen.

I wanted to believe in that theory, but I couldn't.

This note felt different.

It felt like a warning for whoever was going to find the box.

A warning for me.

Human contrariness is a strange thing. I was completely aware of it happening but still had no way to stop it. The note told me not to watch the tapes, therefore I wanted to watch them more than ever.

And not just to spite the note. Not simply out of curiosity. I needed to know how and why this shoebox had gotten into my daughter's room.

I leaned back to look into the den. Kayla bobbed as the characters sang.

My phone pinged. It was just Jax. His message was brief and cryptic.

**I might have something.**

It took me a second to stitch that message back with our earlier conversation. I'd become so focused on the tapes, I'd forgotten about Big Gray. Which was a problem. Kayla's bedtime was in five minutes.

I reached for the phone to answer, and then a thought occurred.

Vinyl records had made a comeback. Not so much VHS tapes. I hadn't owned a player in decades, and I couldn't think of anywhere I could find one. Except...

My thumb flew over my phone.

**Can I stop by? Need a favor. Will be quick.**

---

Jax's store was only a ten-minute drive from home, which was a mercy. Most stores along that strip had been closed for hours, and I was able to park close by. The shops—a long row of connected brick cubes—looked eerie at night, with their windows dead and heavy shadows clinging to their walls. Three of the streetlights were out and had been out for months. People had given up complaining to the council, but I still chewed my lip and held Kayla to my chest as I jogged to cross the ocean of darkness toward the one beacon of light.

Jax's store didn't post any hours in the window because he rarely kept them. He lived in the apartment above the thrift store and was known to welcome people in at six in the morning, still wearing his scrappy pajamas and holding a mug of double-shot coffee. Now, he kept the lights on for me, and threw the door open so that Kayla and I could slip inside.

The shop was pure chaos. I loved Jax, but sometimes I thought he was a hoarder in disguise. He took in items from estate sales and donations and seemed unable to throw out any of them, no matter how worthless. When he'd run out of shelf room, he simply started stacking his finds into piles. The store was claustrophobic, dusty, and still somehow felt like home.

"You know where the toys are," Jax said to Kayla with a wink.

I put her down. She sent me a suspicious glance. It wasn't the first time we'd stopped at Uncle Jax's store, but Kayla must have sensed this wasn't an average visit. Only four, and already too perceptive for me.

"Go on," I said, and she vanished between the shelves in search of the toy section, which I knew would be chaos within seconds.

"I was going to stop by your house," Jax said, dropping his voice so that Kayla wouldn't hear. "But thanks for coming. Saves me the trip."

"What do you…"

He reached into a paper bag he'd left on his counter and pulled out a stuffed, speckled gray chicken.

"Big Gray!" I almost forgot to keep my voice quiet and clasped a hand over my mouth.

"Almost." He slipped the bird back into the bag. "It came in as a donation a few months ago. I figured I'd hold on to it for Kayla, just in case anything happened to the genuine article."

A lot of people around town found Jax unnerving. His tattoos wrapped up his throat to his jawline and featured snakes, skulls, and spiders. Gauges stretched his ears and studs dotted both eyebrows. Only the people who got to know him had the chance to learn how soft he was inside.

We'd become friends in middle school. He'd been a shy boy with thin blond hair back then, and both our families were going through divorces. Jax's had been slightly less ugly than mine. His parents stayed friends, and he went to live with his father in Ludlow for three months every summer.

He moved in with his father permanently when he turned fourteen, but we'd stayed in constant touch. A collection of pen pal letters included photos that documented his first tattoo, and then his second, and showed when he'd started dressing all in black and shaving his head.

He was part of the reason Kayla and I had ended up in Ludlow. When rising prices in our old town had forced me to consider a move, Jax's presence in Ludlow made it an appealing option. It was always good to have a friend close by.

"I'm sure you didn't come *just* for the bird," Jax said, leaning one bony arm on the counter. His mustache twitched as he smiled. "What's up, Tessie?"

"VCR players." I couldn't even ease into it with a preamble. "Do you have any?"

"Oh, *heaps*." He turned to lead me between the shelves. "No one buys them, but everyone wants to donate them. You'll need a connector to make it work with modern TVs too, but I should have one of those…"

He snatched items off shelves, shoveling them into one of the spare boxes he had lying around.

"Do you want something to record and convert it into a digital file? So you can upload it online or share it with friends?"

I couldn't imagine a scenario where that would happen. "No, just the TV connector. I found some old tapes and I want to see what's on them."

"Fair. That's all you'll need." He offered me the box. "I'm going to invite you to stay for coffee or vodka or whatever, but I know you're going to say no."

I sighed. "I'd love to, but—"

"Gotta get the gremlin to bed." He smiled, and it showed off the gap where he'd lost a tooth in a bike accident eight years before. "I hear ya. Hey, Cookie! Time to roll out!"

"She never listens to me like that," I muttered as Kayla came running. She clutched a plastic pony under one arm. I reached for it, but Jax just shushed me.

"That's hers now. And you can keep the player too, if you want." Jax handed me the paper bag with the Big Gray replacement as I crossed to the door. "Safe travels. Bye, Cookie!"

"Later, Biscuit!" Kayla yelled back.

She didn't want to be carried to the car, so I had to run through the shadows in her wake, half afraid she'd vanish into them forever if she got too far ahead.

———

Kayla started looking for Big Gray the moment she got home. I tucked the paper bag by the door, out of sight, and told her to get ready for bed.

She sucked in a breath to argue. Pink color was already starting to seep into her face.

"Big Gray will be waiting for you," I promised. "Just get ready first, okay?"

She clamped her mouth closed, watching with that same suspicion, then turned and thundered up the stairs to change into her pajamas.

That was a new thing this year. She got changed herself and washed her face herself. I know that's the goal of parenthood—to see your child learn how to live in the world on their own—but it still felt like a loss.

While she was upstairs, I took the surrogate Big Gray out of the bag. The bird Jax had found was the right make and model, but it was missing some important details. The real Big Gray had been loved intensely, and he showed it.

I used a pair of scissors to very carefully snip some of the threads on his wing. I was pretty sure I could remember which ones were missing. Then, whispering an apology, I took one of his eyes. When I held him up to the light, I could still see that he wasn't the same tattered, floppy bird my daughter loved. But, when I presented him to Kayla in the dark of her room, she accepted him unquestioningly and made soft cooing noises to him, the way she always did, as she rolled over to sleep.

She'd figure it out pretty soon, I was sure. But it would buy me at least a few more hours to find the actual Big Gray.

The night-light stayed on, as always. I kissed her forehead good night, as always. Then I crept out of the room and back downstairs.

The VCR didn't have a manual, and it took some wrangling to get it to connect to the TV, but the screen turned an eerie white when it did. I dragged the box of tapes down beside me as I knelt in front of the television.

This was going to be a lot of effort for nothing, I figured. It was either going to be some couple's homemade record of their friskier encounters, or the tapes were going to be blank.

The note lay on top. DON'T WATCH. YOU'LL REGRET IT. My mouth twisted as I moved it aside and pulled the first tape out of the box.

*Let's see. Let's see just how bad you are.*

———

The tape clattered as it slid into the VCR's hungry mouth. A green light blinked. I knelt on the rug, staring up at the TV that dominated my whole view. Then I pressed the *play* button.

Static crackled.

A woman's face appeared. She took up almost all of the screen.

"What…" I whispered, leaning close.

Dirty blond hair hung to either side of her face like curtains. Her skin was sallow and waxy and covered with a map of discolored veins. Her lips were bloodlessly pale. Her eyes seemed too large for her slim face, and the eyebrows rested low over them, darkening the blue irises with heavy shadows.

I clamped my hands on my arms as the hairs there rose. Something about that woman got under my skin. She didn't look real. She looked...

My throat caught. She was dead. That had to be it. *That* was why I wasn't supposed to watch the tapes; they held footage of a deceased person. Propped upright, facing a camera, but still unmistakably dead.

And then...

She blinked.

I flinched.

*Okay. Okay. Not dead.*

Even after seeing her move, it was still hard to believe she was a living person. She didn't seem to breathe. I could have believed the tape was paused, except for occasional crackles of static around its edges. The tape was worn from too many viewings; it reminded me a lot of those cartoons I'd obsessively rewatched as a child.

It was hard to guess how old the woman might be. Thirty? Forty? Older? Her skin was waxy and sickly. She repulsed me, and yet, I found myself leaning closer.

The woman shivered, then raised one hand. She extended her index finger toward the camera. And then she began to move it.

Her finger swirled through the air. It was like watching a conductor in front of an orchestra. Or a magician casting a spell. The movements were almost hypnotic to watch, and they went on for nearly a minute before she finally lowered her hand again.

Her jaw began to move, as though she was chewing on something behind her closed lips. Around and around, her eyes staring back at me the whole time. I reached for the remote and increased the TV's volume. Distant crunching noises began to float out of the speakers.

Some kind of liquid bled out at the corner of the woman's mouth. Just a tiny spot. The tape's color was faded and bad, but I thought the liquid might be red.

And then she opened her mouth to show me the contents.

Five small, pale shapes rested on her tongue. They were coated in the same blood that dribbled over her lower lip and down her jaw. They...

*They're teeth.* I jerked back, my hand pressed to my own mouth. *She was chewing on her own teeth.*

As though the woman in the video had heard my thoughts, the corners of her bloodied mouth curved up into a smile.

A piercing scream came from the floor above.

*Kayla.*

---

I moved so fast that my feet slipped out from under me. I hit the stair banister and grabbed it, using it to haul myself upward. Kayla continued to scream, and scream, and scream, and abruptly her voice cut out.

My heart was in my throat, choking me. I hurtled across the upper hall to her room and threw the door open.

The night-light cast a star-speckled blue glow across the walls.

Kayla sat bolt upright in bed, her eyes huge and vacant. The replacement Big Gray was held loosely under one arm. I crossed to her and clasped her face in my hands. It felt hot and sweaty.

"What happened?" I asked. The images were still playing in the back of my mind: teeth on tongue, blood trailing over lips, and it made my voice louder and tighter than I'd meant. "What's wrong?"

Kayla didn't immediately answer. Her eyes trailed down to the toy at her side. "This isn't Big Gray."

I stroked her curling hair away from her sweaty face, trying to draw her focus back to me. "Why did you scream, honey? What happened? Was...was it a bad dream?"

"You were here." A tiny crease formed between her eyebrows as she pulled them together in confusion. "You had Big Gray. Why were you smiling like that?"

I bent closer, until our heads were level. "I was here?"

Her eyes flicked toward the empty doorway. "I didn't like that smile."

"Kayla?" I was scrambling to put together her disjointed words. "Why did you scream, sweetheart?"

The crease between her eyebrows grew as a look of deep betrayal set in. She continued to stare at the doorway as she spoke, her voice on the edge of tears.

"You pulled Big Gray's head off."

---

It took a long time to soothe Kayla enough to get her back to sleep. She fussed around Replacement Big Gray, alternately pulling him closer and then trying to reject him. I whispered soft words as I stroked her hair, then I sang to her, then I tried to read her favorite book, but nothing worked. It wasn't until exhaustion overwhelmed her that she finally slept.

I exhaled heavily as I adjusted the blankets around her and then stood. It was late, not just for Kayla, but also for me. I needed a drink, I decided. I was still rattled from the videotape. Kayla's nightmare was just the icing on the cake.

As I crossed toward the door, something small caught my eye. A tiny clump of tangled threads, no more than five or six, lay near the open door. I picked them up and rolled them between my fingers as cold nausea set in deep in my stomach.

The threads felt a lot like the stuffing from a plush toy.

---

The closest weapon that felt like it might really do some damage was the hammer in my study. I was planning to hang picture frames on one wall and turn it into a feature, but I never settled on an arrangement. The hammer and tin of nails had sat in the corner since the week we moved in.

Even as I collected the hammer, I tried to talk myself down. The threads in Kayla's room might have come from anything, at any time. The stuffing in her puffy parka. Another toy that was loved a bit too hard. I could have even tracked them in on my shoe.

But they aligned with Kayla's nightmare a little too closely, and my maternal instinct—the overwhelming need to protect, to defend—reared up. I flipped the hammer in my hand, testing its weight, then began searching the house.

I'd already looked through Kayla's room: under her bed and inside her closet of chaos. Those were the only places a full-grown human could hide. From there, I paced through every other room, moving slowly and methodically. I kept pausing to listen. The house was still new to me and so were its noises: I heard floorboards groan but couldn't find their source. The pipes somewhere on the ground floor rattled, then fell still again.

The house was a lot larger than our last apartment. It took a long time to really, properly search, but I went through it twice, just in case.

My pacing ended in the kitchen. Through the open doorway I could see the TV room. The screen had frozen on the image of the grinning woman. She seemed to leer out of the gloom, her mouth open to show off the teeth she'd removed.

I placed the hammer on the kitchen counter, frowning. I was almost certain I hadn't paused the TV. I'd been watching the tape when Kayla screamed; there'd been no time to do anything but run.

And tapes weren't supposed to pause themselves.

Slowly, I crossed toward the TV. Chills crept over me as I moved into the darkened room. Static crackled at the edge of the image. And then, a clot of blood dripped off the woman's chin.

*It's not paused. The tape's still running. She hasn't moved this entire time.*

That was well over an hour. A rough, panting noise filled the room, and I realized it was my own breathing. I snatched up the remote control and hit fast-forward.

The woman's image shimmered faintly as I sped through the tape. The teeth on her tongue glistened. Drops of blood built and then fell. My pulse raced, loud in my ears, as my knuckles turned white where I clutched the remote.

Then the tape ended, grinding to a clicking halt. It literally ran out of room to record before the woman shifted.

I threw the remote down and then hit the *eject* button on the VCR. The tape rattled free, and I shoved it back into the open shoebox, then slammed the lid back on.

"What in the hell," I whispered to myself as I rocked back onto my heels. "What in the *hell*."

Was it some kind of transgressive art project?

What sort of person had the patience, let alone the willpower, to stand stock-still for two hours while they bled out through their mouth?

I ran my fingers through my hair. I wished Abe was still with us. Kayla had been young when he'd died, and her only memories were vague and blurry. She didn't miss him quite as much as I did.

He'd always been bad at fixing his own problems, but if he saw I was having trouble with something, he wouldn't rest until he'd made it better.

I needed someone like that now. Or even just a friend who could talk me out of my panic. Instead, I was alone in a house that now felt way too big, and all I had to keep me company were my sleeping daughter upstairs and the box of tapes beside me.

My hand shook as I nudged the lid back off. I should leave well enough alone, I knew. There was nothing to be gained by watching more. But I badly, badly wanted to know if the rest of the tapes were the same, or if they held something *different.*

*Tape #2* scraped against its neighbors as I pulled it free. I glanced behind myself, toward the stairs, just to make sure Kayla hadn't somehow woken and snuck down. All clear. I pushed the tape in and pressed play.

The woman appeared on the screen again. But this view was *different.* She was further away, so I could see all of her body, and she stood in some kind of long hallway with wooden floors and walls. Photos or possibly plaques were hung on the walls; there were dozens of them, and the frames looked expensive, but the camera's angle made it impossible to get a clear look at any.

The woman wore a grimy, off-white nightgown. She was skeletally thin; long, bony arms hung at her side, and although the nightgown went to the floor, I could see bare feet peeking out from under it. She stared straight at the camera as she raised her hand and repeated the same movements she'd made in the first video.

I frowned, leaning closer to the screen despite myself. The lighting was strange. It wasn't coming from any of the bulbs above.

It seemed to be coming from behind the camera. And it was flickering.

"No," I whispered as flames appeared at the edges of the screen. The woman dropped her hand. Heavy smoke rolled out from the growing fire. The building was old, the wood lacquered and stained. I could imagine the stench as the old coatings curled up under the blistering heat. I pressed a hand across my mouth as the wooden frames closest to the camera began to catch fire.

The fire was growing fast. I could imagine the blistering heat that must be rolling toward the woman. Her dress and limp hair drifted in the air currents it caused, but she remained motionless as she stared into the camera.

Flames dances along the floorboards. The walls were on fire. The glass over the framed images splintered; then they fell, shattering into the inferno.

Fire licked across the woman's bare feet. It caught on her dress. It was growing hard to see her as smoke stained the camera lens, but I could make out the coal-red blisters forming on her papery skin.

She didn't so much as flinch.

I wanted to scream at her. *Move, move, run, it must hurt so bad—*

And then the screaming began.

The tape was so old, it sounded like a siren as it rose. The screams didn't come from the woman, though. As the fire burned across her nightgown and blackened her skin, as the screams grew louder and more pained, the woman's lips curled up into a smile.

The screen went blank as the camera broke.

I reeled back. Sweat stuck my clothes to my skin. The video had been so all-consuming, I thought I must have felt the heat rolling out of the TV. It took a moment to realize I was actually clammy cold.

Static continued to dance across the screen. I fumbled for the VHS player and hit Pause. When I blinked, I continued to see the fire—and the woman's unmoving, unemotional face, staring out at me as her own flesh caught on fire.

And…something else.

My stomach churned as I pressed Rewind. I knew I should leave it well enough alone. I already wished I'd listened to the box's warning. But I'd gone too far to call it quits. I had to be certain about what I'd seen.

As I rewound the tape, the scene played out in reverse. Fire retreated down the woman's dress and back onto the old floorboards. The red-tinted light grew dimmer. Rows of framed photos flew back onto the wall.

I hit Stop, then Play.

It took a few attempts to freeze the tape at just the right moment.

There was a point where one of the framed photos landed upright, angled toward the camera, before falling over and being consumed by the flames. In that brief second, its image was just barely visible.

Five individuals, all wearing identical uniforms, faced the camera. They were girls, teenagers, and even though I didn't recognize the uniform it looked like something that might belong to a private school.

A plaque was fastened beneath their unsmiling faces.

*Oakbrook Girls,* the first line of text read. The second line—probably a year or a class—was too small to make out.

I pressed Play again, and I let the photo vanish into the fire as the flames consumed the hall and the woman in it.

———

Kayla didn't want to go to preschool without Big Gray, even though his replacement was tucked snugly into her bag. The nightmare had blown my hope of passing off the impostor, and although Kayla was no longer throwing tantrums at the sight of him, she glared at him with faint mistrust.

I was dead tired. The previous night weighed on me heavily, not just from lack of sleep but from the things I'd seen. When I finally got into bed with the hammer on my bedside table (just in case), images of bloody teeth and fire haunted my dreams.

"Okay," I said to Kayla when it became obvious she wasn't budging without the genuine toy. "How about we stay home today? We can play some games, maybe put on some music."

It wasn't like I was going to be very productive either way.

Kayla sent a shrewd glance toward the stairs that led up to her room. She'd been fighting to kick her shoes off but fell still at my offer. Her small mouth twisted as some internal choice was made. "No."

"No, you don't want to put on music?"

She reached down and awkwardly tried to pull her loose shoe back into place. "I want to go to K."

That was what we had called her old preschool. The nickname had stuck for the new one.

I sighed, holding Kayla's jacket in one hand. "For real? You want to go to K now?"

"Yes!" She was getting agitated again as she fought with the shoe. I helped her slip it back on and fastened the strap, then she leaped up and ran to the door, slamming both hands into it. "K! Now!"

I'd been a mother long enough to not be offended when Kayla rejected my company, but as we snaked through the roads leading to her preschool, I found myself watching her in my rearview mirror. Games and music were some of her favorite things. It wasn't like her to turn them down.

Kayla was staring through the window to watch the trees swish past, and I found myself searching her face for any signs that something was wrong. I couldn't explain why, but this felt bigger than Big Gray.

We were late by the time we arrived, and Kayla's teacher waited by the doors, ushering in the last kids. She smiled and waved when she saw Kayla, and I gave my girl a quick kiss before nudging her toward the school. Kayla made it two steps, then turned back to me.

"Stay safe," she said, before turning again and running to her teacher.

That was something I frequently said to Kayla. I shouldn't have been surprised to hear it parroted back. But there was something in her expression—some kind of intensity that seemed too big for someone so little—that left me cold. I stood in the parking lot long after the preschool doors closed and the sound of yelling children faded.

My gaze drifted across the lot. The preschool was larger and prettier than the one we'd left behind in my old town, with elegant trees casting shade over the play areas. Older buildings dotted the lawn, probably from when the town was first constructed, and although they were no longer used, they were allowed to stand.

One of the buildings had a metal sign attached to its door. The sign was aged and stained and the words were barely legible, but my heart dropped as I read them.

*Oakbrook Primary School.*

———

As I slid into my car, I fished out my phone and called Jax. He answered on the second ring, and I was grateful he was the kind of person who didn't need to waste time on pleasantries.

"Oh, yeah, Oakbrook is *old* news," he said, and each word was accompanied by a crunching noise. He sounded like he was eating toast for breakfast. "Used to be two towns—Oakbrook and Ludlow. They merged, what, eighty years ago? Long time back, way before most people remember. You'll still find some old signs, though, from back then. Some places clung to the Oakbrook name way after the two towns merged."

"Thanks," I said, feeling numb.

"Did the new bird work okay?"

"Kind of." I grimaced. "She knows something's different about him, but I think she'll get past it."

We ended our call, and I slumped back in the driver's seat. If Oakbrook had once bordered the town, that meant the tapes had been filmed somewhere close by. They weren't some novelty brought here as a joke; they *belonged* here. And that made them feel so much more personal. So much *worse*.

I tapped on my phone, searching for *Oakbrook Girls*. The name was generic enough to bring up a menagerie of unrelated links. Even narrowing it down—*Oakbrook Girls School, Oakbrook students*—didn't help much.

It was only when I tried *Oakbrook Girls Fire* that I found something.

It was an old newspaper article that someone had scanned and uploaded to their website. The text was degraded to the point where it was nearly impossible to read, and the website hadn't bothered with a transcript. It did list an address, though.

*I should go home*, I told myself as I typed the address into my GPS. My knuckles were white as I turned the car out of the parking lot. *This isn't any of my business. Throw the tapes out. Don't think about them again.*

But the small threads in my daughter's room and her too-serious request that I stay safe lingered in my mind.

The roads took me past the edge of town. I'd spent a day with Kayla exploring the area shortly after moving in. We'd stopped at the ice cream store, at the three biggest parks, and at the library, between driving down random streets to see what they held. Our explorations hadn't taken us anywhere near the path my GPS directed me toward. I watched the beautiful town slowly degrade into something darker and grimmer as I left the populated center behind.

The roads became narrower, and my car rattled on a surface that was overdue for resealing. The trees were thinner and sicklier. The houses—the few that were about—grew more and more neglected the further I drove.

And then the buildings vanished entirely, and I was left on a path that was barely a car-width wide. Trees pressed in on either side, the leaves scratching across the doors. I'd slowed to a crawl and was breathing too fast. This was the kind of road that felt more than neglected. It felt forgotten. As though no one had tried to come down here in a very long time.

At last, the road ended. My GPS displayed a red dot for my destination: straight ahead, and several hundred meters into the trees.

I left my car behind. There wasn't even a path: I had to climb over exposed roots and duck beneath branches as I pressed into forgotten woods.

And then I stepped past the final tangle of trees, into a place where not even plants wanted to grow.

Bare dirt stretched ahead of me, trampled down until it felt more like rock underneath my feet. An enormous arch stretched ahead. Bronze metalwork formed a name:

*OAKBROOK GIRLS REFORMATION SCHOOL*

Beyond it was a blackened shell of a building.

I tabbed through my phone to find the newspaper article that had given me the address.

The text was old and blurred by the scan. It was a struggle to make out any words, but I fought to piece the fragmented text together.

"Twenty-six deceased in deadly fire…staff, students…cause unknown…"

I remembered the sounds I'd heard in the video. Screams, dozens of them, overlapping. I shook my head, almost convinced I could hear their voices again.

If I was reading the date correctly, the fire had happened more than two decades before.

I stepped under the arch, and my skin prickled like I was covered in ants. Even from a distance, it was clear the building had burned down a long time ago. Sickly vines grew over parts of the structure. Fallen leaves piled up like snowdrifts in the corners. The building must have been massive once—two, maybe even three stories tall, based on the few remaining sections of wall, but the fire had reduced it to rubble.

I stepped through what must have once been a doorway. Even after so many years, the ash was thick underfoot. Each step crunched, announcing my presence, and it was only then that I realized how silent the clearing was. No birds. No insects. I followed the phantom pathways left, and something sharp cracked underfoot.

I stepped back. Old, melted glass littered the ground. I bent and used the tip of my finger to lift a piece of charred wood. It crumbled under my touch, but it was clearly the frame for a photograph.

I'd found the place where the tape was recorded.

All of a sudden, the only thing I wanted was to leave. I staggered through the char and debris and remaining walls and burst out of the building's opposite side.

My breath caught. Ahead, a low fence bordered a stretch of land near the forest, and inside, stones had been erected in the compact ground.

Graves. Directly behind the school. It wasn't hard to imagine who had been buried there.

The school had been built a long time before antibiotics were discovered. If the students were malnourished and uncared for, diseases would have swept through them in waves.

I turned, slowly, to look back at the building. Barely fifty paces separated the graveyard from the school. The wall bordering it was low. Every day, the girls would have looked out the windows and stared into the resting place of previous students.

*What the hell kind of school* was *this?*

---

The middle part of the day passed in a blur. I went home; I tried to work. I must have sat at my idling computer for an hour, staring at the pinned task sheet but without touching any of the items on it. I had a good job; the pay wasn't the best, but it let me work from home and get through the work as quickly or as slowly as I wanted, as long as it was all done by end of week. I'd just have to catch up later.

Then I put on my game face and went to pick up Kayla. I was

hoping to get in and out quickly, but her teacher, Miss Lindsay, caught my arm before I could leave.

"Do you have a moment?" she asked, her voice quiet. I knew that tone; it meant there was something important we needed to talk about. And not in a good way.

I left Kayla in the playroom, then Miss Lindsay and I rounded the corner to where no one could see us. Miss Lindsay pulled a sheet of paper out from her satchel and showed it to me.

"Kayla drew this today during creative time, and I thought I should show it to you," she said.

The drawing showed a room with a bed in it. Kayla's, I knew, based on the gray blob near the pillow that she used to represent Big Gray.

Most of the room was drawn loosely and carelessly, but an unusual amount of focus had been put into the doorway. Black crayons, scribbled over and over, created a dark hall outside. And in the center of the doorway stood a figure.

"I asked her about it," Miss Lindsay said, a nervous smile rising and then fading again. "I couldn't make much sense of her answer. At first, she said it was you, but then she said it *wasn't* you, but someone who was pretending to *be* you. I think. We got muddled around there."

"Okay," I said. But nothing about this was actually okay. The figure in the doorway wore a long nightgown that fell down to her feet. Her arms were stretched out at her sides, the hands ending in jagged lines that might have been claws. Scribbles showed where long hair fell down to her waist. And her face…

Her eyes were points of black, scrawled hard and fast by an unsteady hand. Her mouth was a stretched, screaming, gaping hole.

She looked like a nightmare come to life.

"I just wanted to check in," Miss Lindsay said, her words laced with that awful mixture of patience and concern. "A move across the country must be unsettling for the both of you. I wanted to see if there's anything I can do to help."

She leaned close, one hand extended to offer a hug. How could I explain any of this to her? How could I tell her about the tapes, or about what I'd seen in them, or about the school that was very real and had very really burned to the ground?

I forced a shaky smile. "I think…I think she had a nightmare last night. Something scary came on TV and maybe she saw part of it."

That was close to the truth. The woman in the drawings was unmistakably the woman from the VHS tapes. I'd been careful to play them only when Kayla was supposed to be asleep, but she must have gotten out of bed and caught a glimpse of the video without my knowing.

It was the only explanation that made sense.

Unless…

"I'm going to talk to Kayla," I said, and my mouth was so dry my voice cracked. "Just, just to check in, and, uh…"

Miss Lindsay was nodding, her hand still held out to comfort me, even as I backed away.

"Just to make sure everything's okay," I finished, and I almost ran to the playroom to collect my daughter.

She seemed fine as I buckled her into her car seat. Giggles

broke out of her as she danced two toys across her lap in some epic chase. I waited until we were on the road before I asked, "Hey, Kiddo?"

"Mm." She barely gave me any attention as Princess Strawberry attempted to scale the window.

"Remember that bad dream you had last night? Mommy helped you go back to sleep, remember? Did you *stay* asleep, or did something wake you?"

She hesitated, the princess doll held in the air as though poised mid-leap. "Mommy woke me up."

My attention flicked from the road ahead to watching Kayla in the rearview mirror. "Did I?"

"No, *other* Mommy." Princess Strawberry dove down, impacting fatally into the car seat, her already tangled hair ground into the fabric.

The car slowed as I took my foot off the accelerator. "Have you seen Other Mommy before, Kayla?"

She didn't answer, too focused on tumbling Princess Strawberry across the seat, Hero Horse galloping in pursuit.

"Kayla?" I was starting to sound stressed, and it took all my willpower to get my voice back to something calmer. "Did you leave your room last night? Did you…see something on the TV?"

The toys came to a halt. Kayla wouldn't look at me. A tiny crease had appeared between her eyebrows, her earlier good mood vanishing. She was trying very hard to avoid my questions. Which meant I wasn't going to get *anything* out of her for a while.

A car honked angrily before speeding past. I swallowed, then turned back to the road, my skin crawling.

---

I tried to make that evening as normal as possible. We had Spaghetti Bolognese for dinner, and I had a glass of wine. Kayla laughed and squealed during her bubble bath. I read her two books as she drifted to sleep, the replacement Big Gray clutched against her chest.

Then, once I was certain Kayla wasn't going to stir easily, I went back downstairs.

The bottle of wine, nearly full, sat where I'd left it on the kitchen counter. I picked up my glass and began pouring a healthy measure into it, then stopped.

I always slept heavily after a couple of drinks. And, while that sounded like bliss, it also felt dangerous. What if Kayla called for me during the night? What if I didn't hear her? After everything that had happened...

I tipped both the glass and the rest of the bottle down the kitchen sink. Then I began to check every door and window in the house.

Locked. Locked. Double locked.

I even drew the bolts on the high-up bathroom window, the one that should be too narrow for any human to squeeze through.

Logically, I knew what had happened. Last night, Kayla woke up again and snuck out to the stairwell and saw part of the horrific fire video as I was watching it, then drew those images at preschool.

But it was past ten at night, and all the logic in the world couldn't erase the other possibility. That the woman from the videos had visited my daughter.

"Stupid," I whispered to myself as I checked the dead bolt on the front door. I'd searched the house and all its hiding places. There was no way in or out. At least, not without making a heck of a lot of noise. "You're being stupid, Tess."

The woman was dead. She *had* to be. I'd watched the flames race up her dress and scorch her skin. She'd died in that fire, sometime after the flames consumed the camera.

Almost against my will, I found myself drifting back to the den and the box of tapes. I nudged the lid off with the tip of my shoe. The fire was Tape #2. There were still four others.

I swore under my breath as I took out the third tape. I glanced toward the stairs again, breath held, as I waited for any sound of Kayla stirring or the creak of small feet on the stairs, then pushed the tape into the VCR.

The screen flickered to life, and I thought I was going to be sick.

———————

The woman was still alive.

There was no mistake and no chance of the videos being filmed out of order. I knew because her skin was scarred from the flames. A patch of hair was missing on the right side of her head, and the skin where it belonged was taut and shiny. Bubbles and puckers ran across her chest and up her throat. The scars looked painful, but old.

She swayed, smiling softly, her long gray nightgown flowing in the breeze, her stringy hair clinging to her sweaty skin. She was outside this time, and possibly in a forest. Branches rustled overhead.

The woman held up one finger. Just as before, she moved it through the air ahead of herself in strange, looping patterns. This time, the patterns repeated for more than a minute, her hand dropping lower and then rising again before she was finally satisfied.

Her smile twitched, then she gracefully stepped back and to the side.

The camera focused on a shape behind her. I craned forward, trying to see it through the grainy pixelation. It looked like a man, lying on his back, his body limp.

"What…"

I thought I heard a floorboard creak behind me and swung around, my heart racing. The hallway was empty. I leaned back to see more of the stairwell. No sign of Kayla.

Movement on the television pulled my focus back to it. The woman had returned. The dress gusted around her ankles as she stood over the man. She bent at her waist, her long hair wispy, her head tilting. She was examining him in the same way I'd examine a strange insect on the ground.

Then she reached out. She grasped the man's hands and stepped back, dragging him with her.

A faint sound came through the TV's audio. It was distant and distorted, and it took a moment for me to realize what I'd heard. A groan, coming from the man. He was alive.

The woman continued to pull him away from the camera. He seemed tall; he should have been heavy enough that the skeletal figure in the nightgown would have struggled to move him, but she dragged him as though he weighed nothing.

The man's legs twitched. He was trying to fight, but he'd been robbed of any ability to move. The woman continued to pull, and gradually his body vanished into the gloom between the trees, where the camera could no longer see him.

I held my breath as I waited. The branches high above continued to move in the wind. I could hear faint static, but nothing else.

And then the screams began.

They were horrendous. Pained and full of pure fear, they were like the noises I'd make during a nightmare. The man howled, and I thought I heard the crackle of breaking branches, but it was clear he had no strength left to escape whatever was happening.

I thought I could hear words in the sounds he was making. *I'm sorry, I'm sorry, I'm sorry!*

I clamped my hands over my ears to block the noises out, but they wouldn't stop. It felt like they were scratching at my brain and setting it on fire.

Then the screams were interrupted by the sounds of choking, like his mouth was filling with liquid. Each howl became fainter and thinner as he fought for breath. Until, at last, he had no oxygen left to scream at all.

For several long moments, the only sounds I heard were

something that might have been hands scrabbling at fallen leaves…or might have simply been static. Then, even that noise fell silent.

A ghostly pale shape emerged from between the trees. The woman was back, walking placidly, her bare feet curling over exposed roots and sticks. Her hands were painted red up past her elbows, almost like she was wearing gloves. Red splatter coated her dress and her exposed skin. Her face showed no signs of emotion as she languidly, calmly walked toward the camera.

When she finally stood near enough that her face filled the screen, she stopped. And she smiled.

She reached for the camera and turned it off.

The room seemed to grow darker as the screen switched to static. I sat, stunned and shaking, my knees pulled up to my chest.

The tape contained a murder. That was obvious. But who? And when, and where?

*What do I do now? Do I take this to the police? Do I give them the whole box?*

My hands were shaking so badly that it took three attempts to press the *eject* button. Three tapes remained. I didn't want to see any of them.

I slotted the third tape back into its space, my breathing ragged, then flinched as a floorboard creaked behind me.

Kayla stood at the base of the stairs. Heavy shadows covered most of her face. She clutched Replacement Big Gray to her chest so tightly that the stuffing bulged.

"Mommy?" Her voice was barely a whisper. "The scary lady is back."

———————

I moved on instinct, clutching Kayla against my side. "Where?" I asked, my own voice a whisper.

Her eyes were dark and unreadable. "In my room."

I took a knife from the kitchen. It felt solid and heavy as I raised it ahead of myself and climbed the stairs, Kayla held protectively behind myself.

*Did she see the tape?*

*Was it another nightmare?*

*I locked every door. Every window. I would have heard if someone got into the house.*

But I could feel Kayla's small hands were shaking almost as badly as mine. She wasn't playing make-believe. Something had terrified her.

I paused at the top of the stairs. Kayla's room was the second door to the right. It hung open, but there were no lights inside. Not even the night-light that I'd left on when I read her to sleep.

My movements were small and silent as I crept close to the room. I used the knife's tip to nudge against the door, pushing it further open.

The room was empty.

I crouched, looking under the bed. Still nothing. I crossed to the closet and shoved the door open. The clutter was still endemic. No figures lived inside, though.

It was only as I turned that I saw it. The window was directly above Kayla's bed, and it let in a very thin stream of moonlight.

And pressed into the glass was the smeared impression of an adult's handprint.

---

The police took nearly twenty minutes to arrive. I was waiting on the front lawn for them, Kayla bundled up in a blanket and held in my arms, and I led them straight inside to show them the handprint. The two officers—a man and a woman—searched the house, just like I had earlier that night. And, just like then, they found nothing.

Once we had the all-clear, I put Kayla down and told her to go and play in my study—close enough that I could hear her, but far enough that *she* wouldn't hear *us*—then followed the police back into her bedroom.

"Are you sure you didn't touch it by accident?" the male officer asked, staring at the handprint on the window. He was older and his uniform clung tight around his waist.

"Of course I didn't." I tried not to sound defensive, but that's a lot to ask of a person when they're bone tired and stressed out of their mind and know they probably look like a nervous, frazzled mess.

The female officer leaned over Kayla's bed to reach the window. She touched the smudge with the tip of her finger. I wanted to tell her to stop—that we might be able to get prints off it—but then I realized what she was doing. She swiped her finger, but the smudge didn't move.

"It's on the outside of the glass," she said.

I blinked at the smear, dumbfounded. Kayla's room was on the second floor of the house. "How?"

"Maybe someone was cleaning the gutters and…" The male officer shrugged. "I saw boxes in the study. How long ago did you move in?"

"Six weeks."

"Sure. Might have even been from the old owners. I doubt it's anything to worry about."

*Nothing to worry about?*

The officers were already wandering back into the hallway, and I knew they would be out of the door in less than a minute if I didn't stop them.

Images swirled up through my mind. The charred remains of the reformation school. The drawing the teacher had pressed into my hands that afternoon. The terrified quiver to Kayla's voice.

"My daughter saw someone in her room," I said, but they were already on the stairs to the ground floor and my words barely slowed them.

"I have a daughter just a bit older than her," the younger officer said, and her voice was full of perky optimism that was probably intended to calm me down. "She went through a phase where she was certain there was a monster in the bathroom drain. Refused to go in there, not even to brush her teeth. Took about six months to grow past it. Kids think they see and hear all sorts of strange things."

"Try a new routine before bed," the older officer suggested as he stepped into the downstairs hall. "That's what we did when we were trying to wean mine off the night-light. We put on a song and danced around his room for a few minutes before bed, and that did the trick."

My mouth was dry. The front door was right ahead of them. In a moment they'd be gone, and then I'd have to figure out how to get through the rest of the night with just Kayla and myself and the handprint that definitely hadn't been left by a random person cleaning the gutters.

"There's something else." I hadn't even made my mind up to show them the tapes; the words just spilled out of me. But the older officer paused, his hand on the doorknob, his eyebrows raised just a fraction to show that I had his attention but not for much longer. "I found some videos. They contain…disturbing things. I think one of them is…it… I think it shows a murder."

There was a second of silence, and I knew I had their interest again.

"There's some seriously messed up stuff online," the younger officer began, but I didn't let her finish what must have been a well-rehearsed script about the dark web and snuff films.

"These are old VHS tapes," I said, pointing toward the den. "And I think they were filmed locally. I have them right here."

They shared a brief glance, then followed me.

Faintly, I could hear Kayla playing above us. That was good. I didn't want her to see anything that I was about to show the officers. I turned the corner and stopped dead.

The TV was still on, but the screen was dark. The soft rug in front of the TV contained the VCR and the remote, but nothing else. The box of videotapes was gone.

"They—they were here—" I stammered, hands outstretched, as though the old shoebox was going to magically reappear. My mind spun. *Had the woman from the tapes taken them? No—they already searched the house—we all did—no one else is here...*

Tape #3 should have still been inside the player. I crouched down and pressed the *eject* button. The machine whirred, but nothing came out. It was empty.

The edges of my vision turned white from stress. I couldn't see anything clearly. Had I put them somewhere? When Kayla appeared, I'd been so startled I stopped thinking clearly. Had I moved them?

I stumbled into the kitchen, where I'd retrieved the knife. The countertops were empty.

"They...they were right here," I managed, returning to the den as I stared at the blank TV screen and the empty VCR.

"You're always welcome to bring items of interest into the station," the younger officer said. They were shuffling out of the den and back to the front door, and this time I had nothing to stop them. "I can imagine it's been a stressful day for you, but I think you'll find a good night's sleep will do you a world of good."

They mumbled some other pleasantries as they stepped outside, but I was too stunned to answer properly. The door closed with an unyielding click.

I turned back to the kitchen. On the draining board was the

empty bottle of wine and a single wine glass. The officers knew I lived alone. The single pillow on the master bed would have confirmed that, if nothing else.

I groaned, bending over at the waist. No wonder the younger officer thought I'd feel better after a sleep. I wasn't going to be able to convince them to come back in a hurry.

It would have been different if I'd been able to show them the tapes.

For a moment, I hung there, trying to breathe slowly enough to calm down. The house seemed very quiet. Then an airy, childish song floated toward me from the upper floor.

"*White dress…*" Kayla sang, the words lilting and singsong. "*White dress…one, two, three, four…*"

I ran for the stairs.

———————————

Kayla gasped as I burst into her room. Her round eyes radiated betrayal as they stared up at me.

"Cookie," I gasped, my heart in my throat. "Are you…"

"I was just singing," she said, a defensive pout forming. "*One, two, three, four, five…* and after five comes…"

"Six," I finished for her, nausea filling my stomach as I stared at the open shoebox. My daughter knelt in front of it, her tiny fingers pointing out the numbers on the VHS tapes as she sang her way through them.

"Six," she concluded, triumphant, and her fingertip pressed into the yellowed strip of paper stuck to the tape.

I couldn't stand seeing her touch them. I grabbed the shoebox out from under her, earning another gasp, and then shoved the lid into place so she couldn't look at them any longer.

"Did you take these?" I asked.

She only stared at me.

"Kayla! Did you take these from downstairs?"

I didn't mean to let my voice get so loud. I was just terrified. But Kayla's pout broke into full-bodied sobs. The guilt was instant and icy, and I shoved the box aside so I could kneel and comfort my girl.

At least once or twice a week, my mother had yelled at me about things I couldn't control. I'd promised myself I'd never do that to my own children. And here I was, nearly screaming at my daughter because she'd picked up a box and didn't even know she'd done something wrong.

"I'm sorry," I whispered, cradling her and letting her sob into my shoulder. "I'm so sorry, Cookie. Shh. You're not in trouble. You're a good girl. Shh."

———————

That night, we both slept in my bed. It was a relief. Every time the bad dreams woke me, I could reach out and brush the tiny curls away from her face and watch her deep, steady breathing.

The following morning, I was tempted to keep her home from preschool. We both needed a break, though. A break from the house. From the fear.

I gave her an extra-long hug while dropping her off, but she squirmed free after a moment so she could run inside to see her friends. I waited until she was out of sight, and a few minutes after that, before going back to my car.

Instead of driving home, I followed the road to the strip of old-fashioned shops and parked opposite the secondhand store.

"You look a disaster," Jax said when he saw me.

He wore ratty pajama bottoms and a stained undershirt with holes around the hem, even though it was after ten and the store had customers. At least I'd tried that morning, putting on clean clothes and combing my hair, as though that might help hide the shadows around my eyes.

If I'd had even half a brain left, I would have fired back, but I was out of energy to spare. I simply slumped against the counter. "Thanks."

The jovial banter vanished into concern. "What's happening, Tessie?"

I glanced at the other patrons. They were too busy turning over trinkets and trying to read the tiny price tags to pay us any attention.

"I told you about how I found some tapes, right?"

Jax leaned over the counter, forearms folded on the chipped wood, and nodded for me to go on. I hadn't planned to tell him everything, but all the walls I'd built crumbled in that second, and the full story spilled out of me. The screams echoing out of the tapes' distorted audio. Visiting the burned-down school. The humiliation I felt as the police left.

When I finished, Jax swore, quietly, while running his palm over his stubble.

"I don't know what to do," I admitted. "I'm scared that, if I take the tapes to the police now, they'll think I'm some hysterical, lonely person who's desperate for attention. What if they discount the tapes as some kind of homemade horror film and shove them in a storage room where they're never seen again?" I paused as I picked at the skin around my thumbnail. "And what if they *are* a hoax? What if I'm making a huge deal out of nothing?"

"I don't think you are." Jax frowned at his countertop, the crease between his eyes nearly swallowing the studs. "We know for sure the school burned down. That's a part of the town's history. And that last tape—it sounds way too similar to the guy who was killed in Calk Forest."

My head snapped up. "What?"

Jax grimaced. "Look. It was a long time ago."

"Someone was killed?" Calk Forest wrapped around a large part of the town. It was the same forest I'd walked through to find the school.

"It was way back when I was a kid." Jax looked like he regretted saying anything. "It was a big deal for a while, but everyone's kind of moved on by now. I shouldn't have brought it up."

I narrowed my eyes at him. It wasn't like Jax to be shy about sharing gossip. "Why not?"

"Forget it." Jax turned aside, drumming his hands on the counter. "Come on, I have something that might help you feel safer at home."

He was changing the subject, and I was too tired to fight him on it. Instead, I let him lead me into the narrow aisles and past the other shoppers to reach the corner where he kept the technology. From under a stack of DVDs and a crate of charging cables, he emerged with a large and slightly dusty black box, its glossy exterior covered in photos and promotional text.

"Congrats on your new security system," Jax said, pressing the box into my hands.

"Security…" Now that I could see the box clearly, I realized it was covered in images of cameras attached to brick walls, hallway corners, and trees.

"It's a few years old, but it'll get the job done," Jax said. "Five cameras all feed into a central system. There's no app compatibility, but you can connect it to a computer to watch the feeds, and it'll hold recordings for up to twenty-four hours."

*If anything else happens, I'll be able to see it. I'll have proof.* My throat tightened. "Thanks, Jax."

He grinned that goofy grin that made him look like he was ten again. "Want me to come set it up? I can close the store early."

One of the other shoppers lifted their heads at that, glaring at Jax for even suggesting such a thing.

"I'll be fine," I said, and hoisted the dusty box under one arm. "It'll do me good to have a distraction."

———

The camera system turned out to be a complex behemoth. The setup guide felt like it was written by a sadist. Nothing was labeled properly.

Still, I persevered, only taking a short break to eat two slices of bread and a handful of shredded cheese for lunch.

The box advertised five cameras, but someone must have pilfered one before donating the rest, because I only had four. That was still plenty. One went in the downstairs hallway, facing the front door. Another went in the upstairs hallway, looking down its length. The third went outside, at the house's front, recording the driveway, front yard, and steps up to our front door.

I hesitated with the last one. I knew exactly where I wanted it to go. But putting it on top of Kayla's closet made me feel like I was doing something wrong.

*People put nanny cams in their kids' rooms all the time*, I told myself, stepping back and staring up at the bulky black lens. *She's only four. It's not an invasion of privacy, is it?*

Gall filled my stomach as I remembered the day I discovered my mother had been pawing through my underwear drawer, searching for contraband, when I was twelve. I'd felt humiliated and scrutinized. Like I was living under a microscope, unable to keep any part of myself sacred.

"I'll tell her," I whispered to myself as I descended the stairs back down to the ground floor. It wasn't like it was a secret, anyway. Dark gray cables ran through the house, connecting to the laptop in my still-unpacked study. I'd explain what was happening to Kayla and get her permission before beginning to record. It would be fine. I just needed to keep her safe.

Through the kitchen window, I saw the woods at the back

of our yard, the trees swaying. They'd been a major draw when I bought the property. *What a view! Kayla and I can take walks through it!* But then I'd let them fade into forgotten scenery as the stress of moving and our new daily routine took over.

Calk Forest wrapped around more than half the town. I'd seen its name on maps often enough.

The woods behind my house were a part of it, weren't they?

Was that why Jax had changed the subject so suddenly?

He said he was a child when the murders took place; he would have heard all about it. He would have known where the body was found.

How close, exactly, was that to my house?

I pulled my phone out of my pocket and searched for *Calk Forest Murder*. Unlike my search for the reformation school, this time the answers came quick and fast.

---

"I've never seen anything like it in my forty years," the officer quoted in the article said. "It's monstrous. Whatever did this, it's not human. It can't be."

I sank into the kitchen chair as I scanned news report after news report. Every new detail felt like the twist of a knife in my stomach.

*...local businessman...*

*...peeled apart while he was still alive...*

*...organs suspended from trees...bones tied together like wind chimes...*

Then I stumbled onto a black-and-white photo of the crime scene. I didn't know it was legal to print things like that.

I placed my phone face down onto the kitchen counter so I wouldn't have to see any more. My heart hammered and icy sweat covered my skin. I now understood why Jax had changed the subject when he realized I hadn't heard of the murder. He knew I was already rattled. The death had been gory and vile in the kind of way that shifts how you see the world. The killer—*the woman, it's got to be the woman, you saw her drag him between the trees*—had played with the body for hours.

I picked up my phone and tapped back to see a photo of the victim: James Laker. A rounded, slightly lopsided face smiled out of a photo taken at some kind of family event. The man in the video had been too far away and blurred to properly identify, but I was certain they were the same person. Little factoids had been sprinkled through the article: he'd run the local dry-cleaning business. Forty-one at the time of his death. A wife. Three children.

No suspect had ever been identified. It lingered on as a cold case: the town's darkest secret, something everyone knew about but rarely spoke of.

My eyes were drawn back to the swaying trees outside my kitchen window. None of the articles had pinpointed the location. I was tempted to text Jax for confirmation, but I already knew. The murder would have happened somewhere nearby. And Jax had been trying to spare me from that knowledge.

*It happened fifteen years ago*, I told myself as I went upstairs to unfasten the hallway camera. *Fifteen years is a long time.*

My hands shook as I carried the camera back downstairs and set it up outside the rear door, facing the yard and the distant woods.

The feeds all worked. I spent a minute bent over my computer, checking that the videos were being saved.

It still didn't feel like it was enough to keep us safe.

Every other time I'd gone to the box of tapes, I'd been hesitant. This time, I pulled Tape #4 out without hesitation and shoved it into the VCR.

It didn't matter how bad the videos got. I needed answers.

The screen started out dark. I bent lower, checking that the tape was playing, then squinted at the screen again.

There was a haze of some kind of texture in the lower-right corner. I was pretty sure the camera was recording a space so dark that it couldn't pick up anything. I waited. My palms itched. The texture seemed to morph, slowly, like a writhing snake, but still, I couldn't make out any of it.

And then, suddenly, there was the hiss of a match, and light bloomed.

We were inside some kind of mine shaft or tunnel. The floor was dirt. The ceiling was so low, there must have been less than two feet of space.

The match was held between cracked fingers. The skin around the nails had been picked at until it was nothing but bloody shreds. The veins were mottled red and black with infection. But the fingers were dexterous as they lowered the match and used it to light a small tea candle on the floor.

The woman's face loomed into view. It was hard to see much of anything except for a ridge where her mouth belonged and the white, bulbous orbs of her eyes.

One long, spindly arm stretched out beside her. Muscles and bones bulged under paper-thin skin. The gash that made up her mouth widened, and I saw the glint of teeth, and then she turned and scuttled away from the camera, her head grazing the ceiling as her limbs jerked like an insect's.

I leaned close, my face just inches from the screen, as the scuttling figure vanished into the darkness. Faint static hissed.

For a long time, nothing happened. I stayed crouched there on the rug, even when my muscles began to cramp. I didn't even dare blink. I didn't want to miss anything.

And then pale limbs moved in the far distance. The woman's hair dragged through the dirt as she crept along the tunnel toward the camera. Her eyes glinted in the flickering light. She carried something in one hand, thumping it into the ground as she crept nearer. It wasn't until she dropped it in front of the camera that I realized what I was looking at.

A severed arm landed heavily in the dust.

The woman stared at the camera for a moment before turning away, her body undulating with every angular movement. Within seconds, she was gone again, fading back into the darkness. All that was left was the arm, lying on the ground, near the bottom of my screen.

*It's the man. James Laker. The articles said he was dismembered.*

I stared at the limb, my stomach turning.

James Laker had been a stocky man. This arm was slim and covered in loose skin. Painted red nails glinted at the ends of the fingers.

It wasn't his.

My fingers dug into the carpet.

It wasn't easy to see from the angle, but I thought the arm must have been hacked loose from its owner. Not severed neatly, but ripped away.

The woman reappeared at the edge of the light. She crept back toward the camera, and as she got closer, I saw she was grinning, lines of saliva trailing off the tips of her teeth and over pale lips.

She'd brought a second arm.

I bit down on a moan. This arm was thin, as well, but not a match for the woman. It was marked with age spots and covered in gray hairs. It made a heavy, meaty sound as it fell.

The woman twisted, her off-white nightgown dragging across the floor, then she left once again.

I sat frozen as the remainder of the tape played out. I watched her bring in another two arms. Each of them had been torn free at the shoulder. Each of them was stained with streaks of blood. Two belonged to a woman with red nails. Two belonged to a man whose skin was dappled with age spots.

As she placed the final limb on top of the pile, the woman made eye contact with the camera. I could barely see her: just the whites of her eyes and the shimmer of grinning teeth. Then she raised her hand. And she traced those incomprehensible shapes into the air.

"Who are you?" I whispered at her as her bloodied finger swooped and slashed. Her smile widened a fraction.

*Don't watch. You'll regret it.*

Those five words suddenly felt like an omen. As though watching the tapes had unlocked something horrendous and malevolent. As though I'd opened a door that should have been left closed.

As though I'd summoned her into our lives.

The woman crouched above her pile of severed arms. The light from the single candle shimmered over the edges of her face without showing any of it clearly. But it felt like she wasn't just smiling at the camera. It felt like she was smiling at *me*.

Then the tape abruptly ended, plunging the screen back into perfect darkness, and I realized I was breathing so hard it was making me lightheaded. I pressed Eject and shoved the tape back into the box.

I'd meant to watch through the final three—get them all done in one go while Kayla was out of the house—but the tape had been deceptively long. I glanced at my phone and swore under my breath. I was already late to pick Kayla up.

———

The ten-minute drive to preschool felt surreal. The sun was warm and mellow; my neighbors were out working in their yards. It should have been a pleasant day.

But nothing felt right. Nothing felt *safe*.

Two men gestured as they argued on a street corner. I watched them through my rearview mirror until I turned a corner and couldn't see them anymore. I turned on the local radio station, hoping for a distraction, but the usual songs had been taken over by a news segment. I had to listen for a moment to understand they were talking to a local farmer. All two hundred of his chickens had vanished overnight.

*"Wild dogs might kill a whole coop of hens,"* the farmer said, his voice crackling at the edges. *"But they won't take more than four or five away. The place is just...empty. What happened to the rest of them? Where are the bodies?"*

I slammed my palm into the button to turn the radio off again.

Kayla's teacher was waiting for me when I jogged up to the door. To her credit, she didn't try to make me feel guilty for being late. Instead, she held a scratchy drawing in one hand and had that small, concerned smile on her face.

"I'm sorry," I said, reaching for Kayla and hoisting her up onto my hip. It used to be so easy to hold her like that, but she was getting heavier every week. Eventually, there'd be a day when I wouldn't be able to carry her anymore, and I dreaded it.

Miss Lindsay adjusted her hold on the paper. "I actually wanted to show you..."

I couldn't go through that again. I reached out and took the page without even looking at it. "I've got to run. Late. But—but I'll talk to her. Sorry. Again."

Kayla held onto my shirt as I jogged us both back to the car. Her eyes were inscrutable. "What are we late for?"

"Nothing," I whispered as I slid her into her child's seat. "I just didn't want to talk to Miss Lindsay today."

Kayla giggled at my confession, and that warmed me a fraction. Things couldn't be too bad if Kayla was still laughing.

As I got into the driver's seat, I finally turned the paper over to see the drawing. It was another image of Kayla's room. The door was still open, but the woman no longer stood in the hallway.

Instead, she crawled high up on the wall like a spider.

---

I decided I wouldn't watch either of the final two tapes while Kayla was in the house. Not even when she was asleep.

When we got home, I carefully explained about the cameras and why one was in her room, but she seemed to grow more bored the longer I talked. When I asked whether she was okay with it, she just said, "Yeah," and then, "Can I watch TV now?"

Kayla fell asleep easily. Surrogate Big Gray had been grudgingly accepted as her own. I stayed in her room for nearly an hour after she'd dozed off, sitting in a chair beside her bed with my hands clasped between my knees. Kayla slept deeply, limbs cast out in every direction, her stuffed chicken on one side and her favorite blanket on the other like wards against evil.

There were no similar talismans I could bring when I went to bed. I was exhausted but too anxious to feel tired. The windows were locked. The doors were bolted. But I couldn't stop my mind from running through the house, mentally checking every room for weaknesses.

I left my bedroom door open, just in case Kayla stirred during the night. That was probably the only reason I heard the noise.

It was sharp and high and vicious, and it snapped me awake. I fumbled for the phone on my bedside table. The display said it was after three in the morning. I didn't know how much rest I'd actually gotten, but it didn't feel like much.

I sat in bed, my heart racing and my breath held. Downstairs pipes rattled, and they set my teeth on edge. The rest of the house was silent.

Any other night, I would have assumed I'd heard a wild animal and rolled over to go back to sleep. Instead, I crept out of bed and slipped my feet into my sneakers as I went to check the house.

Kayla slept soundly. Big Gray was clutched to her chest. I didn't dare turn on her bedroom light but used the flashlight on my phone to check the room's darkest corners. Empty.

Next, I crept downstairs. The camera I'd set up facing the front door had a single red light on as proof that it was recording. Feeling foolish, I raised a hand and gave it half a wave. Then I turned and skirted through the ground floor: dining room, kitchen, den, laundry. I checked every door and every window. Still locked.

*It's fine*, I told myself as my heart finally began to slow. *Everything's fine. Go back to bed.*

Then the noise repeated.

It sounded like something between a human's shriek and an animal's wail. Every hair on my body rose. It came from outside, and I jogged into the kitchen and leaned close to the window.

Outside was dark. Very little light made it through the cloud cover, and my phone's light could barely reach outside the glass.

*It's just a wild animal*, I promised myself as I pulled open the kitchen drawers and searched for the flashlight I knew had to be inside one of them. *Maybe an owl. Maybe a cat in heat.*

Except I couldn't shake the sense that the bizarre sound had passed through a human throat.

The flashlight was in the third drawer I tried. I switched it on and pressed it against the window.

A disk of light cut across the lawn. It faded into nearly nothing by the time it reached the trees, but it was still enough to highlight their trunks through the gloom. Dark branches danced in the wind.

And then—

The glint of eyes.

*Human* eyes.

My body turned numb as I stared at her. She stood just between the trunks, facing my house. The filthy nightgown flapped around her emaciated body. Her arms, stained with dirt and I have no idea what else, hung at her sides.

She didn't so much as blink as the light landed on her. But she stared back at me, her eyes glinting as her lips parted into a vicious smile.

Then she stepped backward and vanished into the woods.

I moved without thinking. The kitchen door rattled as I unlocked it and threw it open, then I was racing into the backyard, toward the forest.

"Hey!" I yelled. My voice was hoarse. "Hey, you!"

Long grass whipped against my ankles and left spots of dew in their wake. The cold air stung my arms and made my eyes weep. I was moving too fast to keep the flashlight steady, and its beam speared across the ground and the trees and the sky.

Then I reached the edge of the woods and staggered to a halt.

*What am I doing?*

Was I really going to chase her through the forest when I could barely see? When I had no weapon and no backup? Was I really going to leave the back door to my house unlocked and Kayla vulnerable while I followed someone who I knew was capable of killing?

I backed away from the forest, then turned and started running again. I didn't stop moving until I was back inside the house.

---

The first time I'd called the police, they'd arrived within twenty minutes. This time, it took them nearly two hours. The message was clear: they thought I was wasting their time.

Those two hours gave me a chance to stew.

Kayla was irritable at being woken up, and I didn't blame her. I carried her, bundled up in her quilt and with spare pillows under my other arm, into the study. I let her lie down in the corner with the pillows around her for padding. She was asleep again before I sat down in front of the laptop.

I saved a copy of the surveillance system recordings, then found the file for the camera I'd placed by the rear door.

The screen captured all of the backyard, and a stretch of distant forest. The cameras were equipped with night vision, but they were old models and the quality wasn't great. It was hard to read the details, even when I zoomed in.

I scrolled back through the file until I saw myself running across the lawn. The night vision cast me in a sickly green hue, and every time the flashlight changed direction, the camera struggled to keep up with the wash of light.

I kept rewinding. At last, I reached the point where I'd first seen the woman between the trees. I paused the screen. The flashlight's beam hit the woods like a spotlight, and the night vision pumped up the contrast until it was almost blinding.

She was there, though, clear and unnatural in the harsh light, grinning at the house.

My stomach turned at the sight of her, but it came with a wash of vindication. *I got you. I have proof now.*

*No one can call me a liar after this.*

The police still hadn't shown up. I saved a screenshot of the woman, then began rewinding the footage again. The spotlight vanished. Without it, the scene turned muddy and pixelated.

I squinted. I thought I could barely make out her silhouette through the sickly green glow. I kept rewinding, hoping I might find the point when she arrived.

Two minutes back. Five. Ten. Twenty.

I rewound faster, but doubts were starting to creep in. Could I really see her? There was a band of green pixels that looked like the edge of her head, but maybe I was seeing what I wanted to. The shape could have just been from a tree.

An hour back. Two hours. Three.

I rewound faster.

And then, at last, the screen began to lighten as I reversed through the previous evening. The night vision switched off, trading the uneasy greens for the browns and grays of a low-definition standard camera.

My heart sank.

The woman stood between the trees.

She was hard to see from that distance; the camera reduced her to a few dozen pixels. But she was still unmistakable. As I stared at the distant blur, I began to imagine I could make out the details. Her dress swayed around bare feet. Long hair hung on either side of her thin, scarred face. Shadows were heavy over her unblinking eyes.

I kept rewinding. The woman didn't move. She was as still as a pillar as the day unraveled around her. And then, at last, I saw myself on-screen, magnified monstrously large and staring up at the lens as I adjusted its angle. Then the feed went blank.

*She was there. Back when I installed the camera. She was already there, watching me.*

I tried not to hyperventilate as I paced the office. Kayla slept soundly, and I tried not to think about how the woman would have been able to stare up at Kayla's bedroom window the whole time.

Dawn lit the street outside by the time the police finally arrived. They were the same two officers: Farrow and Jean, I read on their name badges. They looked tired as I let them in, and I had the impression I was their final stop of the night before their shifts ended.

Instead of trying to explain anything to them, I led them straight up to the study and the video.

The older man, Farrow, stared at the frozen image on my laptop for a few seconds before sighing. "And…?"

My mouth was dry. I thought showing them my proof might break through their apathy but, if anything, it seemed to be worsening. "That's the woman. The one my daughter saw in her room."

"This is the first time *you've* seen her, though, correct?" Jean asked.

"It's the woman from the tapes I told you about," I said, my face heating. Kayla stirred in her makeshift bed, and I forced my voice to be softer. "She's killed people."

Jean gave me an apologetic smile. "I'm not sure it's possible to make a positive ID like that. Especially not from this distance. It's not exactly HD, is it, love?"

"Looks like someone might have gotten lost," Farrow said. "Maybe they went out for a late-night walk. They could have just stopped there to get their bearings. Your property ends at the edge of the trees, so it's not technically trespassing."

"She—" My voice caught. I tabbed through the video, rewinding to the day view. "Look. She was standing there for hours. *Hours*. Staring at my house."

Finally, Farrow and Jean exchanged a glance. Farrow raised his eyebrows. Jean shrugged.

"You want us to have a look around?" Farrow asked.

This was their offer of a compromise. They'd take a walk

through the forest, conclude there was nothing out of place, give me some weak peace of mind, and leave.

And I wasn't in any place to reject it.

I'd come close to running into the forest when I'd seen the woman there, but it would have been pure idiocy to step between the trees without some kind of backup. At least the police would give me that. I don't know what I was imagining I'd find, but I just wanted something tangible. Something that would prove she was more than a phantom.

"Okay," I said.

The younger officer, Jean, stayed behind with Kayla. I watched her drop into my office chair and pull out her phone as we left the room. Then I walked with Farrow across my lawn and up to the forest's edge.

I stopped exactly where the woman had stood.

Dawn lit the trunks in an unsettling orange glow. Inside the woods was still dim, and Farrow pulled out his flashlight. I switched on the light on my phone, and we stepped inside.

I shivered and pulled my jacket tighter around myself. Farrow was already diverging from my path. He moved languidly, sweeping his torch across the shrubs. It was clear he was only putting in the time; he'd give it ten minutes, if that, then say we were done.

If he wasn't going to search properly, I would.

I pressed deeper between the trees. Dewy spiderwebs clung to my arms and hair. Sounds came from every direction as small animals and insects moved through the layers of dead leaves. Every crunch and twig snap made me flinch.

And then I saw it.

A gash had been carved into the trunk of a tree, about head height. It was small but looked fresh. Sap trickled from the scar, and when I touched it, my fingers came away sticky.

I stepped back and raised my phone. There, in the distance, was another mark. As I moved toward it, I saw a third. They were leading somewhere. And I knew I was being foolish to follow them deeper and deeper into the woods while Farrow was still trailing behind, but I was desperate.

My pace quickened. A bird whistled in the distance, then fell silent. I was starting to lose my sense of direction, but I refused to slow down.

And then something wet and brittle crunched under my shoe, and I caught myself against a tree as I lifted my foot.

Bright red flesh and white bones peeked out from beneath the fallen leaves.

*An animal.*

*No—a bird.*

Clumps of feathers spread out from the body. It was a large one, but I couldn't tell what kind. Its head was missing. And, from what I could tell, its chest had been torn open.

*Poor thing.* It must have been caught by some wild animal that wasn't hungry enough to finish its meal. I stepped back, wiping my shoe on the ground to try and clear off the blood and scraps of flesh. My torch danced across the fallen leaves, and I saw more feathers ahead. There were a lot of them. More than could come from just one bird. I fell still, my heart running fast, as I watched piles of feathers roll across the ground and build up against trees like snowdrifts.

This wasn't just an animal attack. My mind flashed back to the news report of the farmer's missing chickens. The carcass I'd stepped in looked about the right size to be a hen, didn't it?

I forced myself to go toward them. More bodies began to appear. Each one was identical: Head removed. Chest torn open. Innards carved away.

And then…

A large tree stood ahead. Baubles had been hung from its twisting branches. The carnage condensed around the trunk; what had been just a scattering of bodies further away became piles of them heaped against the roots.

I stood frozen, my mouth hanging open, as my brain tried to process what I was seeing.

The things hanging from the branches weren't baubles. They were the missing chicken heads. Each one had its eyes plucked out. Twine had been run through the holes and then tied to the branches above, leaving the heads to sway in the wind.

Something fluttered against the massive trunk. At first glance the shapes looked like more feathers, but they weren't.

They were small scraps of fabric, pinned to the tree with massive, rusted nails.

I recognized a wing. Legs. A familiar, well-worn felt head.

I'd found Big Gray. The original one. My daughter's beloved stuffed chicken, the one she'd made soft cooing noises to every night before bed, dismembered into a dozen pieces and nailed to the tree.

"Oh…" a man said.

Farrow had caught up to me. His flashlight beam danced across the hundreds of dangling chicken heads. The slackness around his face had vanished. Now, when he looked at me, it was as though he was seeing me for the first time.

───────────

There were no more suggestions that the woman in the yard had been a lost neighbor. No more platitudes about how I'd feel better after a good night's sleep.

This time, the officers stood guard in the hall while I quickly changed Kayla into day clothes. Then they took Kayla and me to the station to file a formal report.

Kayla, groggy and cranky, was taken to a nursery with soft toys and snacks while I was shown into an interview room. They had a form with all my details and asked me to confirm that they were correct. They gave me a cup of coffee. Then they started asking questions.

But they weren't any of the questions I'd expected.

No one wanted to know what the woman looked like. They didn't ask where the tapes were. In fact, they didn't seem to care about them at all.

Instead, they asked me to go over my routine from the previous day. They wanted to know how long I'd been living in Ludlow. How often I went to the south side of town, who I'd been speaking to. Could anyone corroborate my movements from the previous day?

I was tired. I was frightened. And, for a brief few moments, I'd felt relief at being taken seriously. So it took me far too long to realize where the questions were leading.

They thought I'd killed the chickens.

Cold dread washed through me. The officers on the other side of the table were still friendly and smiling. The first questions had been softballs. But the longer the interview went on, the more pointed and accusatory they sounded.

"How'd you know where to find the animal remains?" Farrow asked.

I wanted to scream. I hadn't *known*, I'd just stumbled into them.

I gripped the armrests on my seat until my hands ached. "I didn't touch those birds. I love animals. I wouldn't…"

We were both imagining the scene again, I knew. The gently swaying heads. The mangled bodies, chest walls torn out, broken cartilage exposed.

I wouldn't do *that*.

"There was a murder in the forest," I said, my voice suddenly so tight that it hurt. "Years ago, way before I ever moved here. I have a video of it happening. It was the same woman who was behind my house last night."

"I guess you're talking about Laker," Jean said. She was still pleasant and attentive, but I could feel the chill behind her eyes now. The niceness was all a mask.

"Yes! James Laker. The woman who killed him is back again. And, for some reason I don't know, she's targeting my family."

"You're chasing ghosts," Farrow said. His mustache twitched

as he forced a smile. "The James Laker homicide is technically a cold case, but we have a prime suspect, and that prime suspect is the *sole* suspect. Has been for the entire case."

"Who…" I glanced between them.

"Laker had been feuding with a local man," Jean said. She leaned on the table in a pose that would have seemed casual if she hadn't been watching me so closely. "Traces of Laker's blood were found in his sink and on towels in his trash, but he was never arrested."

"He and his wife skipped town the night Laker was killed," Farrow said. "They packed up their possessions, but they were running so fast they left their luggage in the hallway. We've had an APB out on them for the last fifteen years. No one can hide forever."

I would have been less stunned if they'd pulled the chair out from beneath me. The man in the tape had been too far away and pixelated for me to be *completely* certain, but he'd looked a lot like James Laker. It seemed like too much of a coincidence that two people had been killed in the forest.

Unless…

Could it really be some kind of local hoax? I'd never actually seen anyone die. The woman had dragged the man into the trees and then come back covered in blood.

Blood…or fake blood.

The dismembered arms could have been dupes too. You can buy props that look and feel realistic.

I'd already considered that the tapes might be someone's film project. Maybe someone was fascinated by the James Laker murder and had recreated a fictionalized version of it. Maybe it was all a hoax; maybe the creator was leaving tapes around town to try to garner some media attention for their project. Maybe the woman in the white dress was an actress who strategically wandered through Calk Forest at night to help bolster paranoia.

*No. No one puts this much effort into a prank. I watched her skin blister in that fire; you can't fake that.*

"You didn't answer my last question," Farrow said, tapping his pen on his notepad, the forced friendliness dripping thick off every word. "*How* did you know where to find the chickens?"

My mind fizzled blank. For a brief moment, all I could think of was Kayla, sitting in the nursery as she waited for me.

"Am I under arrest?" I managed at last.

I'd heard that somewhere. Maybe from Jax. They could only keep me if they were charging me with a crime. And, except for the fact that the chickens had been found in the woods behind my house, they had nothing to hold over me.

Farrow and Jean exchanged a glance.

"Am I being detained?" I asked, louder.

"Of course not," Farrow said. "You're free to go at any time. But we're hoping you can help us, uh… understand this situation better."

They weren't on my side. They never had been. Without another word, I gathered up my coat and my tote bag and marched to the door.

It was only when I got to the parking lot, Kayla in tow, that I remembered we'd ridden in the back of the police cruiser. My car was still at home. Shame burned my face as I placed the tote bag on the ground and fished the cell phone out of my pocket.

As I waited for my call to be answered, I glanced down. Kayla was fidgeting at my side; she didn't understand why any of this was happening, but she must have guessed it was serious because she wasn't even trying to pepper me with questions.

On my other side sat the tote bag. I'd brought it into the police station with me, but the officers hadn't even asked about the contents. Inside was the old, discolored shoebox, still with the lines of duct tape around the lid. The six tapes inside barely weighed anything, but their presence felt like a boulder pressing into my back.

The phone clicked, and the ringing was replaced by a tired, "Yeah, huh?"

"Hey Jax." I squeezed my eyes closed. "We're at the police station. I need you to pick us up."

---

Jax didn't ask a single question over the phone, but the first thing he said after his rusting sedan screeched to a halt was "Are you okay?"

"We'll be fine," I said, because I needed to believe it. Jax had somehow had the foresight to throw a spare child seat into the back of the car, and I spent a moment getting it locked into place, then buckled Kayla in.

I directed Jax to drive us to the preschool. It was just ten minutes past opening time. Kayla didn't have her backpack or her snacks, but I'd just have to rely on Miss Lindsay's hard-wearing patience for one more day.

Jax must have guessed that I didn't want to discuss anything in front of Kayla because he cycled through his playlist to find the silliest songs in there and goaded Kayla into singing along with them. She was in a bouncy, giggling mood by the time we arrived at the preschool.

Jax waited in the car while I took Kayla in. I kissed her cheeks and forehead and did my best to smooth her hair into a ponytail that would disguise the fact that it hadn't been brushed. I wondered if she would tell anyone in her class that we spent the morning in the police station. I wondered what kind of questions Miss Lindsay would have for me at afternoon pickup.

"So," Jax said as I slid back into the passenger seat. He glanced toward the footwell, where the tote bag had slumped to reveal a corner of the shoebox. "You want to talk about it?"

"She's real. She was outside my house." My eyes prickled with burning tears as Jax's car rumbled back onto the road. "And I'm scared about what she's going to do to us."

"D'you know what she wants?" Jax squinted against the morning light, his fingernails scratching through his stubble. He was still wearing his pajamas, I realized. "Or, hell, even who she is?"

"No. No idea…"

I blinked.

She was connected to the town. That was now undeniable. She'd been inside the reformation school the night it burned

301

down. She had maybe—probably—killed a local and decimated a nearby chicken farm. She'd been haunting my home ever since I found the tapes. Which meant, wherever she was living, it was probably within the town's border.

I hadn't recognized her. But I was brand new to Ludlow. I needed to show her face to a local.

"Can you take a look at one of the tapes?" I asked.

Both of his studded eyebrows rose.

---

We stopped at Jax's store. Partially because he wanted to change into real clothes, and partially because I didn't want to face my home and the massacre I knew was in the woods behind it.

"There's a VCR back there if you want to set up," he said, locking the door behind us so shoppers couldn't wander in. "I use it to check any donated tapes. It should still work fine."

"You really still take VHS tapes?"

He shrugged as he disappeared up the stairs to his second-floor apartment. Any other thrift store would have started tossing out VHS tapes years before, but Jax had never been able to bin anything, no matter how little value it had.

I found the player where Jax had said, in the back corner of the store. It was dim there, away from any natural light. The towering piles of clutter felt like walls around me, shielding me from the outside world as I knelt.

The player was positioned beneath a blocky cube TV that looked older than I was. The TV made a faint whining noise as its screen came to life, and dust motes danced in front of the artificial light. The player clicked as it turned on.

I chose the first tape, the one where the woman had shown her pearly teeth poised on her tongue. It had the clearest image of her. I rewound the tape to the start, then hit Play.

Seeing her so intimately near again sent shivers through me. Her skin was unblemished and her hair still full, if greasy. She seemed to stare directly into my soul.

"That's her, huh?" Jax said.

I flinched, startled by his sudden appearance. He lowered himself to his knees beside me to get a closer look at the screen, his eyes narrowed as he examined her.

"She was burned in the school's fire," I said, in case it would help jog his memory. "It left scars across her jaw and up into her hairline."

He shook his head slowly. "Sorry, Tessie, I don't recognize her."

I took out my phone anyway. Jax didn't know the woman, but someone else in town might. I took a photo of the screen while the woman chewed on her own teeth. The photo came out with bars of color running across it—the TV's frequencies messing up my phone's camera—but it still showed enough.

"Burned in the school fire, huh?" Jax ran his tattooed thumb across his lip as he continued to watch the screen. "Which school?"

"Oakbrook Girls Reformation School," I said. "Just outside of town."

"Huh." He stood, frowning, and vanished back between the stacks of clutter. "Let me go check something."

On the screen, the woman continued to stare at me, her hair trailing down either side of her narrow face as she chewed.

I stopped the tape and ejected it. As I slid it back into the box, my eyes trailed toward the final two tapes.

They were going to hurt me, I knew. But I was past pretending I had other options. I slid out Tape #5 and pushed it into the player.

The screen went black, then lit up again.

We were in some kind of dark room. The walls were brick, but not the neat kind of brick I saw on houses around town. These bricks were smeared with mortar and some of the lines ran crooked. It was a room that wasn't meant to be seen.

The camera was focused on a wooden chest in the room's center. It looked similar to the crate used to store linens at the foot of my mother's bed. A rusted padlock sealed the heavy lid shut.

The box seemed to shudder faintly.

My breathing was shallow as I leaned closer to the screen. I wished Jax had a bigger TV.

A shadow shifted in the corner of the room. The woman drifted into view. The hem of her nightgown was filthy. Her bony arms swung at her sides as she half walked, half danced across the room.

She circled the wooden chest three times before finally turning and sitting on it, facing the camera.

One bruised and bloodied hand rose. She began to wave it through the air again, like she was casting a spell or commanding an invisible orchestra. Her legs swung as she moved her hand, and her bare heel kicked against the wood.

The wooden chest shuddered again.

And...I thought I heard sounds.

I glanced behind myself. Jax was nowhere to be seen. I reached for the TV's blocky buttons and pushed on the volume to raise it.

Burbling, muffled sounds began to float from the speakers. I pushed the volume higher and higher, a little green bar on the screen's side filling up. Static hissed. And beneath the static...

Sobs. Screams. A voice, begging, futilely.

Someone was inside the wooden chest.

My stomach ached with sudden, secondhand claustrophobia. The chest didn't seem large enough to fit a person. They must have been hunched over, their knees up to their chin. Barely any room to squirm. The wood shuddered as they knocked against it helplessly.

The woman had finished drawing in the air. She sat contentedly, her head tilted to one side and her eyes half closed as a small smile rose. Her heel continued to tap against the wood as though she was encouraging the person inside to keep struggling.

"Tessie?"

Jax was back. I sucked in a gasping breath as I stopped and ejected the tape. My hands were shaking. My eyes were wet. I shoved the tape back into the box and slammed the lid down on it. "Sorry."

"You okay?"

He hadn't seen much of the video. He wouldn't have realized what was happening in it. I swallowed. "I'm fine."

Jax carried something under one arm. He held it up for me to see the cover. It was a leather school yearbook.

"I think we've found her," Jax said.

———————————

"You'd be surprised how many yearbooks we get," Jax said as he led me back to the front counter, where we'd have better light. "People don't always want to keep them, but they still seem too valuable to throw out, I guess. But I remember this one coming in. It wasn't so much a yearbook as…I don't know, almost like records? I thought it was weird because it was leather-bound. Really expensive, yeah? And the name creeped me out too."

*Oakbrook Girls Reformation School.* The letters that ran down the spine were dulled by age.

"She was an adult when she burned the school down," I said, pulling up a spare chair as Jax and I sat behind the desk. "I don't know if she was ever a student there."

"I'll bet she was." He dropped the book on the table and flipped it open. "People don't really go around torching schools unless they hold a grudge."

He had a point. I opened my phone to the photo I'd taken of the TV. Then we turned to the book and its thick, soot-gray pages.

It looked like it might have belonged to a staff member, maybe even the principal. Dour faces stared up at us. Each page was thick and only held six photos. Names and years were written in tiny print below the images. Some of the girls looked as young as ten; others could have been approaching twenty. None of them looked happy or healthy.

Both Jax and I froze on the third page.

"Is that..." he whispered.

A girl's photo stared out at us. Her eyes were heavy-lidded. Her hair hung heavily on either side of her narrow, thin-lipped face. She couldn't have been older than fifteen, and yet, there was an uncanny agedness about her. As though she'd already lived a hundred lives.

My gaze trailed down to the name beneath. *Elsbeth Byrd.*

"Is that her?" Jax asked.

My mouth was dry as I nodded. I opened the browser on my phone and typed in her name.

Results flashed up on-screen. I scrolled through them, slowly at first, and then faster and faster. Then I tried the search again, this time localized to our town. And finally, a third time, with the school's name included.

No relevant results.

*It's the right person, isn't it?* I glanced back at the record book, but Jax was flipping through its pages again. His mouth twitched as he read more names.

She'd been a lot younger in the photo, but I was sure it was the same woman I'd seen in the tapes and the same woman who'd stood in the woods behind my house.

*Elsbeth Byrd.* At least I had a name. I couldn't understand why someone so violently brutal had seemingly left no trace of herself behind. No police records, no newspaper articles. Not even a record of her birth.

"I know Roger!" Jax said suddenly. He flipped the book around to face me. In the last pages were records of the faculty. His finger jabbed into a blurry photo of someone listed as the groundskeeper. "I've never heard of anyone else in this book before, but I know this guy. He lives two streets over from me."

*He was there. At the school. He would have met Elsbeth, even if it was just in passing.*

Jax's eyebrows rose as he anticipated my thoughts. "Wanna go visit him?"

———

Roger Bryce-Feld lived in a small house with a modest garden. The school's photo showed a slim man who couldn't have been older than thirty, but the Roger who answered the door was stooped and shambling and closer to seventy.

Apparently, Jax had helped jump-start Roger's car the year before; they weren't exactly friends, but they were better than strangers. I haltingly introduced myself and tried to explain the reason for my visit. As soon as I mentioned the name *Elsbeth*, the color drained from Roger's face. He didn't say anything but weakly beckoned us into his house.

We sat in a small, sun-bleached kitchen as Roger stared out the window.

"You worked at the Oakbrook Girls Reformation School, yeah?" Jax asked, breaking the silence. He'd brought the record book and laid it on the kitchen table.

Roger breathed deeply, then sighed. "For just under three

years. I hopped through a lot of jobs back then, and I stayed in that one longer than I probably should have."

"And you remember Elsbeth Byrd?" I prompted.

"It's been about..." He paused, swallowing. "About three months since I last saw her in my nightmares. That's the longest I've ever gone."

I exchanged a look with Jax.

"The things that happened to that girl were terrible," Roger said. "The things she did were worse. And I still don't know which came first. Was she twisted into something monstrous by her parents? Or were her parents reacting to what they saw inside of her?"

"What do you mean?" I asked.

"I heard stories. Sometimes from the other schoolchildren. Sometimes from the few people around town who had met her. When she was just a small child, she would catch birds out in the yards—I don't know how, but they say she caught them and squeezed them in her little hands—and bit their heads off."

Chills ran through me. I pictured Kayla, only four, and her plump fingers, which were still learning the dexterity to hold cutlery properly.

"They say her parents were so horrified by what she was doing that they pulled her teeth out." Roger's eyes were watery as he stared at a spot on the table. "And they say, over the next two years, her teeth grew back. So they pulled them again. And they grew back again."

I pictured those teeth. Pearly white and stained red, poised on her tongue.

"They were so afraid of her, they kept her in their basement like some kind of animal," Roger said. "For a while, the neighbors didn't even know the family *had* a child. But then she got out one night—clawed a hole in the door, they said—and she had to be moved."

"To the school," I guessed.

"The Oakbrook Girls Reformation School was for difficult children," Roger said. "*Dangerous* children. The ones that started fires and hurt their parents. It was more of a prison than a school. Parents who were at their limit sent their daughters there to be contained and, they hoped, rehabilitated."

"That's why I didn't recognize the student names," Jax said, jabbing a finger at the yearbook. "Because they weren't from town."

"That's right. I think Elsbeth was the only local girl while I was there." Roger shifted, then sighed again. "It wasn't a kind place. Not to any of them. The rules were strict and the punishments stricter. But Elsbeth had it the worst."

"How?" I asked.

"The other girls hated her. Or feared her. Maybe a bit of both. They said she could put a curse on you just by staring at you, and so they refused to look at her or talk to her. But they would play cruel pranks on her. They hid needles in her dresses. They sprinkled crushed glass in her bed. Once, an older girl grabbed a handful of her hair and used kitchen scissors to cut it off." Rodger shifted uncomfortably. "The next week, that girl was dead. Suffocated while coughing up lungfuls of blood in the middle of the night. They called it a sudden sickness and buried her in the graveyard behind the school. No family came to the funeral, and there was no investigation. No one much cared what happened to those girls."

He was right about that. The school had burned down with all the students and staff still inside, and I'd struggled to find anything on it—not even newspaper clippings.

"Do you think Elsbeth killed that girl?" I asked.

"Oh, I'm certain. She wasn't the only one of Elsbeth Byrd's tormentors who died while I was there." Roger shook his head. "The school tried to send her home, but her parents refused to take her back. She was eventually released into a foster home when she was sixteen. Elsbeth stayed with them until she was eighteen, then she left."

"Where did she go?" Jax prompted.

"I don't know." Roger shook his head. "I didn't *want* to know. People who get too close to her—people who start to know her too well—they're cursed."

I frowned. "Cursed?"

"She haunts my nightmares. No matter how hard I try, I can never forget her face." A bead of sweat formed at Roger's temple. "And I'm one of the lucky ones. You know about the man who was killed in the forest? James Laker? There were rumors he'd had an affair with Elsbeth. He was nearly twenty years her senior and already married, but people claim he met her when he was going door-to-door, passing out fliers for his business. Elsbeth's foster parents tried to chase him away, but it didn't work. And he ended up carved into little chunks and scattered through the woods."

I saw the videotape again. Elsbeth, dragging the faceless man between the trees.

"The police said they knew who did it," I said. "An older couple."

"Oh, yes, they suspected Elsbeth's foster parents. And that's another thing. No matter how many deaths crop up around Elsbeth, the blame always lands on someone else." Roger grimaced. "Always. It's like she's invisible to them. The foster parents managed to skip town before either the police or Elsbeth's curse managed to catch up to them. They were lucky."

*The blame always lands on someone else.* I'd had video evidence of the woman outside my home, and yet, the police had focused on me as the key suspect in the chickens' butchering.

Jax drummed his fingers on the table. "How come I've never heard of her before?"

"Because she likes it that way," Roger said. "Whatever deflects blame off her, works to keep anyone from noticing her too. Except for us poor souls who do something to upset her. She's like a snake in the grass. She's silent. Invisible. You'd never know she was there…until you step on her tail. Then she sinks her fangs into your ankle and there's not a single thing you can do to stop the poison from spreading through your veins."

———

Jax and I were silent as we drove. I chewed on my lip until I tore off little scraps of skin and tasted blood.

*You won't know she's there until you step on her tail…*

Roger had been implying that I'd done something to upset Elsbeth.

The box of tapes rattled in the footwell, next to my sneakers. The note was still inside. DON'T WATCH. YOU'LL REGRET IT.

I'd disobeyed her instructions. I'd opened the box. I'd watched the tapes.

*But that's not fair. Why did I get the tapes in the first place? Why me?*

Kayla and I had only been in town for six weeks. I was certain I'd never seen Elsbeth's face before watching that first video. Had I done anything else to draw her attention? Anything to make her want to hurt me?

"Hey," Jax said. "What do you want?"

We were in a drive-through. A speaker box hissed static outside the window. I hadn't even realized. It was well after lunchtime, I'd skipped breakfast, and my stomach ached as the smell of cooking meat and greasy fries floated through the car's window.

"A burger," I said. Then, "No, two burgers."

Jax ordered those, plus fries, plus drinks. We pulled into the car's parking lot, and I ate ravenously.

All the while, I continued to think.

It probably didn't matter what I'd done to draw Elsbeth's wrath. I just needed to escape it.

She didn't seem like the kind of person who wanted an apology. I was fairly certain, if I tried to talk to her, it wouldn't go well.

*But then...*

The man in the forest. The pile of arms. The unseen figure

locked inside the wooden trunk. Out of everyone she'd targeted, only two people had escaped Elsbeth. Her foster parents. They'd fled town the night James Laker was murdered. Probably because they knew Elsbeth would be coming after them next.

And it had saved them.

My stomach ached, and I wasn't sure if it was because of how quickly I'd eaten or because of how badly it hurt to think about giving up my new home in Ludlow.

I ran the mental calculations. I had just enough in savings to keep Kayla and myself in cheap motels for a few weeks while we found a rental house in some other town. I'd call the real estate agent and ask her to sell our house—and to sell it quickly. Probably for a lot less than I'd paid for it.

I could take the financial hit. We just needed to survive.

"What time's Kayla's school pickup?" Jax asked, sipping from his drink.

"Uh…half an hour…" My mind was still tangled in problems with the home and with the real estate agent. "We should probably…pick her up…"

The agent who sold me the house had been a smiling woman named Gail. She'd been nothing but chipper when I met her at the office, but there'd been something slightly *odd* about her when I was viewing the home. Like she'd been uncomfortable there. And she'd mentioned at least three times how the previous owner had fully renovated the place, as though that was significant.

The burgers were no longer warming and filling. They sat like concrete in my stomach as I fumbled for my phone. I still had

Gail's number saved. I hadn't expected her to answer right away, but the line picked up on the second ring.

"Tess!" She sounded happy, but there was an undercurrent of nervousness in her voice. Almost as though she'd been expecting my call. And had been dreading it. "How's the new home treating you?"

"Fine," I lied. "But what can you tell me about the people who owned it before me?"

There was a slight pause. Then she said, "The previous owner was an investment manager. He did a lot of work to fix it up. Fully new kitchen, new floors—"

"Did he live there?"

Another pause, then she admitted, "No."

I squeezed my eyes closed, my heart hammering. "Who was the last person to *live* in the house?"

"Oh, I don't think I know."

The lie radiated out of every single word. If Gail didn't outright know, she'd at least heard rumors.

"Was it a woman?" I pressed. "A woman who left the house in such a bad condition that the only person who would take it was an investment manager who saw an opportunity to fix it and flip it?"

Silence.

"Was her name Elsbeth Byrd?"

"Tess, I really don't know what you expect from this… I don't, I can't…"

I hung up.

Gail had given me my answers simply by trying to stonewall me. I knew why the tapes had appeared in my daughter's closet.

Elsbeth had once owned my home.

I flipped to the Maps app, and opened Street View. The current version showed my house the way I knew it: clean, modern, all white walls and shiny windows. But as I went back in time, the older versions of that view gave a very different picture.

Just two years before, the house had been dilapidated. Roof tiles were broken, and the walls had cracks running through them. The windows had all been covered; what looked like dirty clothes were taped across each pane of glass. The garden was overgrown and choked with weeds. Piles of trash built up outside the front door, as though the occupant refused to leave the house.

It was unrecognizable compared to the place I now lived in.

Though, maybe that whole stretch of street had struggled. The home next door had a large *Foreclosed* sign out front.

My eyes drifted back to the study's window. It was covered with a filthy cloth, but one corner of the fabric was pulled back. And I swore I saw a pair of gleaming eyes staring at me from the darkness within.

"What do you want to do?" Jax asked. He held his drink in one hand, as though this was just a casual lunch out with a friend, but his eyes looked worried.

"I can't stay there," I said.

"You and Cookie are welcome to crash at my place," he offered.

"It's a mess, but not the biohazard kind yet, and I have a fold-out couch."

"Thanks. But I think we need to get out of town. Right now." My throat ached. "Let's go and get Kayla."

---

I made my plans as we drove to the preschool. We'd get my daughter, then swing by the house to collect my car and pack the absolute essentials. A suitcase of clothes, Kayla's most beloved toys, toothbrushes. I didn't know if I'd be able to come back for the rest. I tried not to think about it too much.

Kayla, at least, was in a good mood when we picked her up. She chattered incessantly about the toys she'd played with, the books the teacher had read, and the things the other children had said. Jax was driving, so I twisted around in my seat to watch Kayla talk. Her cheeks were pink, and her uncombed hair looked sweet as it curled around her face.

I loved her more than I could bear to feel.

We pulled up outside our home. Everything seemed strangely serene, as though that morning had never even happened.

*Maybe I'm overreacting.* It was a good day. Kayla kicked her feet as I unbuckled her from the child seat. The house almost seemed welcoming.

Then I remembered Elsbeth's malevolent smile as the flames crawled up her body, and I knew I was making the right decision.

"Five minutes," I told Jax, who nodded. He was coming with us as backup. We swept into the house. The security camera that faced the front door blinked its red light, showing it was still active. I'd brought the box of tapes and dropped it in the hallway. I'd take our belongings. But I wasn't going to take those videos.

"I learned to write a new word," Kayla babbled, bouncing at my side as I held her hand. "I learned to spell *cat*! Look, it's C-A-T, like this…"

My heart skipped a beat, then skipped another. I watched as Kayla held a finger into the air and traced the letters.

"Did you see? See how good I did it? We all learned it, but some of them kept doing it wrong—"

"Jax," I said, and my voice was barely a whisper. "Can you take Kayla and help her pick which toys she wants to bring? I need a minute."

"Yeah, sure." He must have sensed it wasn't a good time for questions. He held out a hand. "C'mon, Cookie, come and show me your toys."

She bounded away with him, her small shoes smacking against the floor with every pace.

I waited until they were out of sight, then fumbled for the box. The small slip of paper—DON'T WATCH. YOU'LL REGRET IT.—fell free. I dragged out the first tape and ran for the den.

I could afford a moment. The doors were all still locked. The house was airtight. Which meant it was safe. For now.

And I needed to be *certain*.

It was the third time I'd seen the video, but repetition didn't make it easier. Above me, Kayla babbled happily, her voice interrupted by occasional questions from Jax. I rewound the film, my eyes squinted half closed as blood dribbled from Elsbeth's lips, until I reached the section where she raised her hand.

The index finger extended. It hovered there for a second, then it began moving.

*I was right. It's not a spell. She's writing midair.*

I held my breath as I tried to follow the movements. I couldn't make out what the letters were supposed to be. I hit Pause, then scrambled to Kayla's play area.

She had sheets of paper and colored pencils scattered around. I took some of each and knelt back in front of the TV. Then I rewound, raised a piece of paper to the screen, and hit Play.

The paper was thin enough and the TV bright enough that I could still see Elsbeth through it. Barely. I raised a pencil—red, why did I have to pick red?—and pressed it to the paper, right where her index finger was. Then I began to follow the movements, shifting the paper occasionally to try to keep up with her writing.

It took a few minutes and several tries to get it right. Then I lowered the paper. I was looking at a message, written backward as though from a mirror.

THEY TOOK MY TEETH. NOW WE ARE EQUAL.

I tasted bile.

I'd thought the teeth she'd shown me on her tongue were her own, pulled from the gaps in her jaw.

But those gaps had been there for a long time. Back from when her parents had tried to remove her bite.

Instead…

*Did she pull her parents' teeth?*

I hit Eject. The tape rattled as it came out of the player. I stood on shaky legs and faced the stairwell.

It was only then it occurred to me.

I could no longer hear Kayla playing.

---

"Jax?"

My voice shook. I felt like my world was shrinking in on me.

"Kayla?"

The house was deathly, eerily silent.

I ran for the stairs.

The door to Kayla's room was open. I stepped inside and froze. My sneakers sank into carpet that was saturated with spilled blood. Little beads of it bloomed around the sides of my shoes.

*No, no, no, no—*

More blood droplets ran up one wall. They were so fresh they were still shiny. Kayla's toys lay scattered, as though they'd been interrupted mid play session, but there was no sign of her or Jax.

"Kayla!" My voice broke as I tore through the other upstairs rooms. "Jax, answer me!"

From my study window I could see Jax's car was still in the driveway. I took out my phone and tried dialing him. It rang, and rang, and rang, but he didn't answer, and I couldn't hear his ringtone anywhere inside the house.

*How? They were right there—just upstairs—and I didn't hear a thing.*

The computer on the desk was still running as it recorded the camera feeds. As I redialed Jax's phone, I tabbed to get into the saved footage.

The footage from Kayla's room was blank. The camera had been recording, but all it showed was a rectangle of black. I swallowed around the lump in my throat as I rewound it. Hours evaporated, until finally the screen flickered to life again. I pressed Play.

I saw myself on the video feed. I rushed Kayla through her room, getting her into hastily picked clothes.

I remembered the scene. It was from that morning, just after I'd returned from the forest with Officer Farrow. We were about to leave for the police station.

On the video feed, I took Kayla by the hand and led her back into the hallway. The video was still for several long moments, and I imagined us leaving and locking the front door behind us.

Then something near the back of the room moved.

I choked on a gasp as Elsbeth shifted from the darkened corner between the heavy curtains and the wall. Her long, stringy hair hung to her waist. Her hands were coated in blood and soil. She stared up at the camera as a wicked smile split her mouth open.

*She was there the whole time I was getting Kayla dressed. I didn't even see her.*

The curtains had created a perfect little shadowed nook that was just large enough to conceal a person. I felt like I'd fallen into a lake of ice water.

*Is that what happened to Jax?*

*Was Elsbeth waiting in the room when I sent them up to play?*

The grainy, distorted Elsbeth in the video paced toward the camera. Her eyes stared into it. She reached up one hand and her blood-caked fingers fixed around the lens.

A splinter of broken glass sliced across the view, then the screen went black as she crushed the camera.

I took up my phone again. My hands shook as I dialed the police station.

---

They were going to suspect me.

I knew they would. They'd doubted my story the first time they'd visited, when they saw the empty wine bottle. They'd all but accused me of decapitating the chickens. At this point, I was a troublemaker, an attention seeker, a problem.

There was nothing I could do that would make them believe I *hadn't* hidden—or worse, harmed—my daughter. But that didn't matter.

Just as long as they came.

As long as they searched for her.

As long as they *found* her.

I could handle anything else. Just as long as Kayla was still alive.

A man answered the phone, and I told him everything I dared and then some more. My daughter was missing; a stranger had been in my house; there was blood on the carpet. I told him I was sure Kayla was going to die if they didn't get there quickly.

I could only hope they'd take me seriously.

He wanted me to stay on the phone, but I hung up. The hammer was still in the study, and I held it up to my chest as I began to search the house.

As I scoped through the rooms, I looked not just for traces of Kayla and Jax, but for signs of how Elsbeth had gotten inside. She'd been in the forest the previous night, and I'd been obsessive about locking the door behind myself every time we went in and out.

*She used to live here. Does she still have a key?*

That didn't seem possible. The doors were all new as part of the developer's renovations. New doors meant new locks.

None of the windows were broken. The locks were all intact. It wasn't until I got downstairs that I found another trace of Elsbeth.

The camera facing the front door had been broken. Its blinking red light was dead. The lens was cracked. It hung from its cable, a sad, limp, shattered thing.

Tears kept flooding my eyes. They made it hard to see, and I aggressively swiped my sleeve over them to clear them. I could afford to break down when I had Kayla back. Not before.

I stepped outside. Jax's car was untouched. So was mine. I circled around the house, clambering through the overgrown garden. I was looking for footprints or drops of blood. Anything that might show where they'd gone. If there were clues to find, I couldn't see them.

My breathing was ragged. I was starting to spiral as the panic turned to helplessness. I didn't know where to search or what to do. I didn't know how to help my daughter.

*Except…*

I knew where Elsbeth wanted me to turn for answers.

The box of tapes.

I ran back into the house, took the second VHS tape and slid it into the player. Elsbeth stood burning in the hallway of the now-derelict school. Desperation made me mash the buttons as I rewound through the flames. Elsbeth raised her hand. I raised a sheet of paper and pressed it to the screen.

The second video was much harder to decipher than the first. Elsbeth was further away and her movements smaller and harder to trace. I struggled, but a message eventually appeared.

THEY SPOKE WITH FIRE. NOW FIRE SHALL SCORCH THEIR BONES.

More than two dozen girls and their teachers had died in that blaze. None of them were the same students Elsbeth had been at school with. She hadn't cared. The school had been a cruel place to her, and she had treated it cruelly in return.

I hastily ejected that tape and shoved in the third.

Elsbeth stood in front of the forest. I could barely see the man lying on the ground behind her. Again, she raised her hand. Again, I raised a paper and pencil.

HE SAID HE BELONGED TO ME. I WILL NOT LET HIM BE A LIAR.

*The rumors about the affair were right. James Laker was foolish enough to have a fling with Elsbeth when she was just a teenager.*

*Her foster parents fought with him about it; that was the source of the grudge the police were talking about. And then he left her anyway and returned to his wife, and Elsbeth never forgave him.*

Next tape. I tried dialing Jax's number again while feeding the VHS tape into the player. I knew he wouldn't answer. But I was low on options, the tapes were taking up too much time, and I was terrified by what might be happening to my daughter.

This tape had Elsbeth crawling through the dark. When I'd first seen it, I hadn't paid much attention to her surroundings; now, I scoured the barely lit distant walls for clues. It was too wide to be a tunnel. The ceiling was too low to be an attic. The dirt floor meant it was underground.

Elsbeth scuttled toward me, carrying the first severed arm. I fast-forwarded until her collection was complete. Then I began transcribing her message.

THESE HANDS HIT ME. NEVER AGAIN.

I stared at the four arms stacked carelessly on the ground, torn off at the shoulder. Two belonging to a woman, two belonging to a man.

*Her parents? No, she already took their teeth. The foster parents.*

The police said they'd fled town and had never been caught. They'd been in such a rush that they left their luggage in the hallway.

I felt sick as I ejected the tape. Elsbeth's foster parents had *tried* to run. They'd been just a fraction too slow, and she'd caught them before they could get out. Probably just hours after she killed James Laker. His blood had been in the sink drains.

I'd thought I could escape Elsbeth by following their example. But, just like them, I'd made the fatal mistake of waiting to pack.

The fifth tape went into the player. This one had Elsbeth sitting placidly on top of the large wooden chest. It shuddered. She raised her hand, and the fifth message was scrawled into the air.

THEY WANTED ME TO LEAVE. LET'S BOTH STAY INSTEAD.

I shoved that tape back into the box unceremoniously. Unlike with the other videos, I had no idea who the victim in the box might be. A lawyer? A solicitor? Someone who wanted to force her from the house?

No, I realized. The neighbor. I'd seen a house with a *Foreclosed* sign out front when I looked at old street view images. Someone who lived next to Elsbeth had hated the dilapidated state of her house so much that they'd become a nuisance to her.

Did that mean they'd been killed inside this very house? In the video, the wall had been brick, and every room in my current home was white-painted plaster. But the renovations had remodeled just about every section of the house. They easily could have rendered and painted a brick wall, as well.

There was just one tape left. It was the only one I hadn't watched yet. My pulse thundered in my ears as I slid it into the VCR.

Elsbeth's face stared up at me from the darkness. We were close. Intimately so. I could see every scar on her skin. Thin strands of hair hung across her cold, empty face. She looked so much like a corpse.

She raised her hand. And she began to trace words.

For a final time, I placed a sheet of paper over the image and followed her movements.

The final message was written more slowly and carefully than the ones before. Elsbeth lowered her hand. The video continued for just a few seconds, then abruptly ended.

Some of the other tapes had lasted for hours. This one couldn't have been longer than two minutes. But it was somehow more terrible than all the others put together.

I looked at the paper and at my tracing of Elsbeth's final message.

YOU STOLE THE HOME WHERE I WAS BORN.

LET'S BOTH DIE HERE.

---

I rocked away from the TV. Even though her face wasn't on the screen, I swore I could still feel Elsbeth's eyes on me.

The room seemed dimmer, colder. I glanced at the window and realized the sun was lowering behind the hills. It was going to be dark soon, and the police still hadn't arrived.

*Wait…*

I could see a cruiser parked across the street. I ran for the front door as relief bloomed through me, but I staggered to a halt on the driveway.

The cruiser was empty.

"Hello!" I called, craning my neck as I looked up and down the road. "I need help!"

There was no answer. No sign of the officers. None of my neighbors came to their doors. It was almost as though they knew better than to get tangled in whatever was happening.

It made me feel so impossibly alone.

I raised the hammer as I rounded the house, but the backyard was still empty. I took out my phone. The screen displayed a history of my recent calls to Jax, all unanswered. I tried one final time.

And I heard his ringtone.

It seemed to come from miles away, but I'd heard it often enough to recognize it.

The sound was coming from the forest.

"No," I whispered, but I was already stumbling toward it, hammer held at the ready. I didn't want to go into the trees alone. But there was no one else to turn to for help. No Jax; no police. Just me.

The sun was low, and the branches spread enormously long shadows across me as I ran under them. I switched on the phone's flashlight function. It barely helped. But it did highlight spots of vivid-red blood on the fallen leaves.

A lot of spots.

As I ran, the blood flicked up beneath my shoes. A line of vivid red, painted through the forest. More than any human could afford to lose.

I knew where the trail was going to lead me. I barely even slowed down when brittle chicken bones began to crunch underfoot. The heads, suspended from the trees, swung eerily as I pushed between them. Flies hummed around the carcasses.

And then I reached the tree. Big Gray was no longer the only tribute.

Officers Farrow and Jean had been tied to the tree. Their arms were stretched above their heads as though they were reaching for the clouds.

Their eyes had been removed.

Their chests had holes in them the size of my head. Their hearts and lungs were gone, leaving nothing but a gaping view into the inside of a rib cage.

Exactly what she'd done to the chickens.

They must have seen Elsbeth as they parked opposite my house. Maybe it had been an accident. Or maybe she'd lured them deliberately. But they'd chased after her without even waiting to speak to me, and she'd led them into the forest and to their deaths.

I didn't see Jax or Kayla, though. I circled the tree, just in case, chicken bones crackling underfoot, but the other side was bare.

I dialed Jax's phone. It began ringing, and it sounded close. I could barely see through thick tears as I stumbled around, searching. As the final rings faded, I found it. Artificial light shone out from Officer Farrow's open rib cage. The phone had been placed inside. I left it there.

*She wanted me to see them. That's why the phone's here. But Jax isn't. Because…because…*

I felt like I was on the cusp of something important, I just couldn't grasp it.

*The videos were a warning about what was coming. I just didn't realize it until too late. Because I never watched the final video until too late. "You stole the home where I was born. Let's both die here…"*

My head snapped up. I could barely breathe. I'd found the one thing that had been bothering me.

*The home where I was born.*

This wasn't just any place to live for Elsbeth. It was her childhood home. She'd inherited it, not bought it.

And Roger had told me that her parents kept her locked in the basement when she was a child.

I ran back to the house. The hammer kept clipping trees as I passed them. I stumbled over roots, but I didn't dare slow down.

There had been no mention of a basement when I'd bought the house. I'd never seen any doorway or hatch that might lead to it. I'd moved in believing I didn't *have* a basement. Because it had been sealed up during the renovations.

Which meant it was still there. Somewhere. I just needed to find the way in.

I cleared the edge of the forest. The house and its overgrown garden came into view. That snapped another memory into place. The renovations had happened just months before I moved in, but the plants had clearly been growing there for years, maybe decades. The developer had paid someone to pull the weeds and trim the plants but had otherwise left them.

I plunged into the thickest shrubs, pushing thorny branches and waxy leaves out of the way. The further I went, the louder my heart seemed to thunder.

And then I found it. Buried beneath the densest plants, so deep that I never would have found it if I hadn't been looking, was a hatch built against the side of the house.

Not only did the hatch still exist, but someone had been using it. The dirt around its base was scuffed.

I didn't bother calling the police again. Any backups would take too long to arrive, if they came at all. Instead, I aimed my phone's flashlight ahead and pulled on the door.

It groaned faintly as it rose, and a sickening smell wafted out of the basement. I held my breath as I climbed down narrow, steep stairs into the dark.

My light flicked across bare dirt floors and cold brick walls. It wasn't a finished basement; it was little more than a crawl space. I could stand, but just barely; I had to hunch to avoid scraping my head on the ceiling. The only light came from the open hatch and my phone.

My first thought was that this was a cruel, miserable place to raise a child. My second thought was that I recognized it.

The mortar around the bricks was messy. Some of the lines were uneven. This was a space that was supposed to be seen rarely, if at all. But it had been recorded once, in a sickening VHS tape.

I turned, panning my light. The wooden chest was still there, exactly the way it had been in the video. I could picture Elsbeth sitting on top, her bare heel tapping its side. I could picture it twitching.

*The neighbor she forced in there… Are their remains still inside?*

The wooden case shuddered.

I choked on a scream as I scrambled backward. My shoulders hit the wall; trails of dust cascaded through my flashlight's beam.

*Impossible—that video was decades old—they're long dead—*

The trunk shuddered again. I thought I could hear sounds coming from inside. A voice, dry and raspy and broken, whispering to me.

I staggered to the case. My heart filled my throat, suffocating me. The padlock was still firmly fastened on the clasp, and I had no key. But I *did* have a hammer. I raised it, then brought it down, again and again, until the metal broke away.

The lid rose. A ghoul's face lurched up, its eyes bulging, its sunken cheeks stretching as the mouth peeled open.

"Jax!" I screamed and grasped him by the shoulders to pull him toward me.

I'd barely recognized him. Blood coated his face. His cheek had been torn up. His eyes were bulging with terror and were strangely vacant.

I managed to drag him out of the trunk, and as I did, I saw he'd been forced to lie in a bed of bones and scraps of clothes. Elsbeth hadn't even cleared out the first occupant before locking Jax in.

"Kayla," he moaned. His voice was slow and slurred.

"Where is she?" Blood matted the hair at the back of his head. I touched it gently, and Jax groaned with pain.

"Where's Kayla?" I asked, trying to keep my voice gentle.

"Save Kayla," he muttered. "She took…Kayla…"

He didn't know. He couldn't have; he'd been blind in the trunk.

I hooked my arm under his shoulders and pulled him up. He was thin as a pole, but I still staggered under his weight. I pulled him toward the stairs and to the rectangle of light that would lead us outside.

"Come on," I whispered. "Gotta get you out. And then… then…"

A strange noise came from the darkness behind us.

A soft, cooing sound.

I knew it. That was the noise Kayla made when she was playing with Big Gray.

"Get out," I whispered to Jax. We were nearly at the stairs, and I nodded toward them as I let go of him. He staggered but managed to keep his feet. "Find help. Go, quickly."

Then I turned back to the dark.

---

I aimed my light toward the place where I'd heard the noise, but the beam wasn't strong enough to travel far. Fear gripped me so powerfully, I thought I'd never breathe again. But I moved forward. Toward Kayla. Or toward the thing that was imitating her.

Something shuffled across the ground. I still couldn't see it.

"Kayla?" I called. My voice shook. There was no answer.

The ground rose up into a shelf. The crawl space continued. The gap seemed too low for a person to fit, but I already knew what this area was. I climbed into it, and as my head grazed exposed wooden beams, I crawled along the floor just like Elsbeth had in her video.

The cooing noise came again. It was moving further away from me. I knew this was a trap. I still couldn't turn back. Not without my daughter.

My phone was in one hand. The hammer in the other. They made it nearly impossible to move in the cramped space, and every time I tried, my back scraped the ceiling.

Something solid and brittle touched my outstretched hand. I clenched my jaw as I tried to move past it. Out of the corner of my eye, as my scant light flashed in that direction, I saw bones. The pile of arms. Or what remained of them.

A shape rocketed out of the darkness toward me.

I'd been distracted. And Elsbeth moved faster than I ever dreamed a human could. She came at me in a flurry of limbs, half insect and half monster. Long fingernails dug into my shoulder just as I swung the hammer at her.

The hammer hit something solid. I had no idea if that was Elsbeth or the wooden beams. But her fingernails vanished from my shoulder, leaving it burning with pain.

I screamed as I chased after her. I don't know why that was the moment I chose bravery—or stupidity—but I charged in Elsbeth's wake, the hammer swinging wildly through the darkness. It touched nothing but air. I fell still, breathing heavily, waiting.

I couldn't see Elsbeth. I couldn't hear her. But then, from ahead, a strange, creaking sound came. I followed it. And a trickle of very faint light appeared above my head.

There was a hatch in the ceiling. I had to contort my body to fit through it. Then I stretched my phone out, lighting the space, and nearly choked.

I was in the kitchen. There was a basement trapdoor that opened directly into the pantry. It must have been disguised into the wooden flooring; I'd looked inside the pantry every day for the six weeks we'd lived there, but I'd never seen the secret hatch before.

But this was how she'd been getting into my house.

From the kitchen it was a just short walk to the stairs and Kayla's bedroom.

A soft whining sound came from the den. It set every nerve on my body alight. That whine was the sound Kayla made when she was distressed.

Crawling beneath my home had cramped my legs, and I stumbled as I ran to the den. The TV was on. It played harsh white static. And standing in front of it, backlit, were Elsbeth and Kayla.

My daughter was closer. She clutched Big Gray to her chest, and her eyes were wide and red from crying.

Elsbeth stood behind. Her impossibly long hand rested on Kayla's shoulder, pinning her in place.

"What do you want?" I asked. I still had the hammer, but I didn't dare swing it when Kayla was in the way. "The house? You can have it back. We'll leave—right now. Let Kayla go and we'll walk out the door and you'll never see us again."

I could barely see Elsbeth in the gloomy room. The TV behind her lit her hair but left her face in shadow. But I could see her smile. A huge gash of a grin, splitting her face in half.

She raised her other hand. In it was one of my kitchen knives. The blade looked enormous as she pressed it against Kayla's throat.

I ran at her.

Kayla twisted out of Elsbeth's grip, but Elsbeth barely seemed to care. She was focused on me.

The hammer swished through the air as I swung it. Elsbeth jabbed the knife at me. I felt it pierce through the skin over my ribs. I swore I could hear the sound of metal against my bone.

I staggered, and Elsbeth moved deliriously fast, swinging around behind me. The blade grazed my jaw. Then my side, then my thigh. I swung again. And again. And finally, the hammer hit home.

We collapsed away from one another. I felt blood running from a half dozen gashes across my body. Elsbeth stood in the shadowed side of the room, her arms limp at her sides, her head held high. The hammer was embedded in her forehead. Perfectly centered. Slowly, she raised one hand and fixed her long fingers around the handle.

She pulled. The hammer made a sucking noise as it came free. A dribble of blood ran from the indent it had left.

Elsbeth's grin twitched wider.

Kayla crouched on the ground, her hands covering her face. I ignored the screaming cuts across my body. I snatched Kayla up and ran.

Through the kitchen. Into the hallway. I heard Elsbeth behind me, matching my footsteps beat for beat. Every second, I waited to feel the bite of a hammer or knife in my back. But then I hit the door, burst out of it and into the dark night, and didn't stop running until we were on the road and three houses down.

And then I collapsed.

I'd left a trail of blood behind us, and I could barely keep hold of Kayla. I hunched over her, terrified that I'd feel Elsbeth's scabbed hands scratching across my back.

They never came.

Slowly and carefully, I turned. The street was empty. In the distance was my house. The front door was closed.

*She doesn't like to be seen*, I thought, remembering the street view photo with the curtains taped to the windows. *If you see her, it's because she's angry with you.*

Elsbeth had what she wanted, and she was done with us. She didn't need to follow.

Gingerly, I relaxed my grip on Kayla. She stared up at me with terrified eyes.

"You were so brave." I spoke softly as I brushed hair back from her face. "My good girl. You even kept Big Gray with you."

"He's hurt," she mumbled, fingering a spot on his chest that had been torn. White stuffing peeked out.

"Nothing that can't be fixed," I promised.

We sat quietly. Kayla nestled against my chest while I hugged her as tightly as my aching, bleeding arms could and breathed in the scent of her hair.

She was alive.

It was the most precious gift the world could have given me.

A siren wailed. I turned, flinching, and saw flashing lights reflected over the houses. A trail of police cars and ambulances turned onto our street.

Jax had managed to get help.

"Mommy," Kayla whispered.

I followed her gaze toward our house. The windows were no longer dark. They were lit up by a strange, flickering light, and it was growing brighter.

I'd seen that glow before. In the video taken at the school. That was the kind of light that comes from a rapidly growing fire. It seemed impossible that it had built so fast. Maybe Elsbeth had washed the house in fuel. Or maybe the renovations had been cheaper than they looked and the flames devoured them quickly.

My gaze drifted up. Elsbeth was there. She stood in my second-floor study, in front of the window, staring down at me. Her dirty gray dress swirled as the inferno crept closer to her.

She raised one hand. The index finger pointed into the air. And then she began to draw.

It was hard to be certain from that distance, but as the flames swallowed her, I thought she wrote just two words:

MY HOME.

----

Big Gray had been given stitches that matched mine. He sat in Kayla's lap, and Kayla sat in mine, as we said goodbye to Jax in the park close to his secondhand store.

He was heartbroken that we were leaving, but he understood why. Ludlow was no longer a fresh start for us.

"You're going to visit," he promised Kayla as she hugged the toy chicken. "And I'm going to visit you guys. It's not even an hour away."

"Not even," I agreed.

Jax grinned. The doctors said he'd always have a scar on his cheek where Elsbeth had cut him. He said he didn't mind. It blended in nicely with the tattoos and piercings.

I'd spent slightly longer in the hospital and was on orders to take things easy for the next few weeks. Moving into a new house wasn't exactly *taking things easy*, but then, it wasn't like we had much choice. Our old one was reduced to rubble and char. And, even if it hadn't been, no amount of money could have convinced me to return to it.

We were going to a different town instead. A calm place, with good schools, and a river running through it. The insurance company was paying for the loss of my last home, so we could afford a place that was a bit smaller and hopefully a lot less cursed.

The police had spent hours questioning me in hospital. Two of their officers were dead and they wanted answers. At least, this time, none of the blame landed on me. The small army of police and EMTs Jax had summoned all testified to seeing the woman consumed by flames in the second floor of my home.

The tapes had been lost in the fire. My memory of them wasn't enough to be used as evidence in court, but the bones of Elsbeth's previous victims had been found in the rubble, and the unsolved cases were reopened for investigation.

"We should go," I said, sighing, as I checked my watch. I'd strung out the goodbye for as long as possible, but I wanted us in our new home before nightfall. "Come over next week, Jax. We can have a housewarming party."

"Looking forward to it. See you then, Cookie." He ruffled Kayla's hair.

"Later, Biscuit." She stuck out her tongue at him. She was developing so much attitude, so quickly. I loved her for it.

We split up, and I led Kayla back to our car. She bounced, swinging Big Gray at her side, then glanced up. "Should we say bye to *her* too?"

I stared into the trees. Calk Forest bordered one side of the park. For a second, I thought I saw a pale, horrifically thin figure standing there, her long dress swirling around her feet. Then I blinked and it was gone again.

Kayla didn't complain as I rushed her to the car. She didn't ask why I locked the doors the moment we were in, or why I was driving so much faster than normal as I turned toward the road that would take us out of town. I was grateful for that.

The arson investigators had found remains from Elsbeth's victims in the basement of the crumbled house.

And multiple witnesses confirmed seeing her consumed by the inferno. She'd tilted her head back and grinned as the flames engulfed her.

But, for all the hours of scouring through the rubble...

They'd never found Elsbeth's bones.

**THE END**

# ABOUT THE AUTHOR

Darcy Coates is the *USA Today* bestselling author of *Hunted*, *The Haunting of Ashburn House*, *Craven Manor*, and more than a dozen horror and suspense titles. She lives on the Central Coast of Australia with her family, cats, and a garden full of herbs and vegetables. Darcy loves forests, especially old-growth forests where the trees dwarf anyone who steps between them. Wherever she lives, she tries to have a mountain range close by.

**Website:** darcycoates.com
**Instagram:** @darcybooks
**X/Twitter:** @darcyauthor
**Discord:** https://discord.gg/bau65HMHf8